Prai

MW00576540

"*Ashes* uses a poignant cross-country expe... shared history of an interesting pair of estranged brothers charged with fulfilling their father's bizarre last wish. The pilgrimage twists through childhood memories of comic misdeeds and bruising misunderstandings, detours into sibling squabbles, and bounces over the ruts of problematic marriages and ornery children to arrive at an unexpectedly wonderful destination. I loved it."
– Anne Hillerman, *New York Times* bestselling author, *Rock with Wings*

"When two middle-aged, estranged brothers hit the road with their father's ashes in the back seat of the car, what begins as a grueling test of opposites ends up as a heroic testament to love. *Ashes* is a story about disappointment, dysfunctional families, and male aging, filled with observations that are both painfully true and terribly funny. Sometimes raw, always engaging, Steven Manchester's novel is a wry and wise journey through the ruins of the American Dream."
– William Kent Krueger, *New York Times* bestselling and Edgar Award-winning author, *Ordinary Grace*

"Heartwarming and hilarious. Recommended!"
– Ruth Harris, *New York Times* bestselling author, *Park Avenue* series

"Steven Manchester has the enviable ability to capture the intricacies of the human heart through words. *Ashes* is a moving novel of two brothers and their journey back to one another. A must read."
– Heather Gudenkauf, *New York Times* bestselling author, *The Weight of Silence* and *Missing Pieces*

"*Ashes* is a richly developed, deeply moving tale that redefines the modern quest story. Steve Manchester's clever romp, tracing the plight of two brothers on a cross country trek to scatter their father's ashes, makes us laugh, cry and, most of all, think. Cut from the broadcloth of Philip Roth and Kurt Vonnegeut, *Ashes* is a literary triumph of rare depth and pathos."
– Jon Land, *USA Today* bestselling author, *Strong Light of Day*

"Engaging, raw, and very real—*Ashes* is a terrific book about family, redemption, and the difficult things that make us all so hopelessly human."
– Matthew Norman, award-winning author, *We're All Damaged* and *Domestic Violets*

"If you don't laugh reading *Ashes*, then you should go get your head checked."
– Lenny Clarke, actor/comedian, *Rescue Me*

"*Ashes* is a wonderfully character-driven, page-turning tale of two estranged brothers on a personal quest across the country. Their spontaneous road-trip is a bumpy one, full of twists and turns and peopled with all sorts of colorful characters along the way, but it's also touched with humor—enough to amuse and delight the reader through a heartfelt, life-changing journey of self-discovery. Manchester's devoted fans will find much to love in his new novel, which proves he is an author who knows how to keep readers well-entertained, while touching their hearts deeply and profoundly at the same time."
– Julianne MacLean, *USA Today* bestselling author, *The Color of Heaven*

"Simmering emotions erupt as two estranged brothers embark on a cross-country road trip to bury the ashes of their sadistic father. *Ashes* is a brutally honest portrayal of men coming to grips with their own mortality. The surprise turns in the road will keep you glued to your seat, and make this a must read. Masterful storytelling. This is one of Steven Manchester's best."
– John Lansing, author, *Blond Cargo*, producer, *Walker, Texas Ranger*

"Artfully written and full of essential truths, *Ashes* is a journey of two estranged brothers traversing the country, contemplating their pasts, and facing futures unknown—with their cremated father in tow, no less. Always with a rich sense of place and refreshingly honest banter, Manchester will make you laugh and mourn and ponder with characters that feel as if they've been plucked straight from the real world. This is the kind of book that has you soul searching with every word."
– Meredith Wild, #1 *New York Times* bestselling author, *The Hacker Series*

"*Ashes* is a powerful emotional journey. You'll find yourself laughing and crying alongside these unforgettable characters, as you question all you believed about family dynamics."
– Aleatha Romig, *New York Times* bestselling author, *Consequences, Infidelity, and Light* series

"The death of their cruel and violent father brings about a reunion between estranged brothers Tom and Jason Prendergast. In a final act of nasty manipulation, their father stipulates in his will that the brothers must transport his ashes across the country together in order to receive their inheritance. With deeply felt honesty, guts, and humor, Steven Manchester's *Ashes* grants the brothers a bequest they'd never expected. This powerful story of redemption and forgiveness will engross you from its opening pages to its surprising, perfect conclusion."
– Judith Arnold, *USA Today* bestselling author, *Father Found*

"*Ashes* is a poignant and honest look at family, grief, healing, and hope. At times darkly funny and at others deeply emotional, Manchester's newest novel is a story of forgiveness and understanding that resonates long after you have read it."
– Kate Hewitt, *USA Today* bestselling author, *The Fragile Life* and *Rainy Day Sisters*

"Imagine a road trip with two damaged brothers and a box containing the ashes of their lousy pop in the back seat. A perfect blend of heart and hilarity, this dysfunctional brothers' road trip detours into poignant memories revealing childhood scars, making for an immensely entertaining and touching novel. Manchester weaves a smart, honest tale illustrating the bonds of brotherhood, life's disappointments, and the resiliency of the human spirit. Manchester's characters are vivid and believable and his dialogue spot-on; he is the master of witty repartee. Manchester's sharp, edgy humor had me laughing out loud. Turning from gut-wrenching to heartwarming and back again, *Ashes* is a novel that will remain with you long after the last page is turned."
– Lori Nelson Spielman, #1 international bestselling author, *The Life List*

ashes

steven manchester

THE
ST●RY
PLANT

The Story Plant
Studio Digital CT, LLC
P.O. Box 4331
Stamford, CT 06907

Story Plant Hardcover ISBN-13 978-1-61188-242-1
Story Plant Paperback ISBN-13 978-1-61188-259-9
Fiction Studio Books e-book ISBN-13: 978-1-945839-00-9

Visit our website at www.TheStoryPlant.com

First Story Plant Hardcover Printing: February 2017
First Story Plant Paperback Printing: January 2018
Printed in The United States of America

For my brothers, Billy and Randy . . .
two of my greatest heroes

". . . ashes, ashes, we all fall down."

chapter 1

TOM PRENDERGAST AWAKENED. Wiping the sleep from his eyes, he scanned the darkened room. A furious wind knocked on the block of ice that was once a window, violently demanding he rise from his warm bed. He searched for the true master of his life. The alarm clock glowed with the numbers *5:18 a.m.* "I still have another hour," he moaned before his restless memory spit out a bolt of joy that started in his head and tore through his limber body. *It might be another dreadful Monday morning for the rest of the sorry world,* he thought, *but not for me. No sir, Mr. Thomas Prendergast, CEO of Silver Lining Aeronautics, has just embarked on his first official day of vacation!* Pulling the overstuffed comforter under his chin, Tom grinned himself all the way back into the arms of his latest dream lover. A man could not ask for more.

Tom opened his eyes again. For a few minutes more, he lay beneath a mountain of warm cotton while his memory returned in fuzzy bits and pieces. Yesterday, as he recalled, he'd suffered terribly from a relentless toothache. He ran his tongue over a row of straight teeth. *Not a throbbing molar to be found*, he thought. *That's odd.* He quickly switched his mindset to the day ahead. Though he had no need to go near the office, it was still going to prove a hectic one. *There's some last-minute Christmas shopping I need to get done.* He also remembered he hadn't yet finished packing for his tropical getaway. Both thoughts brought a smile. Jamming his tongue into the rear of his mouth again, he thought, *I wish life could always be so busy.*

Drying off from a leisurely shower, Tom chose the day's outfit. He had to wear those stiff suits day-in and day-out, so casual seemed the only option. Avoiding the wingtips and power ties, he located a pair of pleated khakis and a fleece button-down in his vast walk-in closet. Both fit the bill nicely. For whatever reason, he decided to continue with his change in appearance. Rather than slick his hair straight back, as he did each morning, he passed on the usual glob of yellow gel and combed his thick mop to the side. *It's different*, he thought. *I like it.* Two slaps of aftershave later, the room smelled of a mix of melon and musk. Filling his pockets with keys and a bulging billfold, he started for the kitchen.

Tom finished the last drop of fresh-squeezed orange juice and did a double take at the lengthy NASDAQ report. Almost overnight, his Telecomm Italia stock had risen twelve points. It was unheard of, especially since—against his better judgment—he'd accepted his broker's advice to buy. "I swear that Barry Pereira is a diamond in the rough," he muttered, jotting down a note to send the young genius a case of Scotch for his keen insight. Just beneath the note, he did a quick calculation. Broker fees aside, this one deal had reaped—*close to four hundred thousand dollars.* He returned to the note and added, *good Scotch.*

One final bite of dry toast later, a black Lincoln Continental waited patiently just outside the marble foyer. Tom donned his coat and hat, and darted for the open door. Once inside the car, a wave of heat hit his face, removing all of winter's discomforts.

Shamus Donovan looked over the front seat. "Where to?" he asked.

"How about FAO Schwarz, for starters? I'm in the mood to buy some toys."

"But you don't have any wee ones," Shamus blurted, his face immediately burning red at the embarrassment of his thoughtless comment.

Tom took no offense. Instead, he took the time to ponder that very fact. *Lord knows, though I've never settled down—as friends call it—I've spent a fair amount of my adult existence committed to one failing relationship after the other.* At times, friends—as they called themselves—even questioned whether Tom was "too tight" to share his fortune. *Absurd,* he thought. *The problem is . . . I get bored too* quickly. No one had ever seemed to capture the core of his heart. *Tom Prendergast never settles for anything,* he reminded himself, *and I'm not about to start with life's most important partnership.* He stared into space for a few moments. *As far as children go, I suppose a man can never miss what he's never known.* Of course, he sometimes wondered what it would be like to hear a child's laughter spill through the vast halls of his home, but the thought always ended up exactly where it probably belonged—as a vanishing thought. "You're absolutely correct, Shamus," Tom agreed, emerging from his fog, "but there are far too many orphans in this city, and I want to spoil as many of them as I can this year."

"As you wish," Shamus finished, as if giving his blessing. And they were off.

While Shamus headed toward the toy store with its giant teddy bear out front, Tom spent the time admiring the even burn on his Cuban cigar. A gift from a colleague, it was the smoothest tobacco he'd ever tasted.

It was nearly noon when Tom wrapped up his shopping frenzy. Hundreds of Barbie Dolls and an equal amount of superhero action figures made their way toward the register. He purchased every stuffed animal, yo-yo, and sled in the store. Pyramids of board games, sporting goods, and baby dolls were stacked inside one of the dozen shopping carriages being pushed in the giddy man's wake. In record time, Tom had personally selected a mountain of toys. Each time he threw something that beeped, whistled, or cried into a shopping cart, he felt the spirit of giving illuminate his soul. *It's already the best Christmas I can remember,* he thought, feeling his face glow.

Sharing the same truth, Shamus Donovan giggled like a young schoolboy from the first aisle to the last.

Tom threw the gifts onto his platinum card while Shamus shuffled out the door to pull the car around back. Tiptoeing out of the store, Tom ducked into the shiny black car—where Shamus was still giggling.

"To the airport?" the Irish chauffer managed through his glee.

Tom nodded. "Yes, please," he said, grinning. "It's time for *my* present."

As Shamus unloaded the luggage, Tom ascended the stairs of the Learjet. Upon entering the cabin, Christopher Shaw greeted him with a smile. "You're right on time, as always," the pilot noted.

"Let's just hope you can do the same, Christopher," Tom kidded, catching the man off guard. Tom Prendergast was normally so consumed in the details of his business that he seldom spoke, never mind joked.

"I certainly intend to," the young pilot countered, adding, "Kylie has quite a dinner planned for your trip, sir."

Tom's eyebrows danced with curiosity.

"Cracked Alaskan king crab on a bed of . . ."

"Please, Christopher, spare me the details. You'll ruin the surprise." Tom patted the man on the back, stepped into the plush cabin, and removed his wool coat. One look around brought the biggest smile. The plane's interior was comparable to a five-star hotel room, but that wasn't the reason for the joyful feeling. Tom suddenly thought about Sandi. *By the time I get to Hawaii,* he thought, *she'll be comfortably numb on mai tais and primed for a long session of lovemaking.* As the whine of the jet's motors screamed out a final farewell to the Big Apple, he accepted a stiff drink from Kylie, eased back into his seat, and began to daydream about the naughty things he planned to do to his skilled lover.

To the hum of the jet's dual engines, Tom drifted off into sweet oblivion.

When Tom arrived at the hotel, Sandi was already lying naked on the bed, pretending to be asleep. He giggled with the excitement of exploration. Within seconds, his clothes were stripped clean from his body. Mounting her, he kissed her neck, stopping long enough at her ears to make her return his giggle. Without opening her eyes, she flicked her tongue across his . . .

Tom felt a tap on his shoulder.

Still wearing his smile, he opened his eyes, expecting to see Kylie, his gracious stewardess.

Instead, he nearly jumped out of his desk chair. It wasn't Kylie at all. It was his assistant, Sue Nedar. He tried to catch his breath.

"Professor," she said, "I hate to wake you but you have class in fifteen minutes."

Tom's head still felt submerged in the wondrous fog. "Fifteen minutes?" he replied, the throbbing pain of a mind-shattering toothache blurring his vision even more.

Sue tried valiantly to chase away a smile but quickly lost. "Yes, Professor," she said, her voice fighting off laughter. "You need to get up."

As Tom's wits returned, the excruciating pain in his mouth made him want to choke Sue for waking him. *It's not winter*, he told himself, still suspended between his glorious dream and reality. *It's only October . . . and I'm hardly rich.* He tried to shake off the haze before looking back at his grinning assistant. "Sorry about that, Sue. I must have dozed off and . . ."

"That's fine," she said. "Oh, your wife called. She said she's made alternate plans for dinner and that you probably shouldn't wait up for her." Sue quickly avoided eye contact after delivering the message.

Tom cringed. "My wife," he muttered, as if suddenly remembering he still had one of those.

Sue headed for the door. "I'll leave you to get prepared for your class then."

Tom nodded. "Yeah, thanks, Sue." But he never moved. He sat for a few moments, contemplating his life. Although he was a college professor by day and a stock market investor by night, he had yet to satiate his ambitions. *But I'm almost there*, he thought, still striving to prove himself to the world. He knew that the trick behind being successful was preparation. *The best I can hope for is to be completely prepared for when the right opportunity presents itself.*

Tom stood, stretched out his body and, reaching for his worn leather satchel, grabbed for his abscessed tooth. *Oh God*, he thought, cursing himself for not getting to the dentist at the first signs of trouble. He thought about his dream. *Me smoking a cigar? I hate cigars.* After another look around, he shook his head. "Sorry about this, Sandi," he whispered. "It would have been fun."

Professor Tom Prendergast started for the door when he spotted a stamped letter sitting on the corner of his desk; it was addressed to him from Attorney Russell Norman. He caught the attorney's return address. *He's from back home*, he thought, grabbing the envelope to read on his way to class.

After exchanging a friendly nod with Shamus Donovan, the college's finest custodian, Tom made a beeline to the faculty men's room. Three minutes later, he was just outside his classroom door when he froze in place. "Passed away from terminal cancer?" he questioned aloud, looking up from the letter. "Pop died?" He shook his head. *Oh shit*, he thought, *he had prostate cancer and it spread before* . . .

He read the rest of the letter. *The old man's already been cremated*, he recapped, *and the reading of the last will and testament is scheduled for* . . . He stopped. *Will?* he thought. *That son of a bitch had a will?* Though he tried to stop it, his mind instantly returned to his adolescence—where his father glared at him with a look of sheer contempt in his eyes. "You're a dummy," the sadistic man growled, "and you're always gonna be a dummy." The nickname never made any sense to him, as he'd been much smarter than his dad ever since he could remember. Shaking off the hideous memory, Tom folded the letter and placed it into his leather briefcase. Throwing open the classroom door, the heavy buzz went silent. "I don't remember giving anyone permission to talk," he barked, causing a bolt of pain to shoot from his upper jaw straight into his brain. Two deep breaths later, he marched into the crowded classroom like he was heading into a prison block.

Within the belly of the beast—Southeastern Correctional Center—Jason Prendergast reported from roll call straight to his new six-month assignment, Essex III block. Most correction officers dreaded Essex III because it housed some of the more violent animals within the inmate population. But being a veteran sergeant with twenty-eight years of experience working behind the wall, Jason barely noticed. *It's just another day at the office*, he thought. He wasn't fifty feet from his new assignment when the radio squelched once, a night shift officer screaming, "Code 70, medical emergency, Essex III . . . cell seventeen." Instinctively, Jason took off at a sprint.

Sergeant Jason Prendergast was the second man to enter the crowded block. "Move out of the way!" he roared, pushing through a couple dozen inmates congregating outside of cell seventeen. With one final shove, he nearly ran into Inmate Andrew Pires's dangling torso. Pires had hanged himself; his neck was so stretched that his feet were nearly touching the floor. *Dead,* Jason immediately decided, noting that the con's eyes were still open and his fists clenched tight. While the reporting officer—Bobby Couture—was trying to catch his stolen breath, Jason surveyed the gruesome scene. There was a note written on the wall. Initially, he thought it was blood, but a subsequent look revealed that the author had used spaghetti sauce. It read, *To the man who locked me in here for no reason, you better hope there's no afterlife.* Jason looked back at Officer Couture and shook his head. *Looks like the poor kid's going to be sick,* he thought before considering whether to light the fresh cigar that protruded from his mouth. *Nah,* he decided. *I shouldn't. I promised Miranda I was going to quit.*

Officer Couture was dry heaving off in the corner when the penitentiary's only physician arrived on scene and pronounced Inmate Pires dead. Jason turned toward Couture. "Listen, I need you to hold Pires around the waist while I cut him down." Couture looked ready to faint. Jason peered hard at him. "Just do your job," he ordered.

With the unlit cigar dangling from his lips, Jason stood on the toilet. Once Couture grabbed the corpse around the waist, Jason told him, "Watch out, this is all dead weight coming at you." He cut the rope. Both Couture and Pires fell to the floor. Although there was nothing comical about any of it, everyone laughed—everyone but Couture.

"You think this is funny?" the young officer blurted, scrambling to get to his feet.

Jason erased his smile, pulled the stogie from his mouth, and stepped into the rookie's face. "What do you want me to do, cry about this piece of garbage? You show any compassion in this shit hole and you're a dead man, understand?"

As he turned to walk away, he stopped. "Oh, and just so you know, Inmate Pires was in here because he got his rocks off pulling house invasions." Couture's face changed from angry to embarrassed. Jason nodded. "That's right," the caustic man barked, "the stiff you feel bad for used to love breaking into homes, restraining the husbands, and then forcing the poor bastards to watch as their wives and children were repeatedly raped and beaten—the last time to death." Jason placed the cigar back into his mouth, adjusting it between his molars. "So, do you still feel sorry for him?"

Once Andrew Pires was placed into a black plastic bag— without a single tear being shed—Jason called out to the remainder of the block, "Stand for count." The order echoed off the walls, causing fifty-nine hardened, violent men to return to the doorways of their respective cells.

In many eyes, Sergeant Jason Prendergast was the ideal officer. Some said he was incredibly unlucky, though—"always in the wrong place at the wrong time." For reasons unknown, inmate deaths followed him from one block assignment to the next. Through the years, he found hangers, bleeders, and even one child molester who snuffed out his own flame by placing a plastic bag over his face, wrapping it around his neck, and then wedging himself under his bed where he was unable to remove it in his final panic of self-preservation.

Protected by only the small tin badge above his left breast pocket, Jason carried no weapons, except good common sense, his experience, and an undaunted dependence upon his brother and sister officers. Without recognition, he took the same daily risks of personal safety as any policeman, while walking a distinctively different beat. His sole purpose in life was to protect the public by keeping convicted criminals locked behind prison walls. And even when he despised the work, he did his job well.

19

Isolated from reality, every day proved tougher than the one before it. As Jason had learned decades earlier, the self-contained society functioning behind those giant walls was often violent and unpredictable, primarily negative and depressing, but always dangerous. For the most part, it was an abstract and dreary picture painted by the most ruthless people a normal human being would never want to meet. These real-life characters included every type of convicted criminal, from the cold-blooded murderers to the despised child molesters. Individually, the clientele were impulsive. Collectively, they were a roaming powder keg.

Jason was trying to teach Officer Couture that survival was the name of the game and that only the strong survived, while the weak were preyed upon in a shark-feeding frenzy. Jason understood this theory well. His chosen place of employment was where horrors became reality and reality changed from one minute to the next. With the dominant emotions being fear and anger, any and all power was achieved through either deceit or intimidation and force. The good were few and the bad usually became worse. Within this sub-society, a completely unconventional culture was created, forming its own code of morals and values—or lack thereof.

Struggling to maintain law and order within the concrete jungle, Sergeant Jason Prendergast continually penetrated the prison's underworld. Intercepting the inmates' strong desires for weapons and drugs, he was forced to think as his adversaries did. Detecting illicit businesses such as prostitution, loan-sharking, extortion, and gambling, the vicious games never ended. No matter the outcome, violence was woven into everything. Quite often, a grotesque crime was committed such as rape or murder, forcing him to step in and sweep up the remains. Tragically, he'd grown used to it.

As the years rolled by, though, his most challenging task was separating the realities of his thankless profession from the realities of his own life. At some point, the two had overlapped. With the life expectancy of a career correction officer being fifty-four years, it didn't seem to matter all th[ ]anymore. Jason had just turned fifty-two.

The only positive thing to come out of the years of negativity was the knowledge Jason had gained and was able to share. On the first Monday of each month, he gave his time to lecture the future convicts of America. His belief was that if he could help only one, it'd be worth the effort. Most weeks, the number one seemed larger than infinity.

After nearly three decades of working for the Massachusetts Department of Correction, Jason chose to pass on his brutal experiences to those who needed to hear them most—troubled youth.

It was a Monday night. Jason pulled into the parking lot of the Straight Ahead Program—a Christian-based ministry for children confined to lockup within the Department of Youth Services, or DYS—and stared at the eerie building. Surrounded by concertina wire and steel fence, the brick fortress was built in the late 1800s. Shadows moved behind the filthy windows covered by black bars and mesh, little people who blamed their current circumstance on everyone but themselves. *There are some tough cases in there,* Jason thought, *young boys who've been abused and neglected; products of drugs and alcohol, domestic violence, oppressive poverty, and a welfare system that fosters low self-esteem. Most could blame the world and be justified,* he knew, *but for the nightmare they're headed to, that blame isn't going to help any one of them.* Jason took a deep breath and stepped out of his pickup truck. *The only chance they have now,* he thought, *is to take accountability for their behavior and start making better choices.*

As he approached the building, Jason watched as the boys played a violent game of basketball, viciously beating on each other. Every one of them cussed and acted tough. *Doing everything I'd do if I was thrown into this same dark pit,* he thought, moving closer. *It's important to remember that.* Most Mondays, it was the only good reason not to drive away. *They're a pack of little punks, the whole lot of them*, he thought, as he reached the outer gate and rang the buzzer, *but they're scared little punks who need help.*

The lecture started with a prayer, followed by two hours of harsh reality. Jason detailed rapes and murders, anything to scare the delinquent boys into rethinking their futures. At the same time, he did everything he could to show them they were still loved.

"I'm not here to share war stories or to scare you," Jason began and, from the first brutal word that left his lips, he threw his booming voice and grabbed everyone's full attention. "I'm here to tell you the truth about prison." Like a tower searchlight, he scanned his young audience. "I'm here because I care enough to tell you that it's not too late," he roared. "No matter what others have told you; no matter what you may think, yourself—there's still hope. But all of that doesn't matter unless you start to believe in yourself."

With a wave of his hand, Jason gestured around the room. "You can avoid all of this by taking responsibility for your life and by starting to make the right choices. You're the only one who can decide not to graduate from this junior varsity team and go to prison." He shook his head for effect. "But first, no more excuses about your uncle's abuse or your mother's drug problems. It's time to stop acting like *fucking* victims."

Two dozen heads flew up at the unexpected vulgarity.

Now they're listening, Jason thought. "It's time to hold yourselves accountable for what happens in your own lives," he added, peering into their small, hardened faces. "Now how many men do I have in here?"

All hands shot up.

"Then it's time to start acting like fucking men!" he barked.

22

In silence, twenty-four young criminals looked at Jason with equal amounts of suspicion and contempt. *And why not*, Jason thought. Long before he'd arrived, those who were entrusted with their safety and nurturing had betrayed them in the most unspeakable ways.

"So here's how your nightmare begins," Jason explained. "One day, the judge gets sick of seeing your face and hands you a three- to five-year bid to serve at MCI-Cedar Junction, Walpole. And let me tell you right now, it's a lot harder to get out of that place than it is to get in."

His baby-faced audience looked confused.

Jason allowed it—*for the time being.* "Upon your arrival, you'll be shuffled into a concrete room and asked to step onto a blue, one-foot by one-foot square located on the floor. You'll be ordered to strip, but I guarantee you won't be fast enough. Four or five officers will tackle you and take you to the floor to complete the search. This roughing-up is a sort of initiation, or more accurately, a message that when you screw up you can be brought back to the room for a *tune-up.*" Jason nodded. "From the very moment you arrive and, in every sense of the word, you will be tested."

After allowing his words to sink in, he went on. "Upon arriving on the block, the wolves, your fellow inmates, will size up their new prey: you. Once again, you'll be tested. More than likely, some convict will approach you and demand that you take off your shoes or some other article of clothing and give it to him. As I said, it's all about choices, and this is a tough one. If you hand it over, then tomorrow he'll be taking your backside. But if you decide to save face and throw hands with the guy, I promise you'll lose. In prison, strength is found in numbers. Even if you're on top, winning a fight—which is very unlikely given your lack of fighting skills and experience as an eighteen-year-old—other inmates will jump in and finish you off. By some strange occurrence, if you happen to maim or scar your bully, you'll be charged with assault and battery—or even mayhem, which carries a sentence of twenty mandatory years.

All because someone wanted your sneakers and you refused to hand them over." He shrugged. "As I said, it's a lot harder to get out of prison than it is to get in. The chances of avoiding confrontation inside are slim to none. There is a good chance, however, that you'll earn more time while trying to stay alive." He studied their faces. "It's not fair, is it?"

With mouths half-hung in shock, they each nodded.

"But it's not about fair anymore, right?" Jason asked rhetorically. "Remember this . . . because you didn't make the right choices on the street, your entire world now exists in the wrong place, at the wrong time—every time.

"So it's time to stop playing the victim and understand there are consequences for your actions. It's time to take responsibility for everything you do. At seventeen years old, you'll find many people who still have compassion for you and all the horror stories that got you into DYS lockup. But once you enter the adult system, that same folder will get closed and many of those same hearts will become hardened toward you. I guarantee it. It's a matter of self-preservation. In prison, kindness is always mistaken for weakness, and there's no room for it. You'll never find it.

"You'll have enemies on both sides. There are the officers who you'll despise, though—ironically enough—they're charged with your protection. They will tell you when to eat, when to sleep, and even when to take a shit. They'll say *no* to nearly every request you ask of them. All the while, they'll be pressuring you into working for them as an informant."

A few of the boys snickered in a show of disbelief.

"Believe me, at your age, the majority of you will flip," Jason roared, staring down each snickering boy. "Can you imagine a more screwed-up existence?"

No one answered, but Jason could see. *It's starting to sink in.*

"Worse yet, at eighteen you're as close to a female as most of the inmate population has seen in a very long time. Truth is, the vast majority of the population are lifers with nothing to lose whether they rape you or snap your scrawny neck. One of their favorite sayings is 'It doesn't count in prison.' Can anyone tell me what that means?"

A hand shot up. Jason called on it. "It means a dude's not gay if he makes you his wife," the boy said, adding a nervous laugh.

Most of the room echoed his chuckle.

Jason's face remained stoic. "You're absolutely right," he confirmed, nodding. "It means he's taking your manhood."

The laughter immediately ceased.

"And there's two ways that happens. The first is called seduction, which is when an older con promises protection for your sexual favors." Pausing for effect, he shook his disgusted head. "The second way is by gang rape."

His audience looked sick.

Jason capitalized. "Unfortunately, with the amount of overcrowding and understaffing behind the wall, such crimes aren't usually detected until the damage has been done."

He paused again to let them absorb this traumatic truth. Peering into their eyes, he lowered his voice. "As I said, I'm not here to scare you. I'm just here to explain your reality if you do decide to take the next step into adult incarceration."

A small handful of them nodded.

Throughout his shocking spiel, he cursed and used street slang. Then to separate himself as well as maintain order and control, he yelled at the boys. It was a narrow passage to get through. And there was limited time to use humor and storytelling—anything to make a lasting impression. *I need to reach their hearts*, he thought, *the only place where I have any shot at making an impact.* But there was very little time. For what they'd been through, the walls were so thick and high that getting through was nothing short of a miracle. For the ones he could reach, there were only a few precious moments he could stay before he was exiled—most likely, forever.

Jason then explained the prison hierarchy and the different crimes that got inmates convicted. He detailed all the players found behind the wall and their daily games. From con men and thugs to their endless list of victims, he didn't candy-coat a word.

"Okay, the inmates who are on the bottom—you—must unite with others just to survive. Many cons say, 'I came in alone, I'll do my time alone, and I'll leave alone.' That's fucking bullshit! When you're on the bottom, you become the drug runner, or mule; the one who evens the score, or collects the bookie's winnings. If a hit goes down against another group, it'll be you who's ordered to carry it out. You become anything that could land someone more prison time if they're caught. I mean, think about it, why risk more time when you can force someone younger and weaker to do your dirty work, while you slide into the shadows and laugh at some kid's poor luck?"

Those with tough exteriors looked up for the challenge.

Jason went for the heart. "In the meantime, your people on the streets will build walls within themselves because no one can live in two worlds at one time. It's inhuman to keep grieving for someone who is gone but hasn't died yet."

Heads were hung.

Hoping it was due to shame and fear, Jason couldn't tell if he was losing their attention. "But prison's not a fair world, is it? It's the wrong place, at the wrong time—every time, right?"

For the first time, they all nodded in agreement.

Jason concluded, "If you do end up in prison, you will be a much different person upon being released, and these changes will not be good. Only two emotions dwell behind the wall: fear and rage, and you'll spend years becoming very familiar with both. It's called *being institutionalized*." For whatever reason, the last phrase hit too close to home for Jason, causing an unwelcome chill to travel the length of his weary spine.

"And for those of you who haven't figured it out yet, there's no pride in having *done time*. It's dead time. Just ask the nameless men who still wear numbers on their grave markings on Potter's Hill. No one talks about crying at night in his cell. Instead, they make up war stories and brag. I'm telling you, it's all bullshit! If you really want to impress people, then go jump out of an airplane for your country or save people from burning buildings. Get up every morning and go to work to support a family that depends on you. Now that's being a friggin' man. Those are the real heroes, the true tough guys."

Many of the boys were breathing deeply now, fighting off the dark emotions that raged inside them.

"So after hearing all of this," Jason said, "I want somebody to tell me what the good news is."

Not one hand went up.

Jason smiled. "The good news is that you never have to go there." As each boy looked up and made eye contact with him, he nodded. "Not one of you ever has to go to prison. It's really up to you and the choices you make from this moment on."

When he wrapped up, there was muffled applause—along with the promise that he'd be back to look in on them soon.

Jason exited the building. At the parking lot, he looked back. Through the grimy, barred windows, he could vaguely make out the faceless silhouettes of several of his students beating the life out of each other. "We'll try again next month," he told himself.

As he prepared to drive away, he noticed a pile of unopened mail sitting on the truck's passenger seat. The letter on top was addressed from Attorney Russell Norman. *From back home*, he thought, ripping open the envelope.

"Pop died from cancer," he said aloud, "and this is how I find out?" His rising blood pressure made his temples throb; he suddenly felt angry and hurt at the same time. From his earliest memories, it was a combination his dad could easily create in him. Jason took a deep breath and read on. *The reading of the will is scheduled for next week*, he thought, tossing the letter back onto the passenger seat. For a moment, he allowed his mind to return to his childhood where he pictured his father standing over him, snarling. "You're a punk," the old man hissed, "and you ain't ever gonna be anything but a punk." Jason quickly shook off the vivid image and started the truck. Shifting into drive, he glanced sideways at the letter. *They can read the will without me*, he thought. *That son of a bitch never had anything good to offer me anyway.*

As two shadows fought behind the steel mesh–covered windows, Jason stomped on the gas and headed for Mucky's Liquor Store. *I need a drink*, he thought.

chapter 2

ᎧᏗ

TOM WHEELED HIS LATE-MODEL, PLATINUM-COLORED BMW
into Attorney Russell Norman's freshly paved lot and parked
between a brand new Lexus—sporting the license plate *JUS-
TIS4U*—and a custom pickup truck. *Looks like I'm going after
the hillbilly*, he thought when he spotted the faded Massachusetts Department of Correction sticker in the rear window.
His blood turned cold. "It must be Jason," he thought aloud. *I
didn't think he'd come.*

Tom took a few deep breaths, not because he was nervous
about his father's death or talking to any lawyer but because
he hadn't seen his Neanderthal brother—*for fifteen years,
I think*. He paused for a moment to give it more thought.
Although their relationship had essentially vaporized in
their late teens—the result of a fall out that still haunted his
dreams—they'd occasionally wound up in each other's orbits;
weddings, funerals, and the like, enough to remain familiar
with each other's career choices, wives, and children. *But even
that came to an end fifteen years ago*, he confirmed in his aching
head before opening the door. While his toothache-induced
migraine threatened to blind him, he took one step into the
oak-paneled waiting room. His and Jason's eyes met for the

briefest moment. As though they were complete strangers, they both looked away. *And here he is,* Tom thought, disappointed. *This is just great.*

Through peripheral vision, Tom noticed that his older brother now wore a scar over his right eye, just above a bushy eyebrow that could have easily belonged to a homeless Scotsman. A jagged ear lobe, a piece clearly torn away, pointed to a crooked nose that sat sideways on his face—all of it rearranged since birth. *What a big tub of shit he's turned into,* Tom thought, struggling to ignore his throbbing face and head. *He's as fat as a wood tick now,* he thought, grinning, *and he looks like he's ready to pop.* Jason looked straight at him, as if reading his mind. Tom immediately looked away, his rapid heartbeat starting to pound in his ears, intensifying his physical pain. *Unbelievable,* he thought. After all the years and all the distance, his elder brother—by only two years—still scared the hell out of him. *He's just a big asshole, that's all,* he told himself, but he still couldn't bring himself to rejoin his brother's penetrating gaze.

The secretary answered her phone before calling out, "Mr. Prendergast . . ."

Both brothers stood.

"Attorney Norman will see you now."

Tom walked in first, letting the door close behind him—right in Jason's face.

"Still a weasel," Jason muttered, loud enough for all to hear.

"What was that?" Tom asked just inside the door.

"Don't even think about playing with me," Jason warned as he reopened the door and entered the room, "'cause I have no problem throwing you over my knee and spanking you right in front of this guy."

I'm fifty years old, for God's sake, Tom thought, *and he thinks he's going to spank me? I'm surprised the prison even let him out.*

The attorney—his hand extended for anyone willing to give it a shake—looked mortified by the childish exchange.

Tom shook the man's hand before settling into a soft leather wing chair. Jason followed suit.

The room was framed in rich mahogany paneling. The desk could have belonged in the oval office. Beneath a green-glassed banker's lamp, stacks of file folders took up most of the vast desktop. An American flag stood in one corner, while framed diplomas and certificates, bearing witness to the man's intelligence and vast education, covered the brown walls.

Attorney Norman wore a pinstriped shirt and pleated, charcoal-colored slacks held up by a pair of black suspenders. He had a bow tie, a receding hairline that begged to be shaved bald, and a pair of eyeglasses that John Lennon would have been proud to call his own. *There's no denying it,* Tom thought, trying to ignore his brother's wheezing beside him, *he's either a lawyer or a banker. He couldn't be anything else.*

While Jason squirmed in his seat, visibly uncomfortable to be sitting in a lawyer's office, his hands squeezed the arms of the chair. *What a chicken shit,* Tom thought, trying to make himself feel better. Peering sideways, he noticed that his brother's knuckles were so swollen with scar tissue they could have belonged to a man who made his living as a bare-knuckle brawler. *He's still an animal too,* he decided.

Attorney Norman took a seat, grabbed a manila file from atop the deep stack and cleared his throat. "The reason you're both here . . ."

". . . is to make sure the old man's really dead," Jason interrupted.

In spite of himself and his harsh feelings for his brother, Tom chuckled—drawing looks from both men.

"The reason we're all here," Attorney Norman repeated, "is to read Stuart Prendergast's last will and testament." He flipped open the folder.

This ought to be good, Tom thought, while Jason took a deep breath and sighed heavily. Both brothers sat erect in their plush chairs, waiting to hear more.

As if he were Stuart Prendergast sitting there in the flesh, the mouthpiece read, "My final wish is that my two sons,

Jason and Thomas, bring my final remains to 1165 Milford Road in Seattle, Washington, where they will spread my ashes."

"Seattle?" Tom blurted, his wagging tongue catching his tooth, making him wince in pain. Quickly concealing his weakness, he slid to the edge of his seat. "Oh, I don't think so," he mumbled, careful not to touch the tooth again.

Jason was shaking his head. "Hell no," he said.

The attorney read on. "I've always been afraid to fly, so I'm asking that I not be transported by airplane but driven by car."

"No way," Tom instinctively sputtered.

Jason laughed aloud. "This is just great. The old bastard's dead and he's still screwing with us."

The less-than-amused attorney revealed a sealed envelope and continued on. "As my final gift to my sons . . ."

"*Only* gift," Tom muttered, feeling a cauldron of bad feelings bubbling in his gut.

"I'm leaving this sealed envelope for them to share, once and only once they've taken me to my final resting place."

"What the fuck!" Jason blurted.

Every cell in Tom's overloaded brain flashed red. *Don't do it*, he thought. *You don't owe that old man a damned thing.* But every cell in his body was flooded with curiosity. He looked at Jason, who was no longer shaking his fat head.

"Maybe the bastard finally hit it big at the dog track?" Jason suggested.

Tom nodded in agreement but secretly wondered, *Could it be the deed to the land Pop bragged about owning in Maine?* He stared at the envelope. *For as long as I can remember, he claimed to own forty-plus acres with a brook running straight through it.* He stared harder. *Could it be?* he wondered, wishing he had X-ray vision. *A parcel of land in Maine sure would make a nice retirement . . .*

"How 'bout we travel separately and meet in Seattle to spread the ashes?" Jason said, interrupting his thoughts.

"Great idea," Tom said, hoping against all hope that the idea would fly with their father's lawyer.

Attorney Norman shook his head. "I'm sorry, gentlemen, but your father specifically requested that you travel together with his remains to Seattle. Any deviation from this can and will prohibit you from attaining the sealed envelope."

There was a long pause, the room blanketed in a heavy silence. *Son of a bitch,* Tom thought, *this couldn't have come at a worse time.* He turned to Jason, who was already looking at him. "What do you say?" he asked, already cursing his inability to curb his curiosity.

Jason shook his head in disgust. "The last thing I want to do is to go on some stupid road trip with you."

"Trust me, that's a mutual feeling," Tom shot back.

"But I don't think we have a choice," Jason added. "Our fucked-up father wants to play one last game with us, so to hell with it—let's play."

This is insane, but he's right, Tom thought. With a single nod, Tom stood. "Okay, let's have the ashes then," he told the lawyer.

The attorney shook his head. "I don't have them. They're currently at a funeral home in Salem."

"Salem?" Tom squeaked, unhappy that his tone betrayed his distress.

"That's right. You have to take custody of your father's remains from the Buffington Funeral Home in Salem, Massachusetts."

"You must be shitting me." Jason said.

The attorney smirked. "I shit you not," he said, throwing the letter onto his desk.

Salem? Tom repeated in his head. *Just when I thought Pop couldn't be a bigger prick . . .* The migraine knocked even harder from the inside of his skull, making him feel nauseous. Amid the pain, his synapses fired wildly, considering all this would mean: *I'll have to take bereavement leave from school and find someone to cover my classes. I should probably double my treatment with Dr. Baxter tomorrow. And what about Caleb and Caroline?* he asked himself, quickly deciding, *They'll be fine without me for a few days.* Then he pictured his wife's face. *And Carmen, she'll be fine without me for a lot longer than that.* The nausea increased. *Screw her.*

"Are we done here?" Jason asked, obviously itching to leave.

The lawyer nodded. "I'll need proof in the form of a video or a series of photos that you've deposited your father's remains where he wished. Once I have that, the letter's all yours."

"How wonderful," Jason said sarcastically. He stood, turned on his heels, and headed for the door.

Tom also got to his feet. He looked at the lawyer and, trying to ignore his physical discomfort, he smiled. "Don't mind him," he said, shrugging. "That imbecile is exactly what our father trained him to be."

Tom stepped into the parking lot to find Jason waiting for him by their vehicles.

"Just so you know, we're not taking my car on this trip from hell," Tom called out before he even reached him. *Ughhh . . .* he thought, his rotten tooth threatening to drop him to the pavement.

"Well, we're not putting the miles on my truck either."

"Oh, is that your pick 'em up truck right there?" Tom said, adding a southern twang to his tone. "How redneck of you."

Jason took a quick step toward Tom, causing him to recoil just as swiftly. "Sorry," Jason said, grinning. "It's an old habit, I guess. You open your mouth, shit comes out, and all I want to do is shove it right back in."

Tom locked onto his brother's steel blue eyes, trying to maintain his best poker face. "You haven't changed one bit," he said, hardly referring to the man's physical appearance. *Tub of shit,* Tom repeated in his head, taking stock of his estranged brother. Once muscular, Jason was now heavyset. Beneath the dirty blonde hair, he wore a giant chip on his shoulder like some hard-earned trophy. Although there was no sign he was still smoking, the cancer sticks had left him with a rasp that also added to his rough persona. *Maybe he's not such a tough guy*, Tom wondered. *Maybe the whole thing's just some big act.*

"And for whatever it's worth, neither have you," Jason said, looking back at both vehicles. "We'll go halves on a rental then. And I'm driving."

"I don't think *tho*," Tom countered.

"Why are you talking funny?" Jason asked. "You always had a bit of a lisp, but . . ."

"I need to get a tooth repaired," Tom explained, figuring it was easier to tell the truth. "If you think I'm riding shotgun the entire way cross-country then you're crazier than you look."

Jason nodded. "Fine. We'll get the rental car, but we're switching off every eight hours . . ."

"Four hours," Tom interrupted.

"Whatever," Jason said, staring at him. "We'll switch off every four hours or . . ."

"Or?"

"Or I'm not going on this asinine trip and the mouthpiece can burn that envelope and keep those ashes, too."

"Fine," Tom said, fighting through the nauseating tooth pain. "Let's take a few days to get our affairs in order and . . ."

"Affairs?" Jason echoed, snickering. "Now there's an adult word, huh?"

"Well, if anyone should know about affairs . . ."

"After all these years, you still have it all wrong—*traitor*."

Tom winced at the label, trying to act like it had no effect on him. "We'll meet back here on Wednesday to get started," he finished, feeling his face throb. *After I see Dr. Baxter, I need to get into the dentist's office to get this tooth filled . . . or pulled*, he thought, *and it may not hurt to bring some painkillers on this God-awful trip.* "Traveling through the weekend might afford us a clearer road to make better time."

"Fine," Jason agreed, "I'll pick up the rental for Wednesday." He became lost in thought for a moment. "I can't believe the old man's actually making us start in Salem."

35

Tom shook his head. "I can't believe any of this."

Nodding, Jason started for his truck. "See you back here on Wednesday morning at eight."

"Oh, I'm looking forward to it," Tom mumbled sarcastically.

Jason stopped dead in his tracks and spun around. "Listen, you little piece of shit, I'd rather get all my teeth pulled . . ."

". . . the ones that are left anyway," Tom said under his breath.

". . . than travel cross-country with your sorry ass," Jason finished.

"That's a mutual feeling," Tom said, compelled—as always—to get in the last word.

"Good," Jason said. "Just be here on Wednesday."

"Wouldn't miss it," Tom said, feeling like he was eight years old again.

No sooner had Jason barreled out of the parking lot than Tom started back for the funeral home. *Between this tooth and my friggin' prostate, someone should just shoot me and put me out of my misery.* His mind lingered on the thought for a moment, making his head shake. *At least it would save me a cross-country trip with Sasquatch.*

On Wednesday morning, Jason arrived with the rental car, a midnight blue SUV. Tom noticed a dent in the driver's side fender. "Why did you accept a damaged rental?" he asked.

"It was the last one they had with any leg room," Jason answered from the window. "Don't sweat it. It's documented."

Here goes nothing, Tom thought, grabbing two heavy bags from the trunk of his car. As he struggled to lock the faded BMW while lugging the bags to the rental, he spotted Jason grinning at him—amused and unwilling to help. *Douchebag!* After slamming the trunk closed, he slid into the passenger's side of the rental—with two road maps in hand.

Jason looked at him. "That's a lot of lingerie for two weeks, don't you think?"

"Two weeks?" Tom said. "It better not be." He spread out one of the maps on the dashboard.

"What the hell is that?" Jason asked.

"It's a map. They teach you all about them if you can make it to the fifth grade."

"Then you must know all about them, dummy," Jason said.

Tom's breathing became shallow. *Dummy*, he repeated in his head. It was the very nickname his father had given him growing up, the antagonizing, misrepresented label that had helped define him. He struggled to maintain his cool. "That's right, *punk*," he replied. "I do." It was the perfect volley, replying with the despised nickname Jason had been gifted with as a child.

Jason's face went flush, while his white knuckles threatened to fuse with the cracking steering wheel.

Pretending not to notice, Tom returned his attention to the map and explained, "I went to AAA and asked that they chart out our entire trip. Besides mapping out the most direct route, they highlighted the best places for us to stop and . . ."

"Put those friggin' things back in your purse," Jason said. "They're a waste of time." He threw the SUV's shifter into reverse and backed out of the parking spot. "You have no sense of direction. Never have. And besides that, I'm not letting your OCD lead us down the wrong path." He looked at the maps once more. "Just put them away," he snickered. "We have GPS, so there's no reason to use them."

"We are when I'm driving," Tom said, defiantly.

Jason put the car in drive and pulled out onto the road. "Amazing," he muttered. "You're still as anal as ever."

Tom half-shrugged. "Don't you like anal?" he asked. "You're still working at the prison, right?"

Without a reply, Jason popped a cigar into his smirking mouth.

"I hope you don't think you're going to smoke that thing on the ride," Tom said, his stomach already kicking up a plume of acid.

"Relax, lollipop. Don't worry about it." Jason bit down on the stogie, holding it firmly between his teeth. "And the day I need your permission to do anything is the day I hang myself."

Tom shook his head. "We need to discuss logistics."

"Logistics? Another big word."

"Really? Logistics is a big word for you?"

Jason grinned, clearly pleased to have slithered beneath his brother's thin skin.

"The entire trip, one way, is three thousand fifty-five miles. According to my maps, it'll take us forty-four hours and twenty minutes to get there."

"Wow, twenty whole minutes?"

Tom ignored the comment. "Given three meals a day, bathroom and fuel breaks, as well as overnight stops to sleep," he explained, "we should plan to drive at least twelve hours a day, swapping off every four hours as agreed."

"I'm not staying in any bed and breakfast," Jason said firmly.

"Which is unfortunate, considering that bed and breakfasts are usually the most comfortable and least expensive lodging."

"Not doing it."

"All told, we should get there in five or six days."

Jason pressed down on the accelerator.

Straight up Route 24 north, the SUV's wiper blades fought off an annoying drizzle while the brothers silently drove north toward Salem, Massachusetts. It was the last weekend in October, the worst time to visit the infamous tourist trap. Colored leaves of red, orange, and yellow had been nearly stripped bare from the trees; miles of evergreens and hardwood skeletons left behind to brace for another long winter.

En route, Tom called his daughter, Caroline. The call went straight to voicemail. He hung up and immediately dialed his son. Caleb's cell phone also went to voicemail. *These kids are never more than an arm's reach from their phones*, he thought, a wave of sorrow washing over him. *I'll be away for the next week or so, and neither one of them could give a shit.* Feeling vulnerable, he quickly turned his thoughts toward Salem, trying to recapture the joy it had once brought him.

"What the hell are you smiling about?" Jason asked, as they entered the tunnel beneath Boston.

Tom continued to stare out the windshield. "Remember when Pop used to take us to Salem every year around Halloween?" As kids, he and Jason loved ghost hunting—hanging around cemeteries more than baseball fields. In fact, it was one of the two things they shared in common: a deep hatred of their father and a morbid curiosity of the paranormal.

"That was a lifetime ago," Jason grunted.

"It was," Tom admitted, "but the memories are still there." For whatever reason, he felt sorry he'd shared the thought.

Jason shifted uneasily in the driver's seat. "Yeah, they are," he agreed, leaving it at that.

"When we were kids, I used to be obsessed with Salem and why it was so famous," Tom added, as if talking to himself.

"I remember."

While Jason drove, Tom daydreamed about the trials and tragedies of 1692, which had brought great notoriety in New England to things that went bump in the night. He couldn't believe all the details he still remembered and felt the same pang of excitement he felt as a kid. "By all accounts," he recalled aloud, "tensions had been building for a few years prior to the witch trials. Native Americans attacked randomly, causing most colonists to fear for their lives. Along with fatally cold winters, a smallpox epidemic had also been circulating for over ten years. To top it off, Puritans embraced community and were incredibly suspicious of outsiders. These, along with their strong superstitions, made Salem villagers believe they'd been abandoned by God."

Jason looked at him like he'd grown a second head.

"Two young girls, Betty Parris and Abigail Williams, started playing with magic. After seeing a coffin in an improvised crystal ball, each one of them fell ill. At that time, children were seen and not heard, so the afflicted girls . . ."

"Please tell me you're fucking joking?" Jason snapped. "You're actually going to regurgitate some bullshit you remember from high school?"

"Bullshit?" Tom repeated, his face burning red. "History's bullshit?"

"Listen, cut the crap. We both know you're smart. There's no need for you to keep trying to prove it." Jason snickered. "Save it for those who don't know you, because you sure as hell ain't impressing me."

"I ain't, huh?" Tom said, a deep-rooted rage shooting to the surface.

Jason shook his head. "Besides, I know the stories."

"You don't know anything," Tom hissed. "You never have." He matched his brother's snicker. "You're only as smart as the last person you've talked to, Jason. That's all you've ever been."

"Shut your fucking mouth before I shut it for you," Jason barked. "And trust me, I'm okay with it either way."

Tom shook his head. "It's amazing. All these years later and nothing's changed. You did the same thing when we were kids, trying to bully me any time you could." He took a deep breath. "You're still a *punk*."

"I hate that word," Jason hissed, looking sideways. "Only one other person ever called me a punk . . ." He grinned. "Last I heard, his jaw eventually healed."

"Forever the bully," Tom mumbled.

It took a few moments until Jason nodded. "When being bigger and tougher is the only thing you have, it's what you use, *dummy*."

Tom couldn't believe it. He was a tenured college professor who sat on a half-dozen committees, making decisions for the betterment of his community. He held memberships at three prestigious clubs and read at least seventy books a year. He was fluent in French, was learning Vietnamese, but when brought together with his meat-headed brother he was suddenly reduced to a frustrated, inarticulate sixth grader who had absolutely no command over his own feelings, thoughts, or tongue. He just couldn't find the words fast enough; it was as though they got trapped behind some goiter in his throat. *And this never happens with anyone else*, he thought, *ever*. Normally, his cheetah-like thoughts and sharp-clawed tongue were hulking in the shadows, waiting to pounce on anything or anyone that even posed an intellectual challenge to him.

"Punk," he repeated in what sounded like a strained whisper.

"Fuck you," Jason yelled; it was the roar of a lion, disarming Tom for a split second and temporarily paralyzing him with fear.

"Fuck you too," Tom finally managed, as if using a stick to fend off a shotgun.

There was nothing more to say—it was simple and to the point—precisely what they were both feeling.

"You're not that smart," Jason said under his breath, eventually breaking the silence.

"And you're not that honorable," Tom countered, sizing up his brother like he was looking into the seat of a Porta John. "It's amazing how much you offend me," he snarled. *And you're polluting my air space.*

"You don't even know me," Jason hissed.

"True," Tom admitted, "and I don't want to."

"That's a two-way street, dummy," Jason lashed out.

"That's fine with me, punk," Tom hissed and, once again, they were little boys.

Jason bristled again at the old insult, that one simple word turning his face to stone. "Fuck you, dummy," he repeated.

"Clever comeback, Einstein," Tom said.

Jason's white knuckles threatened to snap the steering wheel in half. "Open your mouth again and you'll be eating lunch through a straw, I swear it!" He wiped the spit from his angry mouth.

Shut up, Tom told himself, *you've already pushed a button that can't be unpushed.* He looked sideways at his brother and swallowed hard. *Unless you want to meet the Incredible Hulk, just shut up.*

A thick silence accompanied them through the better part of Massachusetts. *That's fine by me,* Tom thought. The quiet afforded him the time to return to his train of thought—before he'd been so rudely interrupted.

When Tom's distant mind returned to the present, he realized, *I really have to piss.* Unwilling to ask his sulking brother to stop, he peered out the windshield. The drizzle had stopped. As they entered Salem, he took it all in. Brick and cobblestone sidewalks, arranged in a herringbone design, were lined with ancient oak trees. Tom imagined that the narrow lanes looked much like they did in the seventeenth century, when Salem was rocked by hysteria and hate; accusations of devil worship and witchcraft. Still, the town felt quaint, its front doors and weathered stoops sitting two steps from the glistening street.

Having already made arrangements to pick up the ashes the following morning, Jason steered a hard right from Washington Square South into a back alley called Union Street. Tom gazed skyward. The Hawthorne Hotel was six well-kept stories of comfort and the hospitality of yesteryear. Wrought iron fire escapes and streetlamps adorned the exterior. *It'll be nice to check into separate rooms and get away from this donkey,* he thought.

Although it opened in July of 1925, the Hawthorne Hotel had been beautifully preserved, earning its rightful place among the nation's grandest hotels. Salem's famous sights were all within a few short blocks—museums, churches, and other historical landmarks reflecting the town's eerie past were only a hop, skip, and a scream away. Tom stepped out of the SUV and drew in a deep breath. *If Salem's the witch-hunting capital of the world,* he thought, *then the Hawthorne Hotel's the Halloween capital of America.* Here, hordes of tourists celebrated everything that sent shivers up the spine. In spite of his aching bladder, he smiled.

Jason looked like he was going to toss over the keys but pocketed them instead. "Let's meet back here at eight tomorrow morning," he said.

"Are you heading out to check out the town?" Tom asked without thinking.

Jason shook his head. "I couldn't care less about this friggin' place," he groaned.

"I wasn't asking you to go out. I was just . . ."

Jason disappeared into the hotel without another word.

"Fine by me, Cro-Magnon man," Tom muttered to no one. He grabbed his bags from the trunk. "Who needs you?"

Walking past Nathaniel's Restaurant and an art gallery on the corner of Washington and Essex—the restaurant named after Salem's favorite son, author Nathaniel Hawthorne—Tom stepped inside the hotel and hurried for the men's room. After relieving himself, he returned to the lobby, where he took it all in. *Magnificent*, he thought. The foyer was magazine-perfect with its cluttered bookshelves, overstuffed chairs, beveled mirrors, and elegant antique lamps accented in brass. Green plants and detailed cream moldings offset the colors of cherrywood and gold leaf. Persian throw rugs led to a pair of nostalgic elevators. On the right, a gold-encased mailbox betrayed the hotel's age. *Just magnificent.*

After checking in and leaving his luggage with the bellboy, Tom took a closer look around. Among the public rooms: the Tavern on the Green, the hotel's pub, offered an open fire as a nice retreat; a library beneath street level boasted itself as the perfect meeting place; while the Grand Ballroom was a sight all its own—extravagantly decorated for the night's costume ball. Three gorgeous chandeliers hanging from twenty-foot vaulted ceilings lit fifty round tables and a portable dance floor. Windows, fifteen feet high, were decorated in silk valences of beige and cream. Tom glanced out to see that Salem Common Park was only a stone's throw away.

On the second floor, a labyrinth of winding corridors led to the Pickman Room and other colonial hideaways. It was like stepping into a time long forgotten where life remained untouched by progress and its technology. *No wonder Nathaniel Hawthorne was so prolific,* he thought. *Inspiration can be found everywhere here.*

Tom finally settled into a room filled with fine oak furnishings, a four-poster bed, and New England antiques. After getting cleaned up, he took his medication. An hour later, he ventured off to rediscover the haunted world he'd cherished as a boy.

As Tom walked, the unique atmosphere of Salem during Halloween seeped into his bones. Some tourists, with painted faces, giggled nervously at the sights. The more serious, however, wore gothic attire and had clearly traveled north to embrace the dark side. Either way, it was the land of ghouls and goblins where people made their imaginations come to life. Salem was the type of place that could spook a person from their dreams, where the most terrifying nightmares could become reality—as they did back in 1692. He forged on.

One block down, a sign read: *Crow Haven Corner—Salem's First Witch Shop & Purveyor to Witches around the World.* It was the most famous witch shop in all of Salem, and the competing scents of many strange aromas nearly bowled Tom over. While other shoppers purchased everything from mother's wort to frankincense, Tom purchased a plastic baggie of powdered mercury. The label claimed benefits toward imagination and writing composition. *I can use all the help I can get with my poetry these days,* he thought, stepping out of the shop to get some air.

Surrounding yards were bordered in black wrought iron fences, their sharp stakes warning off any unwelcomed visitors. Small English gardens were carefully tended. Even the weeds appeared intentional. The colonial houses, with their small windows, offered a warm feeling of home. Tom was inhaling it all when a door swung open and his hulking brother stepped out of one of the shops. Whether Jason didn't see him or pretended not to, he walked right past him without so much as a look. *It's amazing how much I still despise him, playing me for such a pathetic fool like that,* Tom thought, angry with himself for his brother still having any impact on him at all.

Samantha's costume shop on Essex was the best in town. Tom admired a turn-of-the-century poet's costume, while some hot-looking woman in her mid-thirties paid for a wench's dress. *It looks like someone's in for a fun night,* he thought, recalling when Carmen used to surprise him with similar delights. *But those times are long gone for me,* he sadly realized.

Just up the block, he stepped into the Derby Square Book Store. He'd just started browsing when two words echoed from his belly into his head: *I'm hungry.*

As he walked out, an old lady hobbled in hanging on to the arm of a teenage boy. "Take your time, Brian," she said. "I'm not a young chick anymore."

"Yets, Mama," the lanky kid said.

Although Tom could see that the boy was cognitively impaired, what struck him most was the deep bond shared between the peculiar pair. *What I wouldn't give to have that with my children,* he thought.

Red's Sandwich Shop on Central Street had once been The London Coffee House, a meeting place for the Patriots before the American Revolution, and still served as a landmark. Tom teetered between the taco salad and the lobster ravioli in a spinach cream sauce. *Pasta, it is,* he thought. The meal was rich, but the bill was cheap—recharging his energy level back to full.

One street up, he paused in front of Salem's old police station and jail. An elderly photographer was snapping away when he looked up from his camera and smiled at Tom. "They say if you take photos of this place, you'll be able to see orbs hovering behind those rusty bars when you develop the pictures." He paused for effect. "They say the spirits of the damned are still imprisoned behind these hoary walls."

"I'm sure they are," Tom said, skeptically, and continued walking. Halfway down the sidewalk, though, he stopped to take a few pictures with his cell phone. *I've got to take another leak*, he thought and began looking for a public bathroom.

After relieving himself, he arrived at The Burying Point, the oldest cemetery in the city. From *Mayflower* passengers to the justices of the witchcraft court, many of the famous and infamous rested beneath its lumpy sod. Tom read several faded tombstone inscriptions until locating the one that brought his neck hairs to attention: *I am innocent of such wickedness.* As he started to walk out of the eerie sacred grounds, he spotted a sign: *Open dawn til dusk. No gravestone rubbings.* His mind instantly returned to his childhood, when he'd been scared out of his wits—in this very same place.

It all began as a thrill-seeking joke, Tom and Jason, along with Mike, their half-witted friend, roaming the cemeteries at night in search of the living dead. The Burying Point was the creepiest cemetery in the city and, as such, the source of some legendary stories of multiple ghost sightings. There couldn't have been a more perfect night for a spine-tingling scare.

Strolling through the fields of granite, young Tom fumbled with his tracing paper and charcoal stick, stopping at every other headstone to get the perfect imprint. Most of the stones were cracked and faded, badly decayed from the decades of harsh rains and battering winds. There were others, however, that had endured terrible desecration, having either been defaced or toppled during senseless acts of vandalism. The graveyard was split into two sections. The old section was located at the front of the grounds, with the recently departed planted toward the rear. For a while, the boys lingered in the front. It promised more gooseflesh.

"Get off my land," an angry voice hissed in the distance.

Tom leapt to his feet and dropped his artwork all over the black ground. "Stop it," he yelled at Jason. "You almost gave me a heart attack!"

Jason's mouth hung open, but he said nothing.

Turning his suspicions toward Mike, Tom discovered that his friend's eyes were as big as MoonPies. Mike was obviously using them to scan the area, and he was no longer laughing. Every hair on Tom's body turned to spikes.

"Don't make me come out there," the disembodied voice called again. This time it was closer and much meaner.

Mike screamed. Tom tried to match it but couldn't. All three boys were paralyzed with fear.

Suddenly, the invisible entity let out a shrieking laugh.

Fighting through the freezing numbness of shock, Tom took off at a sprint. Looking back, he saw Jason grabbing as many papers as he could before beating him and Mike out to the street. They were a full block and a half from the cemetery before a word was spoken.

"Tell me we didn't just . . ." Jason started to ask.

Tom was trembling so badly he could hardly speak. He nodded and kept nodding, trying to reclaim his stolen breath. He opened his mouth to say something but nothing came out. He couldn't even think. The brief experience was so unnerving, so unsettling that he couldn't decide whether it was reality or merely their wild imaginations.

Without a word, Mike high-tailed it out of there.

"Mike!" Jason yelled after him, but the petrified boy kept running—never once looking back.

Tom and Jason tried to rationalize in whispers. "Something's not right with this," Jason said, taking a knee on the sidewalk. "I think somebody's playing with us."

Tom had finally recovered the air he'd lost in his lungs. "It's not like . . . like we can tell anybody," he stammered. "Who would believe us?"

Jason shook his head. "This is bullshit, Tommy," he blurted. "I'm going back." He stood and started marching down the sidewalk.

Still perplexed by the disturbing experience, Tom's heart and mind were instantly thrown into mortal combat. Like his older brother, he was attracted to the mystery of the supernatural. But the thought of a confrontation with some angry apparition terrified him. *Go with Jason*, he screamed in his head and, one deep breath later, he was able to coax his legs to start moving.

As the anxiety levels turned Tom's goose bumps into sandpaper, he discovered his brother hunched down in some bushes just outside the cemetery gates.

"Shhhh," Jason whispered, his index finger pressed to his smirking lips. He pointed toward something with his other hand.

In the distance, an old man—presumably the cemetery's groundskeeper—was half-concealed behind a large elm tree, scaring away a new band of thrill-seekers.

Jason stood and looked at Tom. "So you came back," he said, impressed.

Tom nodded, never feeling more proud about anything in his young life.

"I told you there's no such thing as monsters," Jason said, laughing.

"Except for Dad," Tom said, still overjoyed he'd found a fraction of his brother's courage to return to Jason's side.

Jason nodded. "True. Except for Dad."

As Tom returned to the present and left the decrepit cemetery, he decided that besides author Nathaniel Hawthorne, his favorite Salem son was Giles Corey. The man had been accused of practicing witchcraft and was subsequently pressed to death beneath a pile of stones on September 16, 1692. The jailer of that time had jammed Giles Corey's swollen tongue back into his mouth with a walking stick before asking for the man's final words. "More weight," Corey had replied.

Many of the accused back then were weighted down and placed in water, Tom recalled. *If they floated, then they were a witch and would be hanged. If they sank, then they were free from the conviction.* He shook his head. *Either way, they were condemned to a horrible death.*

Horse-drawn carriages and vendors peddling their goods filled Salem's bustling streets near the Pickering Wharf. Boris Karloff's Witch's Mansion, Terror on the Wharf, and Salem's Museum of Myths and Monsters beckoned the brave at heart. These fake haunted houses charged top dollar to have college kids dressed in torn jackets and rubber masks leap out at you and scream loud enough to jumpstart your heart. Salem had become a tourist trap where trinkets and souvenirs helped create visions of bubbling cauldrons and diabolical spells. Tom was filled with a sense of simple joy, watching the herds of people. The wide eyes of children absorbed each detail, while the natural suspicions of their parents kept them close. *I love this place,* he thought, laughing to himself. For too many reasons to count—most of which seemed foolish at the moment—it had been years since he'd been to the haunted city. *It's already the most fun I've had since I can remember,* he thought.

As an aspiring poet, Tom found Nathaniel Hawthorne's *House of the Seven Gables* to be breathtaking. He gawked at the place and, when he could gain control over his jaw muscles, he recited a passage from the famous author in his head. *Half-way down the by-street of one of our New England towns, stands a rusty wooden house, with seven acutely peaked gables, facing towards various points of the compass, and a huge, clustered chimney in the midst.*

One mile later, Tom arrived back at Salem Common Park. He approached the statue of the city's founder, Roger Conant. In his conservative puritan dress, the settler's dead and distant eyes stared sternly from beneath the brim of a pilgrim's hat. He was faded and weathered from a century of battering winds and punishing New England winters. He'd clearly stood in this very spot for far too long, guarding the park before him.

And he's paid dearly for it, Tom thought. The statue's face was pock marked, his flowing cape oxidized to green.

There was an unusual nip in the air. A soft but consistent wind howled through the clusters of shedding trees that populated the sparse grounds. Tom looked around, thinking, *I can't believe this place is so abandoned.* Suddenly, it hit him. *Everyone's at the hotel's costume ball.* It was the most famous in the world. *So much for getting a good night's sleep*, he told himself.

Beneath the frugal light of a half-moon—and an avenue of sturdy oak trees that danced in the late autumn wind—Tom strolled through the park. In the distance, he swore he spotted his brother's massive silhouette sitting on a park bench. He walked a few feet more to be sure. *What a piece of work*, he thought about his brother. *You couldn't care less about this place, huh?* He studied Jason's large outline. *After all these years, you're still just an uncultured gorilla.* Shaking his head, Tom turned his back on the unfriendly shadow. *I need a drink*, he told himself, *and another piss.*

chapter 3

IN THE MORNING, with a pounding head and cottonmouth—
the result of too many vodka and tonics—Jason awoke. It took
some time for reality to register. *I'm in a friggin' hotel room*, he
thought, looking around. "On some bullshit quest to . . ." He
stopped. Even his whisper sounded like a scream.

After getting dressed, he hustled to get behind the wheel
of the SUV.

"I thought I was driving today," Tom said, approaching
the driver's side door.

"The trip starts today. I got the first leg," Jason said, his
own voice making his head feel heavier. "Just get in," he said,
adding, *you useless toad*—but only in his throbbing head.

As they drove in silence to Buffington Funeral Home
across town, Jason could feel the dead weight in the passenger's seat looking at him, smirking over his physical discomfort. *I hope you have another tooth that starts aching*, he thought,
returning the smirk.

"You feeling okay?" Tom asked.

Jason shook his head, slightly. "Recovery time isn't what
it used to be," he admitted, feeling like a wrecking ball had
kissed him on the forehead.

"I remember when I could—"Tom started.

"I can do everything I used to do," Jason interrupted defensively. "But just once," he added, grinning.

"Sure . . . and a lot slower."

Buffington Funeral Home was very quiet and just as clean. As Jason walked, he noticed that the carpet was so thick it gave a slight bounce to each step. For whatever reason, he found it amusing. Past one parlor—empty of any caskets— and then another, he led Tom to the end of the hall before they reached the door marked *Director's Office.*

"Come in," a muffled voice called out, answering his knock. Jason threw open the door and stepped in. A scarecrow of a man with a pencil-thin moustache stood up from behind an antique maple desk and extended his hand.

Tom shook the man's hand before gesturing toward Jason with a tilt of his head. "We're the Prendergasts."

"Of course, of course," the scarecrow said, wiping his hand on his pants leg. "If you'll excuse me for a moment, I'll retrieve your father's remains." He scurried out of the room.

While the undertaker was away, an awkward silence took hold. *This is going to be a long week,* Jason thought, trying to sit still in the straight back chair. He looked at Tom. His little brother's bright eyes had long been extinguished. *It looks like life's ground him down a bit too,* he surmised. Tom's face was taut, as though he'd had some work done. *Which figures,* Jason thought. *Always the narcissist.* Tall and fit, Tom wore glasses with frames that were clearly selected to betray his intellect. Beneath the salt-and-pepper hair, although he appeared tired, his chiseled features allowed him to remain handsome. Jason took a few deep breaths, trying to ease his hangover. He glanced at Tom again. *I'd better accept the fact that I'm basically traveling alone.*

Tom sighed a few times, shaking his head.

He's probably thinking the same thing I am, he thought, laughing to himself, *except he's so animated, he should come with his own theme song.*

Too much time had passed before the mortician returned to the room, holding a plain wooden box. While he checked Tom's identification and requested a sign-off—which Tom was happy to provide—Jason couldn't help but stare at the box. With no engravings or shiny placard, it was nothing more than a lackluster walnut box. *Cheap and simple*, he thought, *appropriate enough for the life the old man lived.*

While Jason completed a different piece of documentation, the funeral director lifted the wooden box and extended it toward Tom.

"Ummm . . ." Tom said, balking. While his wide eyes filled with fear, he refused to accept the box.

What a sissy, Jason thought, snatching the box out of the man's manicured fingers. "No need to fear the old man anymore, little brother," he told Tom, before shaking the square box up and down a few times. Amused by his brother's bleached-white face, he half-shrugged. "Feels like laundry detergent to me," he added, shaking it hard again. "The old man doesn't weigh more than five or six pounds now." He shook it one more time and grinned. "Even you could take him in a fight now, Tom."

The undertaker was clearly mortified.

Jason looked at him. "I must seem crude," he told the man, "but our father was a grade-A prick." He couldn't help it; his mind immediately returned to one of the countless nightmares he'd been forced to live through as the child of a masochist.

Jason and Tommy were wrestling when the old man staggered into the living room. They immediately stopped the horseplay. Expecting to get yelled at or even slapped upside the head, Jason was surprised when Pop grinned and took a seat in his ratty recliner instead. "Teaching him how to fight, huh?" he asked.

Oh no, Jason thought, already sensing this was going to end badly. He shrugged. "We're just messing around, Dad."

Cracking open a fresh beer, his father took a sip before continuing. "It's your job to teach your brother to be a man, you know . . . not just mine." He settled back into his chair and took a long draw off his beer. "Go on then," he said, "and teach Sally, here, how to protect himself."

Tom's face turned white, as though the old man had just doused it with bleach.

"But Dad . . ." Jason started.

"Do it!" the man screamed, nearly catapulting himself from the chair—spilling his beer as he did, making him even angrier. "I want you to show Tommy what it feels like to be in a real fight. This way, he won't be so damned scared when some punk takes him on."

Jason didn't want to do it; the last thing in the world he wanted to do was hurt his little brother. But knowing there was no choice, he turned to Tom and shoved him to the floor.

"Get up and fight!" the old man screamed.

Tom lay there in shock before getting to his knees; tears were starting to roll down his cheeks, landing on his quivering lips.

"Punch him in the face," the old man told Jason.

"What?" Jason gasped.

"You heard me, punk," he said, sliding to the edge of his recliner. "Either you do it, or I will." He took another sip of beer. "And I won't go so easy on him," he promised.

"But . . . but . . ."

Putting his beer can on the floor, the drunkard placed both hands on the chair's armrests, preparing to get up.

With the sharp instincts of a protective older brother, Jason threw a jab that landed straight on Tom's cheek, collapsing him like an abandoned puppet.

"Get up and fight!" the old man screamed at Tom.

Tom got to his knees again, his eyes now filled with such pain that it tore Jason's heart in two. Surprising everyone, Tom punched Jason back, landing a decent shot square on the mouth and drawing blood. Jason couldn't decide if he was more surprised or happy his brother did it.

Clapping his hands together once, the old man sat back and watched the remainder of the struggle like he was at the Friday night fights.

While Jason slapped his younger brother, throwing the occasional punch—as softly as possible but enough to keep their maniac father out of the fray—Tom flailed his arms, screaming in rage and crying out in a terrible mix of frustration and pain.

A minute or two went by before Pop downed the rest of his beer and got up. "Lilies," he groaned, having already grown bored of the spectacle.

For a while, Jason and Tom lay on the floor—both bloodied and wheezing.

"I'm sorry, Tommy," Jason whispered. "But if I didn't hit you, then he . . ."

"I know, Jason," Tommy said between sobs. "I know."

Jason returned to the present to see Tom staring at the box, his brother's eyes betraying the unspeakable terrors of a young boy.

Tom still fears Pop, Jason thought, *and it doesn't matter whether the old man's flesh and bone or ashes.* Stuart Prendergast had penetrated his brother's subconscious, where a scared eight-year-old boy still dwelled. Jason gave the box another good shake. *After all those years of vulgar insults and terrible beatings, the monster's been reduced to a half-dozen pounds of ash,* he thought, his mind trying to wrap itself around the permanence of it.

Speechless, Tom continued to stare at the box of ashes.

Let's just get this over with, Jason thought and, tucking the brown box under his arm, he headed for the door. "Let's go," he barked.

Tom followed him as far as the bathroom, where he disappeared.

At the rental, Jason tossed the wooden box onto the backseat. Tom shot him a look of disgust but never commented. "There's no way I'm holding him in my lap the whole trip," Jason said. "But be my guest."

They both climbed into the SUV.

Tom shook his head. "I think I'll pass." He took out a map and struggled to spread it out.

"What the hell do you think you're doing?"

"Plotting out our route," Tom answered, ignoring Jason's scowl.

"I already told you, we have a GPS," he said. "We could even plot our route on one of our cell phones." He shook his head. "The technology's so easy now that even you could use it."

"Map reading is a lost art form," Tom said, running his index finger across the yellow highlighted line.

"Don't be a mama's boy," Jason said.

"I wouldn't know how," Tom fired back, turning to face his brother. "We would have had to have had a mother for that to be possible." He shook his head. "No such luck on that one."

"You got me there," Jason said sadly. "No such luck is right."

Tom returned to his map. "It looks like the best route to take is I-90, the turnpike," he said, "and shoot right across Massachusetts into New York."

"Sounds good to me," Jason said, avoiding further debate that would only make his head feel worse. *Get along to go along*, he decided. *Besides, there's no way in hell we're taking the turnpike.*

Obviously satisfied, Tom folded up the map and eased back into his seat. As Jason turned onto the road, he looked at his brother again. *Of all the brothers in the world*, he thought, *I ended up with a sniveling little weasel. Go figure.*

They were barreling south when Tom turned the radio knob to the NPR station.

Jason reached over and changed it back to the country music station. Adjusting the unlit cigar in his mouth, he struggled not to light it. The frustration of spending time with Tom was already causing the temptation to feel overwhelming. *Just consider it a test of will*, he told himself, rolling the stogie until it sat comfortably in the opposite corner of his frown. *I promised my girl I'd quit, and I haven't broken a promise to her yet.*

Tom waited a minute or two before turning the knob again.

"Are you fucking kidding me?" Jason snapped, his blood pressure instantly catapulted into the stratosphere, making the veins in his neck pulsate.

"I need to stay informed," Tom said.

"Then buy a newspaper," Jason replied, his jaws locked down on the stogie—threatening to chomp it in half. "There's too much bad news in the world, and I get enough of it every day at work."

"Well, I hate country music."

Every time Jason talked to his brother, it was like pressing *play* on some annoying recording he didn't want to hear. "Why?" he asked. "At least you know what to expect with country music." He took a deep breath, trying to calm himself. "My wife's run off; my truck's broke down; my dog's up and died."

Surprisingly, Tom laughed. "I'm sorry," he said, "but I won't be able to listen to country and western the entire trip."

Jason thought about it. "How 'bout this then, whoever's behind the wheel controls the radio. The passenger can either get some sleep or suffer through it."

Tom nodded. "Fine, but the volume has to be set at four, no matter what station is on. Okay?"

Oh, dear God, Jason thought, *he's still a negotiator too*— remembering when they'd traded baseball cards under the shade of a weeping willow tree all those years ago. "Fine," Jason agreed, checking the next road sign. They'd already made progress.

While the twang of country music softly filled the cabin of the SUV, Tom called his daughter, trying unsuccessfully to gain some privacy through a turned torso and muffled voice. "Caroline, it's Dad. I've been trying to call you. I've even texted you a few times, but you haven't returned my calls or texts. I hope there's nothing wrong. Call me, please." He hung up and immediately called his son. "Caleb, it's Dad. I'm already on the road. I've been trying to reach you. Please call me back as soon as you receive this. I'm waiting on your call." With a heavy sigh, he hung up.

Looks like the kids don't want anything to do with him either, Jason thought. He looked at his brother, whose face showed signs of pain . . . *which really stinks.* And then it donned on him. *He hasn't called Carmen.* Jason cleared his throat. "So are you going to have to check in with the kids every few hours?" he asked, commencing his probe.

"I wish," Tom said, staring straight ahead. He shook his sorrowful head. "Nope, those days are done. They won't even know I'm gone until they need money."

Damn, Jason thought, his brother's honesty taking him aback. "Well, that sucks," he said. "What about Carmen?" he asked, refusing to walk on eggshells around a sore subject that was not his fault. "No call home to her?"

Tom stared out the passenger side window for a moment before shaking his head. "She's busy right now," he mumbled, still avoiding any eye contact. "She's got a lot going on."

Jason studied his brother's profile. *That's bullshit,* he thought.

"What about you?" Tom asked, obviously changing the subject. "No girlfriends to call?"

"Nope. I'm in between failed relationships right now." He grinned. "There's just Miranda, but she's drowning in wedding plans. I'm sure I'll hear from her before too long." He shrugged. "I'm learning that weddings cost a lot of money."

Tom's head snapped sideways. "Miranda's getting married?" he exclaimed, his tone changing from solemn to excited.

"Yeah, and I think her mother's behind a lot of her ideas for the wedding. It's going to cost me half my retirement." He took a deep breath and exhaled just as deeply. "Janice is brutal with Miranda. She feeds on the poor kid's time like a vulture ravaging a fresh carcass."

Tom nodded. "How poetic."

"Screw you," Jason barked, instinctively feeling both insulted and defensive.

"It was a compliment," Tom said, being sincere.

"If that's your idea of a compliment, then you should keep them to yourself," Jason said, unsure how to recover from his outburst.

"Not a problem," Tom said, closing his eyes for a few minutes.

Perfect timing, Jason thought, taking the exit to I-95 South, toward Providence, Rhode Island.

They were halfway into the turn when Tom opened his eyes and began craning his neck, searching for a road sign. "What the hell are you doing?" he asked. "The turnpike's the quickest way."

"According to the GPS, 95's our best bet right now," Jason lied nonchalantly. "We can cut through Providence and pick up 80 in Connecticut. Trust me, between the new construction and traffic on the pike, we'll make better time on 95." He grinned. "Besides, there's more to see along the way."

"To hell with the scenery," Tom said, clearly frustrated. "I just want to get there the quickest way we can."

"The way the crow flies, I get it," Jason said.

Tom glared at him, unconvinced.

"Go to sleep," he said. "That's the quickest way."

Tom continued to stare.

"Go ahead," Jason said, passing the *Welcome to Rhode Island* sign, "I'll wake you up in Seattle."

"I wish," Tom said.

"Me too," he said, adding the word *hamster* in his mind.

Shaking his head, Tom closed his eyes again. "Get off at the next exit," he said. "I need to use the bathroom."

"You can't hold it?" Jason asked. "What are you, five years old?"

"Take the next exit," Tom repeated, his eyes still shut.

Jason pulled the cigar from his mouth and looked at it. *Don't friggin' light it*, he told himself. *You promised Miranda.*

One bathroom break, a full tank of gas, and a handful of scratch tickets later, they passed the big blue bug, Ocean State Theatre Company and Los Andes Restaurant on their way through the land of quahogs and coffee milk. *Nearly two states down,* Jason thought, *and a whole damn country to go.* He bit down hard on the soggy cigar, speeding toward the Constitution State.

They weren't five exits into Connecticut when Jason thought, *I should have gone to the bathroom too.* The hangover had dropped from his head all the way down to his worn digestive system. He couldn't hold it in any longer and farted. *Oh my God,* he thought, nearly choking on his own stink. He looked at his brother and waited—struggling not to laugh.

Tom's eyes suddenly flew open and his body sat up erect. For a second, his furrowed brow searched for an answer—and then he gagged. "You rotten bastard," he said, fumbling to find the power window button. "I think you got some in my mouth."

Jason laughed hard. "Now that's the language I want to hear from you." He choked on his own laughter. "At what point does a gas become a liquid?"

"You're so repulsive."

"Another big word," Jason teased. "How many points do you get for that one?"

"You're so nasty," Tom countered, his face hanging outside the window like a Labrador retriever's, his eyes watering in the cold wind.

"Sorry," Jason said, grinning. "I was just trying to slip some gas past a solid. We should probably stop soon."

60

"Before you shit your pants?" Tom asked.

Jason shrugged. "Tough to tell," he said. "That ship might have already sailed."

"So nasty," Tom repeated.

"The good news is I have to make one quick stop in Connecticut anyway," Jason said, "to make a deposit."

"You're kidding, right? I don't want to extend—"

"Listen," Jason interrupted, the funny moment evaporating between them. "I don't want to be around you either. But I need to make a stop."

Tom pulled out his map and studied it.

Here goes nothing, Jason thought, as he turned on the directional, taking exit 92 toward the Foxwoods Casino.

As they drove deeper into the woods of Mashantucket, Connecticut, Tom looked at him from the passenger seat—contempt oozing from his retinas.

He looks just like Dad, Jason thought. He looked back in the rearview mirror—*as if the man in the wooden box could go anywhere.*

"I knew it!" Tom squealed, his face turning crimson. "You said you needed to make a deposit."

Jason shrugged. "It'll probably be more like a payment than a deposit," he said, trying not to laugh.

"What the . . ."

"Relax," Jason interrupted. "We needed to stop for lunch anyway." He checked his watch. "We'll be back on the road in two hours."

"Two hours?" Tom repeated, his voice raised three octaves.

As Jason opened his mouth to offer another smart-ass comment, Foxwoods appeared in the distance—like Emerald City shimmering on the horizon. *Ahhh*, he thought, *home sweet home.* Speeding up to the valet attendant, he hopped out of the SUV. Tom's mouth was still hanging open in shock. "It's better than two days," Jason said, flipping the keys to the kid.

"What about the ashes?" Tom asked.

"Leave them in the car. I doubt anyone's going to steal them," Jason said, starting for the casino's front door. He looked back and smiled. "And who gives a shit if they do?"

"You son of a bitch," he heard his brother say as the glass doors shut behind him.

"Enjoy the alone time with Dad," Jason muttered.

Greeted by the Rainmaker—a twelve-foot statue of a Native American warrior kneeling with his bow and arrow aimed at the heavens to bring down the rain—Jason picked up the pace. *I can already use some time away from Tom*, he told himself, but even he knew there were darker forces at work here. Making his way through the immense lobby—bouncing off of a few people texting on their cell phones as he went—he hurried downstairs to try his luck.

With its six casinos, Foxwoods had thousands of slot machines, hundreds of table games, and the world's largest bingo hall. With no need for any directions, he made his way to one of the nonsmoking casinos—the unlit cigar still dangling from his lips. *Better safe than sorry*, he thought. Past the slot machines and keno parlor, he made a beeline toward the table games.

There were plenty to choose from: acey-deucey, baccarat, blackjack, Caribbean Stud, craps, roulette, and more. He circled like a starving seagull until finally finding an opening seat at his favorite stop—the blackjack table, with unlimited maximum bets allowed.

Okay now, he thought, *let's win a few bucks here and send Miranda off in style*. He placed two one-hundred-dollar bills on the green felt table and received a short stack of twenty-five-dollar chips. The dealer swept her hand across the table, as if blessing the holy ground, and the betting began.

Jason was dealt the ace of spades on the very first card. *Now that's what I'm talking about!* he thought, feeling so much adrenaline course through his veins that he felt high. With a smile, he slid another twenty-five-dollar chip forward, doubling down on his bet. His next card was the queen of hearts.

"Blackjack," the dealer announced, paying Jason double his bet.

And I'm only getting started, Jason thought.

It didn't take long before he was down four hundred dollars. For reasons unknown, it bothered him much less than it should have. While the dealer shuffled some new decks, Jason looked around and smiled. *I love this friggin' place.* Cocktail waitresses delivered drinks tableside, while the fast-paced action had men and women of all ages and ethnicities yelling, cheering, and using every prayer they knew to take home the big pot. *It's exactly what the doctor ordered*, Jason thought, as wave after wave of adrenaline rushed through his thirsty veins.

He went down another hundred before he even bothered to check his watch. *Shit*, he thought. *It's been almost three hours.* Unable to cash in his final few chips, he bet it all on the last hand. As the day's luck would dictate, the dealer hit twenty-one. "Of course," he said and stood up on legs that were fast asleep.

As he limped past the poker room on his way out of the casino, he took a quick peek in. *If I only had the time*, he told himself, imagining the rush of getting in on a no-limit game of Texas Hold'em. *Good thing, I guess*, he thought. *It's too rich for my blood now anyway.* Still, he imagined dueling it out with a table of high rollers and making it to the final round.

The fantasy vanished just as soon as he spotted Tom's sour face peering out the driver's side window of the SUV. *Oh crap*, he thought. Tom glared at him and didn't look away. Jason could picture the capillaries ready to burst in the whites of his eyes. *Crap.*

The valet attendant was hovering and didn't look happy.

"He didn't tip you, did he?" Jason asked, gesturing toward his brother.

The kid shook his head.

"Of course he didn't," Jason said, pulling out a ten-dollar bill and handing it to him. He then approached the driver's side window. "Hey, are you sure my time in the driver's seat is already done?"

"You're so done," Tom hissed.

All righty then, Jason thought, deciding he had no right to argue the point. With a nod, he hustled around the vehicle and jumped into the passenger's seat. "Did you get to eat?" he asked nonchalantly.

Tom sped out onto the road. "I had the buffet," he said, sighing heavily. "Actually, I could have had the buffet three times."

"Yeah, sorry about that. I lost track of time."

Without accepting the apology, Tom switched the radio station to NPR news. "Considering the old man was a gambling degenerate, you think you'd know better."

Jason ignored the comment. "I didn't get a chance to eat," he said, treading lightly. "Do you think we could stop and hit a drive-through real quick?"

"Sure," Tom said. "We'll stop again when we need gas."

Jason leaned over and checked the red needle on the fuel gauge. It was more than three-quarters full. *Little brother's still passive-aggressive*, he thought, closing his eyes and hoping to get some sleep. *But I'm sure he'll have to take another piss before long*, he told himself, grinning.

Jason was just about to nod off when he heard his brother's irritating voice. "You have a gambling problem, don't you?"

Without opening his eyes, Jason grinned. "Oh, you don't know the half of it."

"And I don't care to know! It's your problem, and I have no interest in making it mine."

"Then why are you asking me?"

"This is the last time we stop at a casino, that's all."

"We'll see about that," Jason said, smiling wider. "Even you have to sleep sometime, Benedict Arnold."

"Screw you," Tom hissed.

For miles and miles, they passed one fast-food sign after the next.

What a bastard, Jason thought. *All of a sudden, the knucklehead can hold his bladder.* His stomach rumbled loud enough to be heard. *I swear I'm going to snap his pencil neck if we don't stop soon.*

Tom cleared his throat, drowning out the NPR classical hour for one magical moment. "How bad's the problem?" he asked, his voice laden with genuine concern.

"What problem?" Jason asked, squirming in his seat.

"The gambling problem you inherited from Dad."

Jason opened his eyes and looked at him. "Don't you ever compare me to him again, do you hear me?" he snapped.

Tom nodded.

After collecting himself, Jason explained, "I've always been an adrenaline junkie . . . the thrill of the chase, you know? I used to get my fix breaking up fights in the joint, but I'm too old and tired for that shit now."

"You're retired?" Tom asked.

"Not physically, no . . . but when you work behind the wall you can either react to everything you see or turn a blind eye." He nodded. "That shit hole's taken enough from me, so I've strapped on the skates. I'm hoping to coast to the finish line."

"How much longer?"

"Two years," Jason said, sighing heavily. "An eternity. Besides making the final payments to the college Miranda attended, I'm paying for her entire wedding."

Nodding, Tom put on the directional. "I'm getting hungry too," he said, obviously fibbing.

He probably just needs to use the bathroom, Jason thought, preferring to stay on the safe side.

While Jason devoured his value meal—plus one double cheeseburger—in the passenger seat, Tom shook his head. "If you keep eating like that, you're not going to be around much longer."

Jason swallowed a mouthful of cheeseburger and shrugged. "I'm not sure it matters. According to the statistics, I only have a couple years left anyway."

"And why's that?" Tom asked.

"The average life expectancy of a retired correction officer is fifty-four, due to stress-related heart disease." Jason shook his head in disgust. "It's the perfect souvenir for all my years of heartlessness."

"And you have two years until you retire?"

"Two years and seventeen days," Jason corrected him. "But who's counting?"

"And then someone's spreading your ashes?"

Jason nodded. "According to the statistics," he said, stuffing a fistful of fries into his mouth. "Though I think I'm going with the traditional morbid burial."

Tom shook his head. "You realize you're not helping yourself by being so unhealthy, right?"

Jason shrugged and, as he ate, he watched Tom text both his children again. Each time Tom checked his phone for a reply, his breathing became more rapid. *They're not going to get back to him*, Jason realized. *They obviously don't respect him.* Tom looked at his cell again before firing it onto the floor in a rare display of rage.

"Don't you pay for their phones?" Jason asked, jamming another handful of french fries into his gob.

"Yes."

"Then I don't see the problem," he said past the mouthful of fried potatoes.

"What do you mean?"

Jason chewed a few times—his mouth wide open—before swallowing. "If they can't return your calls or texts, then there's obviously something wrong with their service, maybe even their cell phones." Shrugging, he took a sip from his giant soft drink. "If I were you, I'd cancel right away. I mean, why keep paying for something that doesn't work, right?" He smiled. "It doesn't make sense to keep throwing good money after bad."

Tom sighed heavily. Looking back at the wooden box of ashes, he shook his frustrated head. "I just don't get it," he said. "The only thing the old man ever really gave me was the ability, the need, to be a good dad. I've always used Pop as a template, doing the exact opposite of whatever he did."

Jason chuckled. "You're not alone there," he said, feeling surprised they shared something in common.

"Every time I faced some situation or challenge," Tom added, "I'd ask myself—what would the old man do? And then I'd go the other way."

"Perfect strategy," Jason said, thinking, *I took the same damn approach.*

"I've never struck my children," Tom added, "and I tell them how proud I am of them all the time. Love was always a given, but respect had to be earned, you know?"

"Amen to that, *brother*," Jason said, immediately feeling awkward; he couldn't believe the word had actually come out of his mouth.

Tom never caught it, or at least never let on—allowing him to wiggle off the hook. "And I've never held anything back when it comes to expressing my feelings for them." He nodded. "I thank Dad for that."

"That's some seriously twisted logic, but I can definitely relate to it." Jason thought about it for a while. "You can give kids everything they need—teach them, protect them. But at a certain point, it's all on them. They need to make their own decisions and become accountable."

Tom nodded, but his eyes were a million miles away. "I helped them do their homework, remembering how I used to struggle through my own," he said, a hint of guilt in his tone. "I figured they worked hard in school all week, so why trouble them to cut the grass—like we had to when we were kids." As if he were talking to himself, Tom rambled on. "And you know what, I still gave them an allowance because, what the heck, I was their dad and that's what dads do, right?"

"I get it," Jason said. "I wish I didn't, but I get it."

"We rode our bikes or walked everywhere we needed to be," Tom continued, "but not them. I'd never let that happen to them. So I drove them everywhere. When they had a problem, I solved it for them. When they had a need, I filled it. And wishes, well, I made sure every one of them came true. And unlike our father—the stingy slave driver—I gave them everything."

". . . everything but wings to fly on their own," Jason said. Tom's head flew up, defensively.

"Listen, I'm not judging you, because I did the same damned thing with Miranda," Jason said, shaking his head, "but people won't give our kids free rides in the real world, they just won't. In fact, they'll be lucky to get the right directions if their GPS breaks down." Although Jason was too old not to tell the truth, he was still young enough to attempt kindness in its delivery.

"I think about all the trouble life will throw at them," Tom interrupted, "and I feel guilty that I allowed them to relax on the couch and play their video games in the safe little haven I created for them."

"Don't I know it," Jason admitted. "But like I said, at a certain point they have to forge their own way. The most we can do is make sure they know they're not alone, that we're right there beside them to offer our love and support." He nodded. "The rest is on them." Finishing his pail of soda pop, Jason added, "But no one says we have to tolerate them disrespecting us." He shrugged again.

Tom reached down, picked up his cell phone, and gave it a look. "It's unbelievable," he said, "how they screen my calls, ignore my texts. They have no idea how valuable our time is together and that we only have—"

"Whoa there," Jason interrupted. "Don't tell me the old man's passing has got you all melancholy and shit."

"Not at all," Tom blurted. "I just wish it wasn't so easy for my kids to dismiss me."

"If they're adult enough to have cell phones," Jason said, "then they should be held accountable for disrespecting the man that provides them the privilege."

They'd passed three exits before Tom juggled the steering wheel and his cell phone, and called his kids again. Both messages were brief but direct. "It's Dad. Call me back or I'm canceling your phone."

Good for you, Jason thought. One exit later, his own cell phone rang. He looked at the number. "Shit," he said, cringing. "It's the ex." The phone rang again.

"Well, aren't you going to answer it?" Tom asked.

"Screw that," Jason said. "Janice is just looking to spend more of my money." He shrugged. "Besides, if your kids can get away with not answering their phones, then I shouldn't have to talk to anyone I don't want to talk to either." The phone rang again, and went unanswered.

"Screw you," Tom said.

Jason's laughter drowned out the final three rings.

chapter 4

IT DIDN'T TAKE LONG BEFORE JASON WAS SNORING LOUDLY. Sixty exits later, they were still on I-95 southbound. Tom slowed the SUV to take exit 69 to pick up I-80. *At least we'll avoid the traffic in New York*, he thought, peering into the rear-view mirror. There were no cars behind them. Glancing back at Jason, he grinned. *Payback's a bitch*, he thought and slammed on the brakes halfway down the on-ramp, nearly catapulting his brother through the windshield.

The seat belt did its job and body slammed Jason back into the seat. He gasped for air. "What the hell?" he said, his eyes as big as whoopie pies.

Although it begged to be freed, Tom concealed his smile. "It was either a raccoon or a possum, I'm not sure," he said. "Whatever it was, we just spared the poor thing's life."

Jason studied his brother's face for any hint of a crack in the truth; his glare had clearly been perfected in three decades behind a prison wall.

Tom stared out the windshield. *Just breathe normally*, he told himself.

Jason leaned back against the passenger window again and closed his eyes.

"I think it was a raccoon," Tom said aloud, and did all he could not to burst out laughing.

"You're a real dick," Jason said, his eyes still shut. "I was having the best dream."

"I could tell," Tom said. "Your hands have been buried down your pants for the past half hour."

Jason chuckled. "I've noticed you haven't talked to Carmen once since we left. What's going on?" he asked.

"Mind your damn business!" Tom snapped. *You don't want to know,* he thought, focusing on the road ahead. *I don't even want to know.* For years, there had been sporadic glimpses of tenderness, of passion—just enough to keep clinging to a love affair that had ended long ago. *It's been so cruel,* he thought. His marriage was like a grapevine that showed enough color, just enough life, that it was foolish to abandon it altogether, cutting it away to allow for new growth. He shook his head. *It's like Carmen woke up one morning with a peanut allergy and hasn't touched me since.*

Tom's cell phone rang, yanking him back. With one eye on the road, he looked at the caller ID. *It's Caroline,* he thought. *She's finally calling me back.* "It's a miracle," he said before answering. Out of the corner of his eye, he saw Jason grin.

"Hi, Dad. Sorry I haven't gotten back to you sooner. I've been really busy with school and everything, so that's why—"

"I don't want to hear the excuses, Caroline," Tom interrupted. "There's no excuse for screening my calls."

"You know, Dad, it's different nowadays. People my age don't talk on the phone. We text."

"Right, which is why you haven't returned my texts either."

There was silence on the other end. "I'm sorry," she finally whispered.

"You know, Caroline, I don't care what you say is normal for your generation. When I try to contact you and you don't return my calls or texts, it's disrespectful—period."

"I said I was sorry," she said.

"Apology accepted, sweetheart. But let's stop the games, okay? Even if you can't talk on the phone, it doesn't take long for you to send me a text to let me know you're getting back to me and that you're okay. I realize you guys are older now, but I still worry about you, you know?"

"I know," she said. "But you don't have to." She paused. "Love you, Dad."

He smiled. "And I love you, too." He nodded. "I'll call you in a day or two. In the meantime, if you happen to speak to your brother, tell him to start looking for a part-time job. He's going to need it to pay for his cell phone."

"I will," she said. "Bye, Dad."

"Bye, sweetheart." Tom hung up and looked at Jason, who was still grinning. *I should thank him*, he thought, but he just couldn't bring himself to do it.

They weren't two more miles down the road when Tom's cell phone rang again. He glanced quickly at the caller ID and snickered. "What do you know," he said, "it's Caleb, checking in." He let it ring a few more times before answering. "Well, if it isn't my long-lost son . . ."

They reached unfamiliar country just beyond Connecticut. After a short jaunt through New Jersey, skirting past the peculiar smells of Newark, they entered the Keystone State— Pennsylvania. According to Tom's calculations and a confirmation from the GPS, they agreed to stop overnight in Lock Haven.

"Fairfield Inn and Suites is probably a safe bet for a clean room at a decent price," Jason said, already punching the Spring Street address into the GPS.

"First class all the way," Tom said, thinking, *I haven't stayed in a motel since making tenure at the college.*

"I was hoping to share a room with you in the Poconos," Jason countered, rolling his unlit cigar from one side of his mouth to the other, "but this'll have to do."

They pulled into the Fairfield Inn and Suites' half-empty lot and parked. "What are we going to do with the old man?" Tom said, looking over his shoulder into the backseat.

"Well, we can't kill him. It's too late for that."

Tom stared at the box. *I don't want him near me*, he thought, *in life . . . or death.* After all these years and all the effort he'd put into distancing himself from his childhood, he could still picture his father's crooked smile—the man's teeth as twisted as a mangled Swiss army knife—as he told him, "Don't you dare cry, dummy, or I'll give you something to cry about." Although he fought hard not to return to his childhood on Maple Avenue, his mind traveled back at warp speed.

The old man kept chickens for their eggs, which accounted for more than fifty percent of their meals—scrambled eggs, over easy, hard-boiled, soft-boiled, and, on special occasions, omelets filled with meats like deviled ham or Spam.

After a full Saturday morning of cartoons and a gallon of cherry-flavored Kool-Aid, Pop announced, "Get in the car. We're going to the grain store before these chickens start eating each other."

Normally, Tom loved visiting Chase Grain, where he could dip the giant metal scoop into the wooden bin that held the cracked corn and then pour it into a thick paper bag. But he had to pee—badly. "But Dad . . ."

"Get in the car now!" the man barked.

It was an old Chevy Nova, a two-door the old man had purchased off of a fellow gambling degenerate that owed more debt than he could pay, forcing him to forfeit the car for a fraction of what it was worth. It had once been a custom machine, some real American muscle, but that was long before Pop got his greasy fingers on it.

His father held the Nova's split front seat for Tom to climb in. Tom scurried into the backseat, his bladder already aching him. Pop fired up the beast, the loud exhaust leak causing Tom's eyes to sting and water from the fumes—even though he was somewhat used to it from hanging around the racetrack.

They weren't to the end of the street when Tom's bladder was already screaming for relief. "Dad, I have to go," he called over the front seat.

"You should have gone before we left."

"I tried to, but you said I had to hurry so . . ." The sensation got more intense. Tom crossed his legs and then his eyes and finally his fingers that they'd make it to the grain store before he flooded the backseat. *Even if I run behind the store and pee there,* he thought, *Pop'll be okay with it. He does it all the time.* The pain was getting worse when he looked up to find his father staring at him in the rearview mirror—and grinning. *I'm not going to make it,* he thought, panicked. "Please pull over, Dad," he pleaded. "I'm not going to . . ."

"You piss on that backseat, boy, and I'm gonna make you clean it with your tongue."

Jason shook his head in the passenger seat. "He has to go bad, Dad," he said.

The old man glared at him. "You mind your own damn business. Your brother's not a baby anymore, and we've got to stop treating him like one. He can hold it."

As tears formed in Tom's eyes, he grabbed his crotch and squeezed tight—doing all he could to plug the dam.

They finally pulled into the grain store parking lot. The old man parked the car and shut off the ignition. It sputtered twice before coughing one last breath and going silent. Slowly, the old man climbed out of the car and pulled back the front seat so Tom could climb out. "Let's go," he growled. "You have to piss bad, right?"

As Tom crouched to get out of the car, the pressure on his bladder proved to be the final straw. He peed his pants right then and there, right in the parking lot beside the car. While his father watched the dark wet spot spread across the front of his jeans, Tom thought, *At least I didn't wet the backseat.* It wasn't much to be grateful for, but at least it was something.

"He fucking pissed himself," his dad grumbled. "The baby pissed his fucking pants." His hand lunged forward, grabbing for Tom's earlobe and pinching it hard. "Let's go," he said and started walking toward the store, dragging his horrified son behind him. "Let's go tell Charlie that you messed up his parking lot."

"No!" Tom squealed, sounding like the baby he was accused of being. "Please, Dad, don't make me do this. I'm sorry, but I couldn't hold it anymore. Don't make me . . ."

But they were already in the store, with the old man announcing loudly that his son had just "pissed his pants like a baby." Pointing down at Tom's crotch, his dad laughed while he told Charlie, who stood shaking his head behind the high plywood counter.

Tom was so overwhelmed with emotions—shame, humiliation, rage, hate—that he just stood there like a lifeless zombie. *I hate you so much*, he thought, repeating those five words over and over in his head until they became his mantra, the cruel cadence of his miserable childhood.

"Listen," Jason said, breaking off Tom's horrid memory, "I've babysat the old man up until this point. Tonight, he's all yours." He thought about it. "We'll switch off every time we stop to sleep. This way here, he gets to spend an equal amount of quality time with each of his boys."

They both climbed out of the SUV. Tom opened the rear door and grabbed the box like it didn't bother him in the least. *I should have never agreed to go on this God-awful trip*, he thought. *Whatever's in that damned envelope, it can't be worth it—forty acres or not.*

Stretching out his back, Jason looked around. "Where are all the Amish?" he asked.

"In the country," Tom answered sarcastically.

"That makes sense," Jason said, either missing the sarcasm or completely ignoring it.

With luggage as well as his father in hand, Tom checked in first. While the young girl—Tammy, according to her name tag—ran his credit card, he looked behind him. The foyer was splashed with an orange and green floral design, the carpeting just as bright with the same chaotic patterns found in a casino. *I hope it doesn't give The Gambler any ideas,* he thought, looking back at his brother.

Jason checked in next. "So tell me, what's there to do here in Pennsylvania?" he asked Tammy.

Smart move, Tom thought. *Let's hear about all the landmarks and famous places we're never going to visit.* "We're not on vacation, you know," he told his ogre brother.

Jason smirked. "I would have never been able to tell," he said sarcastically, before turning back toward Tammy. "You were going to say?"

"There's Dutch Country in Lancaster County. We have Hershey Park and Penn State," she listed excitedly, "and there's also Independence Hall in Philadelphia—"

"Perfect," Tom interrupted. "Let's backtrack and head south to Philly. We can see where the Declaration of Independence and the Constitution were signed, and then go get a cheesesteak at Gino's."

Oblivious to the cocky wit, Tammy nodded. "That's great."

"We can even stop at the Eastern State Penitentiary," Jason said, contributing to the fantasy. "From what I hear, they have an unbelievable museum."

Tom felt a strange mix of frustration and amusement but continued with the game. "Then we can stop at Gettysburg on our way to Pittsburg. The Steelers are actually home this weekend, playing the Patriots."

Tammy grew more excited with the amazing itinerary.

Jason turned to her and shrugged. "You know, I'm not sure we have time to see any of those places, Tammy," he said, putting an end to the foolishness. "But I do appreciate . . ."

Her face instantly changed from joy to disappointment. "We have an indoor pool," she blurted, trying to salvage their stay in Pennsylvania.

"Perfect," Tom said, looking at Jason. "Maybe you can do some skinny-dipping later?"

Jason shook his head. "I'm too heavy for skinny-dipping now," he said. "But I could do some chunky-dunking if we get back early enough."

Both Tom and Tammy laughed.

After completing his check-in, Jason turned from the counter. As he slid his credit card back into his wallet, he said, "So we'll get cleaned up and then head out for dinner?"

Tom couldn't tell if it was a question or a statement. He was too tired to come up with an excuse believable enough to get out of it. "I suppose," he said, coming to the dark realization that neither of them had any choice but to surrender to this twisted quest and all the awkwardness that came with it.

It was a typical low-budget hotel room. There was a queen-size bed, a flat-screen TV, and a window with a view of nothing—just some brick buildings and a small range of green hills beyond them. *Too bad we aren't in Philly,* Tom thought.

After placing the wooden box of ashes on the floor near the door, he started to unpack. *No need,* he quickly decided. *It'll be easier just to live out of the suitcase for these one-night stops.* He ran the shower hot, turning the narrow bathroom into a steam room. Before undressing, he checked his cell phone. *No new messages from the kids. Maybe I should text them?* He shook his head. *No,* he decided, *it won't help anything if I start badgering them.* Taking a seat on the edge of the bed in his boxer briefs, he then thought about Carmen. *My sexual needs are an itch that—somewhere along the way, many moons ago—she no longer had any interest in scratching. What happened?* he still asked himself. *Did I lose my mojo? Insufficiencies she once overlooked for other reasons?* He shook his head at the absurdity of it. *Carmen had gained some weight and began avoiding mirrors like they were dentist visits. And then, all of a sudden, she went on a diet. No, it wasn't a diet,* he told himself, *it was some obsessive-compulsive mission I've never seen the likes of before.* His wife began eating less and working out several hours a day, while Tom watched the weight melt right off of her. *At first, I was so proud of her,* he thought, still feeling foolish for being so blind. And then came the new hairstyle and wardrobe. Carmen began going out with the girls all the time, and late into the early morning hours—*which she'd never done before.* He shook his head again, feeling both angry and ashamed. *That's when I started wondering whether she was seeing someone on the side.* He stood, pulled off his underwear and headed for a much-needed steam bath. "Oh man," he said aloud, trying to clear the golf ball from his throat. *So many questions to answers I never wanted.*

After showering for as long as he could take it, Tom threw on a new pair of khakis and a pressed button-down shirt. Without water, he took two of his new pills and swallowed hard. "Let's go," he said aloud and, with the wooden box in hand, locked the door behind him.

Walking past the hotel's tiny gym—containing a couple treadmills and a rack of dumbbells that looked like they'd never been used—he thought, *Maybe Jason can get in here after dinner and burn off a few calories.*

With the cigar sticking out of the middle of his face, Jason was already waiting in the foyer dressed in his best redneck duds. He wore a worn NASCAR T-shirt, faded jeans, black biker boots, and a denim jacket. *Who still wears a jean jacket?* Tom thought, giving his brother another once-over. *It looks like Goofy does.*

"What?" Jason asked, sensing something was wrong.

"Nothing," Tom said. Although it wasn't easy, he held his tongue.

"What's up with the box?" Jason asked. "You don't want to leave the old man alone in the room?"

"Don't worry about it. He's my responsibility until tomorrow night, right?"

"Yeah, but do we really have to take him to dinner? That's kind of nasty."

"Don't worry about it."

As they walked out to the SUV, Tom said, "I know you're trying to save some money, so . . ."

"Because of Miranda's wedding," Jason quickly explained.

"Right, so I looked online and found a place that serves home-cooked meals. It's called Dutch Haven."

"A little piece of Dutch Country, after all," Jason joked. As soon as they jumped into the SUV and fired it up, he plugged the place into the GPS. "Here it is," he said, "just a few minutes away."

"Hey, there's a gym at the hotel," Tom mentioned on their way to the restaurant. "In case you wanted to work out." *Porky,* he added in his head.

Jason stared at him for a moment. "Whenever you want to test me to see if this is all baby fat, just let me know."

Tom shook his head. "I'm sure it's all muscle underneath." He paused for effect. ". . . very relaxed muscle, but muscle nonetheless."

The vein in Jason's neck bulged. "How 'bout we both go to the gym after dinner and see who can bench press the most weight? And just to make things interesting, whoever loses has to pay the fuel tab the rest of the way. Deal?"

Or we could try our skills at a game of intellect, Tom thought, but said nothing; he only shook his head.

"Deal?" Jason barked, pulling the soggy cigar from his mouth.

"I'd never bet with you," Tom replied, thinking quickly. "I'm a lot of things, but I'm no enabler."

"Yeah, I didn't think so," Jason said as they pulled up to a red light.

A teenager with his pants hanging down below his butt and his blue boxer briefs hanging out walked at a painfully slow gait in front of the SUV.

"Look at this kid with his head jammed right up his ass," Jason said, the cigar back in his mouth.

The light turned green, but the kid walked slowly—smirking at Jason and Tom.

"Now that's what you call a *punk*," Jason said, jumping out of SUV. Before Tom could object, he called out to the disrespectful youth. "Hey, do you need some assistance crossing the street?"

The kid twisted up his face before flipping Jason the bird.

"Glad to help," Jason said, running after him.

Here we go, Tom thought, *this is where we both get locked up.*

The kid appeared confused about being bum-rushed and that brief moment of hesitation was all it took to remove his options. Jason grabbed the kid by the elbow with his right hand while sweeping his left wrist across the kid's right forearm in one swift move. Before anyone knew what was going on, Jason had the kid's arm secured behind his back and began walking him—the tips of the boy's toes barely touching the ground—to the other side of the street. Once they reached their destination, Jason let his arms go and then slapped the kid hard on the backside, shocking everyone watching the spectacle.

Tom tried to make out what Jason was telling the terrified punk but couldn't. Nose-to-nose, Jason clearly offered the nodding teenager a few words of wisdom before returning to the SUV.

"Did you actually spank that kid?" Tom asked, as his brother buckled his seat belt.

"The window is narrow," Jason explained. "It's better for that kid to get scared for a few seconds than to spend a lifetime rotating through the prison system." He shook his head. "If he can disrespect strangers like he just did, then trust me—he's on the wrong path."

Tom was at a loss for words.

"Granted, no one should be beating on their kids," Jason said, "but a slap on the ass never killed anyone. And that kid's parents obviously dropped the ball with him."

Tom shrugged, still unsold. "I don't know if I agree with that."

Jason grinned. "I'm betting that a few slaps on the ass from his parents could have saved him some harder slaps on the ass from some frisky cellmates."

"But he's not in prison," Tom said, thinking, *Jason's even crazier than I thought.*

"Not yet, but he's on his way."

"What about the people who might have witnessed that show you just put on? Don't you care what they think?"

"I've reached a point in my life where I couldn't give a rat's ass about what anyone thinks. In fact, sometimes I worry what my attitude will be like in another ten years."

I can understand that, Tom thought.

"By then, I might even be telling people what's really on my mind, and won't that be something?"

"I hope I'm not around for that," Tom joked.

"I doubt you will be," Jason said, his smile erased.

They pulled up to the restaurant to find that Dutch Haven looked like a single-family home, painted yellow with green awnings. As they got out of the SUV, Tom retrieved the wooden box from the backseat, amused that it seemed to bother his stouthearted brother.

"That's just nasty," Jason said, as he put his cigar onto the SUV's dashboard, saving it for later.

And if anyone knows nasty, Tom thought.

Beyond the horseshoe bar, a quaint dining room—with half walls of exposed brick—was crammed with small brown wooden tables, four blue banquet room-style chairs surrounding each one.

"Looks like we missed Mexican night," Jason commented, as the pretty hostess—somewhere in her mid-twenties—escorted them to their table.

"But you've made it for steak night," she said, handing them each a menu. "Enjoy, gentlemen." For whatever reason, she looked down at Jason's feet.

"I wear a size fourteen shoe," he said, grabbing the seat facing the entrance. "You know what that means, right?"

Here we go, Tom thought, already feeling embarrassed.

The girl smiled wide but walked away before he could reveal the big answer.

"It means I haven't cut my toenails since 1987," he said under his breath. As the curvy hostess continued toward her podium near the door, she took Jason's eyes with her. "It's like watching two baby pigs fighting under a blanket," he said, referring to her backside. "So cute."

Still shaking his head, Tom placed the box of ashes on one of the empty chairs and tucked it back under the table. *Out of sight, out of mind,* he thought. When he looked back up, he noticed that Jason was still staring at the girl.

"Beauty and the beast," Tom muttered, picking up his menu.

"You can go to hell," Jason said, redirecting his attention back to his brother. "And I'm more than happy to arrange the trip."

"And you can kiss my ass," Tom countered, his eyes diving into the menu. "And I'm equally happy to arrange the meeting." He snickered. "Go ahead and stare at her, if you want," he said. "But trust me, she doesn't even see you."

"And why's that?"

"Because you're invisible to women at this stage in the game," Tom explained.

"Speak for yourself," Jason said, insulted.

I am, Tom thought. "We're both invisible," Tom continued, adjusting his approach. "If the police came in right now and announced there had been a gruesome murder committed in this restaurant, and asked that girl to describe us, she wouldn't be able to do it."

Jason glared at him.

"The only difference between you and me," Tom concluded, "is that I know it."

"You're one cynical bastard, do you know that?"

"I'm a realist," Tom concluded, looking back at the girl. *She has no idea we're even men*, he thought sadly.

Their waitress—an older, tired-looking woman—arrived to take their order. "Okay, Big Foot," she said to Jason, "what can I get you?"

Jason laughed. "Let me get a cold beer, whatever you have on draft, and give me the tallest glass you have." He quickly scanned the menu. "Let me start with the cheese planks." He looked up. "How's the monster burger?"

"Filling," she answered matter-of-factly.

He nodded, still reading the menu. "You know what, let me go with the tavern steak, medium rare, smothered in mushrooms, onions, and peppers. And can I have mashed potatoes with gravy instead of the fries?"

She nodded, writing the order into her small pad. She looked up, turning to Tom. "And you?"

"I'll have the French onion soup, followed by the almond chicken salad."

"And to drink?"

"A glass of white wine, please."

She penned it into her book, grabbed the menus, and hurried off.

"If you're not gay, then you've got a lot of people fooled," Jason joked.

"So you're a homophobe too?" Tom said. *I'm not surprised.*

"Not at all," Jason said, his face turning serious. "And you know what, I'm so sick and tired of walking around on eggshells over who's gay and who's straight."

Looks like I hit a nerve, Tom thought, happy for it.

Jason peered hard at him. "Just because someone's gay doesn't mean I have to be gay too, does it?"

Tom said nothing, thinking, *This ought to be good.*

"Gay, green, ten feet tall—it makes no damn difference to me," Jason said. "But I've had enough of the political correctness bullshit! I mean it. I really don't care who's straight or gay, male or female, black, white, or orange. An asshole is an asshole and a decent human being is a decent human being, and that's the only criteria any of us should be measured against."

"I agree," Tom said, surprised by his brother's point of view.

"You do?" Jason asked, looking equally surprised.

"I do," Tom admitted. "I may have used some different language to get my point across, but I definitely agree."

"Well, thanks, professor."

While they ate, Jason chewed with his mouth open again, making Tom's skin crawl while assassinating his appetite. "Please don't do that," he said.

"Do what?" Jason asked.

"Eat with your mouth open."

"I'm not," Jason said, closing his mouth tight to finish chewing.

Tom took a sip of wine. "So you're living alone?" he said, starting a discreet fishing expedition. "What's that like?"

"It was a loveless marriage, for sure, but at least I wasn't alone—well, not in the physical sense anyway," Jason said, revealing he'd endured periods of loneliness since getting divorced. "But I do admit that it can really suck coming home to an empty house."

Tom's skin prickled at the possibility for himself, so he decided to curtail the discussion. "Then get a dog," he jokingly suggested, picking at the last remnants of his salad.

Jason thought about it. "Not a bad idea, but I'm out all day and . . ."

"Just get a damned dog," Tom repeated. "It might stop you from blowing your brains out some night."

"Did I say I was thinking about suicide?"

"Well, I would be thinking about it if I were you."

"You're such an asshole," Jason said, before laughing aloud.

Tom joined in the laughter; it was a rarity and neither one held back.

After paying half the tab and polishing off his third beer, Jason wiped his mouth and stood. "I need to go land a mako shark," he said. "If you need me, I'll be in the men's room."

"That's great."

A minute or two later, Tom's bladder sent a clear message to his brain: *Relieve me, please.* He was stepping into the bathroom when he caught Jason coming out. "Did you spray?" he asked.

"I did," Jason said, grinning. "Now it smells like shit *and* potpourri in there."

"Great," Tom repeated, disgusted.

They were just pulling into the Fairfield parking lot when Tom felt a bolt of panic rip through his body—from his chest to his feet, then back up to his head. *Oh shit, I left the box at the restaurant.* He pulled the SUV over and turned to Jason. "We need to go back to the restaurant," he said, dreading his brother's reaction.

"Why? You want to get an order of cheese planks for the room, don't you?"

"Not quite," he said, feeling like a seven-year-old having to confess. "I forgot the box."

Jason looked at him for a moment before bursting into laughter.

Tom couldn't help it and laughed along with him. Pulling a U-turn, he stomped on the accelerator.

Parking in front of Dutch Haven, Tom jumped out of the SUV. Jason got out too.

"What are you doing?" Tom asked. "I'll be right back."

"Oh, I'm coming with you," Jason said, his laughter turning to tears. "I wouldn't miss this for the world."

The older waitress was still cleaning off their table when Tom approached—with Jason standing in his shadow.

"Did you forget your doggy bag?" she asked, looking at the table. "But you didn't have . . ."

"No," Tom said. "We came back for our dad." He pulled out the chair and grabbed the wooden box. "He was so quiet through dinner we forgot he was even with us."

The woman's jaw dropped. "That's awful," she said.

Jason's laughs roared through the room, drawing everyone's attention.

"Sorry," Tom said, not knowing what else to say.

Jason laughed harder. "Just awful," he scolded his brother through his convulsions.

The breakfast bar at the hotel—with its vaulted ceiling, freshly painted walls, and bench seats—featured fruit, cereal, breakfast pastries, and toast, as well as milk and an assortment of juices. While Jason wrestled with the broken waffle maker, Tom watched in delight over his brother's childlike struggles. *It looks like the Missing Link has yet to master his gross motor skills*, he thought, chuckling to himself.

With Jason behind the wheel, they hadn't left the parking lot when he turned to Tom. "We need to hit a drive-thru," he said. "I need eggs and cheese or my body will shut down."

"Actually, what you need is a cardiologist."

Two breakfast sandwiches and a hash brown later, Jason turned back onto I-80.

"How did you sleep?" Tom asked for no other reason than to break the silence.

"Like normal," Jason said, looking exhausted. "You?"

Tom shook his head. "I couldn't get comfortable."

"Was Dad digging into your back?"

"Not quite. The old man was in the closet."

"I've always had my suspicions," Jason joked.

Tom chuckled. "Nah, I just have a lot on my mind. This trip came at a bad time for me. There's so much going on right now."

"I hear you there."

"And that bed . . ."

"Crash out then," Jason said. "I got the wheel for the next four hours anyway."

Tom closed his eyes. "So how did you feel when you found out Miranda wanted to get married?" he asked, yawning.

Jason sighed heavily, clearly tormented over it. "I've never felt so torn my entire life. Her boyfriend, Mario, is a good kid. He really is. He even came to me, asking for my permission to pop the question."

"Good for him," Tom commented.

"Yeah, good for him," Jason muttered, shaking his head. "The way I remember it, once I figured out he was trying to ask for my blessing to marry my little girl, my mind fought against my heart. I knew what I needed to say to him, but it was one of the hardest things I've ever done."

"Really?"

"I'm still not ready to let my baby girl go." He shrugged. "Like I said, Mario's a great kid, but no one's good enough for Miranda."

"You're really screwed up," Tom said. "And trust me, I'm an expert at screwed up."

Jason's brow creased. "You wait, brother," he said. "You just wait until you go through it with Caroline."

Brother, Tom repeated in his head. It was the second time Jason had called him that—without a hint of contempt. He grinned, thinking, *I hope I'll be able to handle it better than you.* He eased back into the passenger seat. The draft of tires on the open road was causing his eyelids to grow heavy, lulling him to sleep.

"I wish I knew what to get Miranda for a wedding gift," Jason said.

Tom grinned. "How about *the wedding?*"

"Great idea, but a little tough to wrap," Jason said. "Why don't you crash out for a while. We'll stop when I can't go any further."

Tom nodded. This suggestion wasn't made because Jason wanted to be rid of his company but born of real concern. *This is strange*, Tom thought, before putting the seat all the way back. He rested his elbow in the frame of the back window, with his forehead resting in his open palm, and watched as the scenery whipped past. The tops of trees began blending into a sort of natural fence. The darkening sky above it was nearly cloudless.

Jason put on the radio and immediately found a country and western station, but he kept it lower than normal.

That's considerate, Tom thought, taken aback even more, *which is different.* As he stared out the window, he allowed his mind free reign with all the controls off. Daydreaming, vegging out, whatever you called it, he no longer felt the weight that accompanied focused thought. Instead, his mind jumped from one mental glimpse to another, landing nowhere in particular. It felt different, good—free. As his eyelids grew even heavier and the green trees and shadowy sky melted into one blurry landscape, he could hear the constant whoosh of the car barreling down the highway, disturbing the air. Through peripheral vision, he looked at his brother. *Amazing*, he thought. *For someone I can't stand, I've never trusted anyone more.* He closed his eyes; although he was at total peace, he was still aware of his surroundings. He thought about his motionless body lying prone just a few feet above the road—being catapulted forward. The car rose and fell, jerked to and fro on the road; these were subtle movements but he could feel each one, each crack in the asphalt, each dip in the road.

Yawning again, he considered Jason's overreaction to Miranda getting married and smiled to himself. *I wonder why money's such an issue for Jason and me . . .* he thought before the world went black.

Like two panting puppies, young Jason and Tommy—carried by their father's fast-moving shadow—hurried into the smoke-filled arena known as the dog track.

"Go get me a race program and a sharp pencil," Pop told Tom, handing him a single dollar bill. Tom ran for it like he was on a mission from the pope. The program only cost seventy-five cents. *Whether the old man didn't know that or didn't care about the quarter, he never asked for the change*, Tom recalled. Day after day, week after week, Dad studied that program, which he affectionately called "the Bible."

"It's not all luck," the old man claimed. "You gotta know what you're doing." But his dad didn't seem to have either luck or enough knowledge when it came to succeeding at the racetrack. "You have to look at the odds against the dogs favored to win, see which ones have won a few races and stay away from those that haven't run in a while." He looked Tom square in the eye. "Remember, males peak at two years old and bitches at three."

Tom giggled.

Past the rectangular-shaped bar, there was a giant window with two doors on each side that led to stadium-style seating. Rows of men—and the occasional woman—sat with their heads down, studying their own race programs. Most of these men wore soft hats and smoked cigars or cigarettes while studying hard until the bell rang, and then they were on their feet, yelling out the same profanities his father was so versed in.

Although Tom never knew its proper name, there was also a glass booth—with two chain-smoking ladies sitting behind the glass, accepting stacks of money—where Dad bought all his tickets, most of which he ripped up and threw into the air while cussing out someone who wasn't there.

The giant room where they spent most of their time was engulfed in smoke; it took a while for Tom's young eyes to adjust to the constant sting. A door that led to some bleacher seats just outside the glass room also faced the oval track. Jason and Tom were constantly in and out, alternating their discomfort between the cloud of smoke and angry yelling, and the bitterly cold air or sweltering heat.

Tom loved the greyhounds—tall, sleek, majestic-looking creatures that wore different-colored bibs. He could see the rib cages on some of them, making him hungry. They all wore muzzles and Tom felt bad for them—and not just because of the muzzles.

A white rabbit—or at least something that looked like a white rabbit—was fastened to a steep pole that circled around the inside rail of the track. Just as it flew in front of the dogs' numbered gates, the bell rang and the gates opened all at once. A straight row of greyhounds bolted out at once, all bunched together. Bumping into each other, they sprinted toward the mechanical rabbit they could never catch.

A man with an auctioneer's voice called the race over some old, muffled speakers that cracked and whistled. Tom could hardly make out every third word. "Turns one, two, three, and then the home stretch . . ."

Sometimes, as the dogs raced, one of them would stumble and fall, making Tom feel even sorrier for them. For reasons he couldn't quite understand or articulate, he felt really bad for them most of the time. *Poor dogs*, he'd think, *chasing something they can never have.*

On warm days, he and Jason would watch the races from the apron just in front of the fence that separated visitors from the dirt track.

During one such afternoon—while all of his neighborhood friends were riding their bikes and having fun at home—he watched as the mechanical rabbit slowed, jerking violently before it came to a complete stop. The dogs quickly caught up to it but couldn't do a thing but get up on their long hind legs and paw at it. Tom imagined them whimpering through their leather muzzles and felt bad for them—as usual.

After the final race's results were announced over the broken speakers, the old man would storm out of the place—always drunk and normally upset.

It was a sweltering August afternoon. Pop had had a few more draft beers than usual and was drifting from lane to lane on the ride home. He'd also thrown a few more losing tickets than normal into the air and was in an extra-foul mood.

"It looked like Benny cleaned up pretty good tonight," Jason commented nonchalantly from the passenger seat.

Without warning, the old man backhanded him, making Tom's testicles retreat into his torso, while his breathing became rapid and shallow. But Jason didn't cower or make a peep. Instead, he leaned his face in toward his father, as though he wanted another one. And Pop obliged, whacking him even harder this time. Jason took that one like a man too, a trickle of blood now dripping from the corner of his mouth. Tears welled in Tom's eyes as he forced himself to witness the rest of the brutality.

"You want to fuck with me?" the old man screamed, slowing the car and pulling over into the breakdown lane.

"I'm done being scared of you," Jason replied, making Tom recoil deeper into the backseat and himself.

"Well, you should be," the old man hissed before stopping the car and wailing on Jason with everything he had—the cracks and thuds making Tom feel like he was going to vomit.

But Jason never made a peep.

When there was nothing but the old man's heavy breathing, he gasped, "You had enough, punk?"

"I don't know," Jason said. "You tell me." He wiped the blood with his sleeve, his eyes never leaving his father's sadistic stare.

The old man balled his fist and pounded Jason square on the nose, breaking it clean.

Even from his fetal position, where Tom felt helpless, he could see there was blood everywhere. *Please don't say anymore,* Tom begged his brother in his mind. *Please shut up.*

But Jason looked back at his father and held his gaze.

The old man threw the shifter into drive and pulled back onto the road, looking more disturbed than Tom had ever seen him.

Tom's body jumped in the passenger seat. Without realizing they'd hit a pothole in the road, he immediately understood that he'd fallen asleep in the car. For a few moments, he kept his eyes closed, allowing the present to return in its own sweet time. *Unreal,* he thought. There was no logical way to explain it. For the most part, he disliked his older brother, but he also felt completely safe in the gorilla's company. *Come to think of it, I haven't fallen asleep in a moving vehicle since I was a kid.* He just never trusted anyone enough behind the wheel. But here they were, speeding down the highway, and he'd fallen into such a deep slumber that he was able to dream—recounting some crazy day from many moons ago.

Tom slowly opened both eyes and wiped the drool from his chin; he moved once and felt a sharp pain travel the full length of his back; it was the price for being rolled into a ball on the passenger seat. Yawning twice, he tried to stretch out the kinks in his back. "Do you remember all those weekends we spent at the dog track?" he asked Jason.

"Remember them? I thought we lived at the track when we were kids."

They both laughed.

Suddenly, Jason's face twisted up. "I hated that place almost as much as getting pinched with a bag of weed."

"Will you just shut the hell up," Tom snapped. "I'm not the only one who screwed up when we were young. You also . . ." He stopped, knowing that another opportunity to put the past into the past was lost to them forever. *Unreal*, he thought, struggling to straighten out his cramped back.

chapter 5

WHAT A FRIGGIN' JACKASS, Jason thought, looking at his smug brother in the passenger seat beside him. *He still thinks I betrayed him too.* He took a deep breath to calm himself. He searched his pocket for a new cigar. *Son of a bitch, I'm out,* he thought. *I went through an entire pack without lighting a single one of them.* He took another deep breath. *This is just great.* He let the truth of the situation marinate for a while. *Maybe it's time to do away with them altogether and snap that crutch in half?*

"I hated that dog track too," Tom muttered, talking to himself.

Jason nodded. *Not half as much as I did,* he thought. *I'm the one who suffered most of the old man's wrath.*

The dog track was where Jason and his brother had spent a fair share of their childhood. From a boy's perspective, the place was massive—and awesome. A green carpet peppered with cigarette burns led up two stairs to a rectangular-shaped bar where scantily clad waitresses—their faces painted thick with makeup—buzzed around the room, balancing dozens of drinks on small round trays.

While some gamblers phoned in their bets for the simulcast races, betting on other tracks that were being broadcast on a bank of black-and-white TV's, Stu Prendergast always made a beeline to his usual seat in the large glass room that faced the dirt track.

Week after week, year after year, his lessons remained the same: "When betting the dogs, you have to consider weight, and light dogs don't run well in the rain. Positioning in the gate can mean everything; dogs can get trapped in the middle of the pack and not be able to move until it's too late to win, show, or place." He shook his head. "And I've lost many a race with some sure winner pinned on the rail." Whenever one of the dogs was heavily backed and then the odds on him sharply reduced just before the race, Pop got up and hurried toward the ticket window to adjust his bet. "Someone knows something we don't," he'd claim.

Jason remembered one man—dressed in a worn maroon jacket and matching fedora, with a green feather protruding out of the hatband on the side—sat on the end of the second row of gamblers. Dad always ogled him with equal amounts of respect and hatred. "That's Benny," he'd say. "He's one smart son of a bitch . . . the best handicapper in the business." This confused Jason the first time he'd heard it because the grumpy gambler in the maroon coat wasn't confined to any wheelchair, nor did he show any signs of a disability. "But the selfish bastard wouldn't share a tip if his mother's life depended on it," Pop complained. "He'd rather keep it all for himself." His dad would then look at him and Tom, and shake his disheveled mop of hair. "Betting the dogs is how that man makes his living. Can you imagine a better job than that?" Jason was still young, but he could list at least a half-dozen jobs off the top of his head.

They were at the track so often that the dog handlers started waving at the boys—who always waved back.

As Jason got older, he'd go to the ticket window with his dad to place the night's bets. Usually, they got in line right behind Benny—who whispered his wagers to one of the girls behind the glass. Pop always tried the same thing. "Let me have exactly what he bet," he'd say, grinning.

"You know we can't do that, Stu," the girl would say. "What'll it be?"

Placing a short stack of bills onto the counter, sliding it into the half-moon cut in the glass, he'd rattle off. "Six and five for the daily double. First race, give me number seven to win . . ." And the order went on, with the girl punching in the bets as fast as the old man could spout them.

Although Jason struggled with long division in math class, he'd been schooled well in this art and knew exactly what each bet denoted: A quiniela meant first- and second-place winners could cross the finish line in either order; a trifecta was one, two, and three in exact chosen order; twin trifecta was for two races; a perfecta or exacta meant first- and second-place winners in precise order. Across the board, bets referred to win, place, and show, whereas a two-dollar bet cost the old man six dollars. A superfecta referred to four greyhounds crossing the finish line in their exact chosen order, while a jackpot was where a better picked the six winners from all six races. "It's a sucker's bet," the old man grumbled, but he always placed it.

At the end of the second race, a miracle happened. The old man had won the daily double and one hundred and thirty-five dollars to prove it—strutting around like a peacock that hadn't lost twice that much in the last three weeks. Although Jason wasn't great at math, even with his limited skill set, he could tell the old man was hardly winning anything.

Jason did his best to pay attention, and he even tried to enjoy the spectacle. The dogs' names were always interesting; Rusty's Bucket, Critter, O'Ryan's Belt, Thor, and North Wind. "That dog must be fast," Jason said, referring to North Wind.

The old man shook his head. "That's what they want you to believe. I bet you a quarter he comes in last."

The bell rang, and less than a minute later, North Wind crossed the finish line in second place, causing the old man to tear up a ticket and grumble a string of obscenities—never paying the twenty-five cents.

Jason was still young and, although he didn't know all that much about anything, he did know his father—although sometimes lucky—wasn't very good at picking the winning dogs.

While some men grabbed the waitresses' behinds and other men passed out drunk, he and Tommy ate potato chips and Slim Jims—which the old man claimed was "meat." This always angered Jason, not for himself but for his neglected brother.

At the end of the races, a few men always cheered, celebrating their winnings, while the rest of them cussed and tossed their ripped tickets into the air. More times than not, Pop was the leader of the second group.

Jason watched Benny at the end of the row; whether he won or lost, he never reacted either way. *That's one cool character*, Jason thought.

Most days, they stayed for all six races. Sometimes, Tommy fell asleep and Jason would cover his brother with his jacket. They normally went home hungry with a miserable man who was happy to find any reason to slap them around—especially if Jason praised Benny for his gambling prowess, which he sometimes did. As Jason recalled, *It was worth the beating just to get under the old man's skin like that.*

A hundred or so miles of highway later, Tom was snoring loudly again—rolled up in some twisted ball on the passenger seat. "I've missed you, Sandi," he mumbled in his sleep. "Come back to bed, baby."

Sandi? Jason thought, grinning. *I doubt that's his nickname for Carmen.* He took the next exit, in search of fuel and scratch tickets. *And maybe I'll have a quick look at their cigar selection.*

As the vehicle pulled into the gas station parking lot and slowed, Tom awakened. "Where . . . where are we?" he mumbled, wiping the drool from his chin.

"We're making a stop at a place you're going to love."

Tom's wits were returning. "Looks like the crow's veered off course again, huh?" he commented, clearly getting aggravated.

Jason chuckled. "It'll be good for you. You could learn the value of spontaneity in your life."

"Now who's using big words?" Tom sighed heavily. "You're unbelievable," he said, looking out the side window, trying to figure out where they were.

"There's no crying on road trips. That's a rule, you know."

"I wasn't crying," Tom said, looking back at his smirking brother.

"Whining falls into the same category."

"Screw you."

"The answer's no," Jason countered, surprised by his brother's pathetic comeback. "You don't have that kind of money."

Without another word, Tom turned back toward the passenger window, sighing once more.

Oh my God, Jason thought, stunned. *No razor-tongued counterattack?* Long ago, he'd stopped hoping to match wits with his braniac brother and win. But he just did. *Maybe all those years in the prison have paid some dividends after all.* He laughed to himself. *Now I'm starting to sound like him . . . even in my head.* It was scary. *Maybe Tom's not as smart as he pretends to be?* he wondered.

"You're so unbelievable," Tom hissed. "We agreed to—"

"We stopped to get gas, jackass," Jason interrupted, "and they have a bathroom, which is obviously your favorite place in the whole world."

Tom glared at him, his sleepy eyes still glazed over.

He's too tired to match wits, he realized, disappointed he couldn't take credit for the verbal victory. *Damn it.*

In silence, they drove through miles upon miles of road construction, with not a single worker to be seen.

Several oncoming vehicles flashed their high beams at Jason. He immediately slowed the SUV to five miles under the speed limit.

"What's going on?" Tom asked.

"What do you mean?"

"Why is everyone flashing their lights at us?"

Jason looked at him in disbelief. "To warn us that there's a cop up ahead, probably concealed in some bushes or something."

"People still do that?" Tom said.

"Evidently, you don't," Jason countered just as they drove past a state police cruiser tucked into the shadows of an overpass bridge.

They finally reached Youngstown, Pennsylvania. It was a stone's throw from the Ohio border, but Jason decided it was time to stop. *I'm starving,* he thought, looking over at Tom, *and I'm surprised he hasn't pissed himself yet.* He reached for the GPS monitor, suctioned onto the windshield, and touched the *Restaurant* icon—a crossed fork and spoon. "There's Arby's, IHOP, Denny's, Cracker Barrel," he read off the list.

"No way," Tom said. "Besides, it's my turn to pick the restaurant."

"You picked breakfast."

"No, breakfast came with the room to save us, or you, money. We can eat the franchise garbage anytime. We should pick a place we'll never eat at again."

"Fine," Jason said, "but I want real food . . . maybe Italian."

"And that's me picking?" Tom said.

"Then pick," Jason said, his voice louder than called for.

Tom scrolled through the screen. "I have it. Carmella's Café on East Western Reserve Road. It's an Italian joint." He pressed *GO* on the screen.

He picked Italian, Jason thought. *The little guy's making amends.* "Great," he said. "Let's go exercise our dinner muscles."

Tom looked toward the backseat. "The old man's all yours today."

Jason nodded. "And he can stay locked in the back where he belongs." He grinned. "Since he's been on his best behavior so far," he added, grinning wider, "I'll keep the window cracked a few inches so he can get some fresh air."

Tom choked on a stifled laugh.

From the moment they stepped over the threshold, the dim lighting and rich smells brought Jason back to Hanover Street in Boston's North End. Carmella's had a warm atmosphere, and he immediately imagined someone's nana slaving over a giant pot in the kitchen out back.

"I'm sorry, but we just closed the patio last week," the raven-haired hostess announced.

"Whatever you have will be fine," Tom told her.

They were seated at a small table beneath an oil painting of the Tuscan countryside, with Jason ensuring his back was to the wall. She had no sooner stepped away when a young busboy—a smiling skeleton wrapped in tanned skin—delivered a basket of bread sticks with olive oil, crushed garlic, and red pepper for dipping. After filling two glasses with water, he nodded. "Your waitress, she'll be right over for you," he said in a thick accent.

"Shouldn't he be at school?" Tom asked rhetorically.

Jason shrugged. "At least he's working."

Without a word spoken between them, they studied their menus. Before long, the waitress appeared at the table, smiling. "For today's specials, we have the tortellini carbonara, the pantacce tuscane alfredo, grilled salmon, and our authentic black pepper calamari."

"Wow, that sounds great," Jason said, fumbling with the thick menu, "but I think I'm going to go with the loaded fried cheese." It was a half-portion of fried provolone cheese with ricotta cavatelli, onions, bell peppers, mushrooms, and their house sauce, served with sweet sausage.

"More fried cheese?" Tom asked, as if the waitress wasn't even there. "No wonder you're only going to live a couple more years."

"It comes with a side salad, *Mom*," Jason said, making the waitress smile and Tom blush. He looked back at the woman. "And let me have a bottle of Italian beer, whatever you carry."

"*Mom*," Tom repeated, snickering, "now there's someone you should have definitely had in your life. At least you would have learned—"

"Someone we both should have had in our lives," Jason interrupted, his face serious.

With a slight nod of agreement, Tom cleared his throat. "Pecan-crusted walleye, with a side salad as well," he ordered, closing the thick menu.

"And he'll have the house wine," Jason said, poking fun at him.

"That sounds perfect," Tom said, handing his menu back to the nodding waitress.

As they ate, Tom asked, "Do you remember anything about her?"

"About who?"

"Mom."

Jason took a drink and shrugged. "I do," he said, "at least I think I do. It's been so long that the memories are really fuzzy." He thought about it and smiled. "I remember she had curly auburn hair, and I also remember her smell."

"Me too," Tom said. "I can't describe it, but I'd know it right away if I ever smelled it again."

Jason nodded. "As I recall, Mom and Dad were always fighting. I never knew what they were arguing about, but I was old enough to know they didn't like each other very much."

Tom laughed. "Who could like the old man?"

"What about you?" Jason asked. "Do you remember anything about her?"

Tom drew in a deep breath and exhaled. "The memory's so blurry I'm not even sure it actually happened, but I remember that when I was upset she used to place both her hands on the sides of my face and move her thumbs back and forth, rubbing my cheeks just under my eyes." As his eyes began to mist over, he tried to shrug it off. "It had the most comforting effect, calming me like nothing else ever has."

Jason nodded again, taking a bite of his food.

"So what do you think's in that sealed envelope?" Tom asked, changing the subject.

"Knowing the old man, a pipe bomb," he said, thinking, *A giant wad of cash from the dog track, I hope.*

They both laughed.

"Actually, I was thinking . . ." Jason's phone rang. He looked at the screen and threw up his index finger. "Sorry, it's Miranda. I have to take it." He suddenly realized how much he felt homesick for her.

Tom took the opportunity to jump on his own cell phone and began texting.

"Hi, sweetheart," Jason said, placing the small phone flush against his cauliflower ear.

"How's the trip going so far with Uncle Tom?" she asked, sounding like she wanted to laugh.

"We haven't killed each other yet, but we still haven't made it out of Pennsylvania."

Tom smiled. "Tell her I said hi," he mouthed.

Jason nodded.

"Dad," Miranda said, "Mom and I were talking and . . ."

"Oh boy."

"Be nice."

"I am nice. What's up?"

"We thought it would be so amazing to have a quartet playing during the receiving line and cocktail hour."

"How much?"

There was a pause. "Twelve hundred for two hours."

Jason took a deep breath and, looking at Tom, shook his head. "Are you sure it's what you want, sweetheart?"

"I do, Dad."

"Go ahead and book it then. I'll cover it."

Tom smiled wider.

"Thanks so much, Dad," Miranda squealed. "You're the best."

"Make sure you tell your mother that."

"Yeah, I don't think so," Miranda said, laughing. "Thanks, Dad. I love you."

"I love you too, sweetheart. I'll talk to you in a few days. Bye." He hung up.

Tom's brow creased, while both palms of his hands turned skyward. "You didn't tell her I said hi."

"What's the difference?" Jason said, taking the final sip of beer. "She doesn't even know you."

"Listen, you're the one who refused to play a role in my kids' lives, so I . . ."

"Whoa, whoa, whoa," Jason said, sliding to the edge of his seat. "That was a two-way street. My daughter barely remembers she has an uncle, or at least an uncle who gives a shit about her."

"And my kids don't even remember they have an uncle," Tom said, his words garbled from emotion.

Jason opened his mouth to speak but knew he was just as wrong as his finger-pointing brother. "That's it, I'm done," he moaned, pushing away from the table and rubbing his swollen abdomen. "I'm tapping out."

Tom nodded. "Me too," he said, calling for the check.

On the way back to the SUV, they passed a fine-art studio and peeked into the front window. Tom pointed out a large oil painting by artist Brian Fox being displayed front and center; it was a racehorse in full stride with a jockey sitting atop its muscular back. The animal was exquisite; every muscle and sinew flexed in the sunlight. "Just look at the detail in this canvas," he said, "it's amazing."

Jason glanced at it for a moment, thinking, *Yeah, it's nice.*

"Brian Fox is a rare talent who can awaken a person's soul to the beauty that surrounds us," Tom said, frozen in place. ". . . remind us of the more important things in life, you know?"

"What?" Jason said, turning to face his brother.

"Look at the eyes in that painting, Jason," Tom said. "Go ahead, take a moment and study the horse's eyes."

Although reluctant, Jason did exactly that.

"What do you see?" Tom asked, his voice just above a whisper now.

Jason continued to scan the large canvas, carefully taking in the rich details. "They seem real, like he's looking right at me." He leaned in closer and felt an unusual tingling sensation in his chest. ". . . or through me."

"Exactly!" Tom said, clearly proud of himself. "I don't know too many artists who can create a connection like that."

Jason nodded a few times before slowly stepping away from the window.

"Now there's an idea for a nice wedding gift," Tom suggested, a few feet down the sidewalk.

"I'm not sure Miranda likes horses," Jason said.

Tom shook his head. "Brian paints more than just horses," he said. "You should see some of the portraits he's done."

Suddenly, a lightbulb flickered to life in Jason's tired mind. *A portrait,* he thought. *I can't think of a more personal gift. I wonder how much Brian charges for . . .*

"You're considering it, aren't you?" Tom said, grinning.

Jason shook his head. "Not really," he fibbed.

"Excuse me," a female voice called out from the shadows. They turned to find a young prostitute smiling at them. *She's stoned out of her mind*, Jason instantly surmised, *and she can't be any older than drinking age.*

Ignoring Tom, the strung-out girl approached Jason to solicit his business. "What do you say?" she mumbled. "Do you want some company?"

"Sorry, darling," he told her. "I appreciate the offer, but I don't think my wife would appreciate me spending time with a creature as lovely as you."

She faded back into the shadows just as quickly as her tormented smile.

When they hit the SUV, Tom asked, "Why were you so polite to the prostitute?"

"Prostitute?" Jason said, feeling defensive. "I didn't see a prostitute at all. What I saw was a poor girl addicted to drugs, willing to do whatever she has to do to feed her addiction." Jason stopped at the passenger side door. "Do you really think she wants to be a whore, Tom? You don't think she had bigger dreams than that at one time in her life?" He shook his head from side-to-side. "My guess is that somewhere along the way, and many times over, she was faced with some difficult circumstances and ended up making some terrible decisions. Then, one morning, she wakes up and there's no more decisions to be made—she's a junkie with a habit so greedy that she's selling her body to pay for her next fix, a reality neither one of us could ever imagine in our worst nightmares." He looked at Tom long and hard. "And I'm guessing the worst part must be having to deal with all the self-righteous, sinless assholes passing judgment on her without knowing one single thing about how she got where she is."

"Are you calling me an asshole?" Tom asked, his face turning pink.

"You're not judging her, are you?" Jason asked, concealing a slight grin. It was extremely rare for him to outwit his little brother and he savored the moment. *It's a question of compassion*, he thought, *and there's no way Tom can outmaneuver me on that front.*

Tom remained quiet, pondering the unexpected lesson. "You're right," he said after a while. "I'm no one to judge," he confirmed in a whisper.

"Me either," Jason admitted, letting him off the hook for the first time since they'd left Salem. *Welcome to the world, little brother*, he thought. Feeling like a stuffed pepper, he collapsed into the passenger's seat.

They drove in silence for a long while—some real hard miles—through Ohio. As they passed signs for Cleveland and then Toledo, they struggled to maintain even small talk. "So, LeBron finally brought a championship to Cleveland," Jason said.

"Who?" Tom asked.

"The NBA star," Jason explained. "He went to Miami and . . ."

Tom's eyes retained the blank gaze of a pigeon.

"Forget it," Jason said, preferring to suffer through another talk radio debate.

"Capitalism?" the caller squealed. "Don't even get me started on that. While the masses fight to avoid starvation, the chosen few gorge themselves on greed."

"There are some who say capitalism is the very reason America stands head and shoulders above the rest of the world," the radio host countered. "Without the dangling carrot, we'd be living in Russia with no real incentive to wake up every morning."

"We need to put more money into programs," the caller said.

"Like welfare?" the radio host asked, laughing aloud.

"Yes," the caller said. "My mother needed it once, before she met my stepfather, and she still says it saved our family from living on the streets."

Jason shook his head. "Fine," he barked at the radio, already aggravated. "But welfare shouldn't be a career choice.

Everyone should have to leave the cave in the morning, hunt or gather, and bring home dinner—not expect delivery."

Tom lowered the radio's volume and offered a subtle nod. "Granted, I'd rather we give a hand-up than a handout, but it's the responsibility of our entire society to educate and subsidize the minority so they're not condemned to poverty." He shook his head. "No matter what it costs, even welfare isn't enough for many people who are struggling."

"Are you all right in the head?" Jason asked. "Welfare as a temporary solution? Absolutely. But as a family tradition? No way! The entire program is a complete waste of money, and no more than a means to keep people down."

"So we sort of agree," Tom said.

Jason gawked at him. "If you say so," he said, "but I don't see it."

"The entire system needs to be revamped," Tom said.

Jason nodded. "Now we agree."

Tom turned the radio up again, while Jason tried to ignore the banter.

They forged on through a small stretch of Indiana, where a sign for South Bend glistened in the twilight.

"Go Fighting Irish," Jason said.

Tom put on the directional. "We should stop," he blurted.

"You want to go see Notre Dame?" Jason asked, happily surprised.

"No," Tom said. "We don't have time."

"Of course we don't," Jason said sarcastically.

"Well, we don't."

"Why?" Jason asked. "It's not like Pop's in any hurry." He leaned over and looked at the fuel gage. *There's still plenty of gas.* "Why are we stopping then?"

"I have to go really bad," Tom said.

"You always have to go *really* bad," Jason said, feeling amused. "Why don't you just piss in one of the empty bottles on the back floor?" He grinned. "It's not like Dad's going to yell at you."

"Go ahead and laugh," Tom said. "You have no idea how much it sucks to have . . ." He stopped.

"Oh, I don't huh? What do you think; you're the only one who's gotten older?" Jason asked, shaking his head. "All of the doctors' appointments now, monitoring my high blood pressure and dangerous cholesterol levels." He shook his head again. "It's become like a part-time job."

"Try having prostate issues," Tom countered. "It's like I have the bladder of a canary now."

They both laughed; it was sorrowful and funny at the same time.

"You get any of those blue pills yet?" Jason asked.

Tom hesitated in answering.

Jason laughed. "If it stays at attention for more than four hours, I'm supposed to contact a doctor, but I should probably be calling a videographer to capture my last moments of glory." He laughed. "Those damned pills; I can't get off half the time—which poses its own set of challenges. 'Is it me?' my last girlfriend used to ask. 'Is it because I've put on weight?' And there goes the mood. Either that, or I perform like a champion, feeling like a complete fraud the entire time."

"Fraud," Tom repeated, his grin erased.

Jason caught it but decided not to question it—*not yet.* "And I can't have sex in front of a mirror anymore," he added, "not for years now. At a certain age, it should be the law that you can only have sex if you're blindfolded. My big belly. Her big butt . . ."

Tom smiled, but it was a fake smile.

Jason decided to forge on. "A few months ago, I was in full bull-rider mode."

Tom chuckled at the clever reference.

"She was moaning and groaning, and then there was silence. She turned her head, looked back at me and—with the piston still firing—asked me, 'Is everything okay?'"

"Ahhh, the kiss of death," Tom said.

Ashes

"Exactly!" Jason said. "I should have just called it quits right then and there."

Tom shook his head. "Once it gets mental, you're all done."

"Exactly," Jason repeated. "My mind started racing. *What's wrong with you? Why can't you finish? 'Is it me?'* she asked. I switched positions to buy me some time. 'There's nothing wrong,' I told her. She played along, even enjoyed all of the extra attention, I think. But when I hopped back on to finish the ride . . ."

"Your head was spinning," Tom finished.

Jason nodded. "I went for a little while, but I knew right away that I could have gone all night. She finally said, 'We can stop anytime, you know.' 'I think it might be my prostate,' I told her. 'I'd say it's working well enough,' she said. 'Maybe it's working a little too well,' I said and rolled off." Jason shrugged. "We laughed it off and everything was cool, but somewhere in the back of my mind an evil seed had been planted and I knew this wasn't going to be the last time I'd have that problem."

Tom nodded. "I know exactly what you mean."

"So I guess the moral of the story is balance," Jason said.

"How's that?" Tom asked, pulling up to a fast-food restaurant to use their bathroom.

"Too much Viagra and you can't seal the deal. Not enough and you can't even take a seat at the table."

They both laughed.

"And then there's the weight," Jason said. "If I didn't go to the gym, I'd turn into . . ."

"You go to the gym?" Tom asked, acting shocked. "You'd never know it."

Jason punched his little brother in the arm. And from the look on Tom's face, he'd punched him too hard. As Tom sprinted from the SUV, Jason leaned back. It was quiet. *This is nice*, he thought. *I hope Tom takes his time.* He closed his eyes and . . .

Drip. Drip. Drip. The leak of the broken water pipe pounded in Jason's head like one of Satan's own war drums. Before long, the rhythm of the throbbing pain rocked his thoughts straight to hell.

Twenty-eight years, he thought, *twenty-eight wonderful years spent swimming in the cesspool of society, surrounded by everything from murderers to child molesters—each one an innocent man. What bullshit! They'd slit their own mother's throats for a smoke. Hah, I guess it is funny. I haven't met an innocent man in this hole yet. And everybody's a tough guy. Yeah, everybody's gotta try his hand at the top seat. It's not like years ago, like when I first walked in here. There was honor then. Guys knew how to throw hands, and the one who wanted it more came out on top.*

Not today, though. Today, the skinners, the diddlers, all the twisted freaks travel in packs, each one lugging a blade. Each one bragging about some fabricated bank robbery or kidnapping, anything to conceal the truth. The young gangbangers, the bikers, the bugs—groups of racists who roam this concrete jungle like a pack of famished werewolves.

Shit, everybody's gotta take a weapon into battle. Broomsticks, shards of glass, razor blades, anything to give them the edge. But not me. No, I've always relied on just my hands.

And respect—damn, that went through the barbed wire long ago.

Even the guys who stayed strong—stayed solid—have no problem dropping a dime when there's something in it for them. They call it survival. I call 'em rats—and there's more of the two-legged kind than the four-legged bastards I share my dinner with.

But me, I'm almost there. Two more and I wrap . . .

Drip. Drip. Drip.

As panic filled Jason's body and threatened to freeze his legs in place, he searched for an open door. *But all the doors are locked and there's no way out,* he thought. *I . . . I can't get out.*

Panting and gasping for air, Jason woke himself up.

Tom was staring at him. "I thought you were heading toward the light," he said. "For a while there, I really thought I was going to lose you." He shrugged. "And I was kind of all right with it."

"That's nice," Jason said, wiping the spittle from his lower lip.

"In fact," Tom continued, "I kept telling you to go to the light. But every time it looked like you were about to pass over, you gasped for air again."

"That would have been fine with me," Jason said, yawning. "I can use the rest." He half-shrugged. "Besides, I have some good people waiting on me."

"Where you're heading," Tom teased, "I'm guessing you might feel some warmth on your face before you ever see a flicker of light."

Jason shook his head, trying to knock the rest of the cobwebs away. "I can't believe we're already there," he said.

"And where's that?" Tom asked, looking out the windshield for something he might have missed.

"Heading for the backstretch."

"You don't know that," Tom said, his eyes instantly changing—becoming sad.

"I don't, huh? Mom passed away early, and Dad was only a couple decades older than we are right now."

"Speak for yourself," Tom said, clearly uncomfortable discussing the time they had left.

"I'm not afraid of death," Jason said. "I'm just afraid of how I might be remembered."

"It all comes down to labels," Tom said, "which is why I hate labels."

Jason was confused. "Labels?"

"If I tell people I'm a professor, then they conjure up some vision of what they think a professor is—or should be—and that's exactly who I become to them, nothing more. As a dad, I'm the provider and protector, nothing more. Husband, brother—whatever. Before long, some little person will be calling me Grandpa, and everything I am, all that I'd done before that point, is gone—at least to my grandchild."

Jason's eyebrows danced up near his hairline.

Tom shook his head. "How you're remembered depends on who you're remembered by, that's all."

"That's very profound."

"Thanks."

"And very depressing."

Grinning, Tom pointed the car straight down I-80 toward the Windy City.

"What hotel did you book for us in Chicago?" Jason asked.

"J.W. Marriott on West Adams Street. It's on the central loop."

"That sounds expensive."

"It is," Tom said, "unless you know how to book a room using AAA discounts and whatnot."

"How much?" Jason asked, growing tired of the question.

"Two hundred seventy-nine dollars for the night."

Holy shit, Jason thought. "Can I have my debit card back now?" he asked.

"Why don't I just hold onto it?" Tom teased.

Jason extended his hand. "Give me the card before I shake you down for it."

Tom handed it back.

Jason was quiet for a moment. "Why are we going into Chicago anyway? I'm guessing it's a lot more expensive than staying outside the city. And aren't we going to lose time having to fight through all the traffic?"

"Don't worry about it," Tom said. "You only live once."

"You only live once?" Jason repeated, surprised. "What the hell's gotten into you?"

"Nothing," Tom said, obviously withholding something.

"Okay, but just so you know," Jason said, "I'm not leaving Chicago until I get a deep-dish pizza."

From the exterior, the J.W. Marriott Hotel—constructed of chiseled granite and glass—appeared to consume an entire city block. Jason whistled, making Tom grin. There was a parade of limousines parked beneath three fluttering flags out front. After parking the SUV in the garage beneath the hotel, they entered the exquisite lobby—with Jason carrying their dad under his arm—to find an ornate black staircase adorned in wrought iron railings and polished brass. The vaulted ceiling, easily thirty feet high, showcased a modern chandelier that made the slick marble floor glisten. It was the grandest of lobbies, accented in red and gold, and furnished to magazine-advertisement perfection. Jason whistled again. *So this is how the other half lives?* he thought.

After checking in, the brothers headed straight to their rooms. Beige walls and red carpeting framed a massive bed—with a padded headboard—and a rich mahogany-accented bathroom. Jason looked out the floor-to-ceiling window, realizing he was standing in the middle of a metropolis of modern glass-and-steel skyscrapers situated among carved stone buildings of breathtaking architecture. *Damn*, he thought, feeling small in the big city.

After getting ready for dinner, he swung by the hotel's swimming pool, which could have been located in Mykonos, Greece; the tile, the walls, the pool—everything was painted white and sky blue.

Tom was waiting in the lobby, wearing dress slacks and a sports coat. His face dropped when he saw Jason. *What now?* Jason thought. "I secured the old man in the room's safe," he said before Tom could speak.

"That seems a little overkill."

"Well, he's precious to me."

"I can tell."

Jason grinned. "Actually, I've never had reason to use a room safe before."

Tom pointed down at his sneakers. "Fancy footwear," he said. "I didn't realize we were going to a monster truck rally after dinner."

You little prick, Jason thought, but his tongue got twisted in his mouth—as it always did when dealing with his brother. "Book covers, brother," he finally managed. "You should have learned better by now." Somehow, he could never seem to articulate what he was thinking or feeling quickly enough. *Maybe I should just crack him in the head?* But he was afraid to slap Tom around like he did when they were kids. *I don't think I'd be able to stop.*

Changing the subject, Tom asked, "Do you know why they call Chicago the Windy City?"

"No, but I'm sure you're going to tell me."

"It got its nickname from its windbag politicians."

Jason stared at his brother. "Hello irony," he said.

Ignoring the comment, Tom asked, "Have you ever seen the city?"

"I've been through here a few times," Jason said.

"Yeah, but have you ever *seen* it?" Tom asked, putting on a disarming smile.

From the windows of a yellow taxi cab—which Tom swore was the "only way to experience it all"—Jason saw the Jay Pritzker Pavilion, LaSalle Boulevard and Board of Trade, the Wrigley Building Clock Tower, and the Buckingham Fountain for the first time.

"If we had time," Tom said proudly, "we'd visit the Art Institute and the Adler Planetarium. The aerial view from the Skydeck is really something to see, and so is the Navy Pier, which is like a city within a city."

"How's the nightlife here?" Jason asked.

"It's been a while for me, but years ago we used to go to Lincoln Park." He nodded. "It was amazing."

As they headed toward Gibsons Bar and Steak House on North Rush Street, they spotted a homeless man panhandling at a stoplight. Tom grabbed a few dollars from his pocket and started to roll down his window.

"What the hell are you doing?" Jason asked him.

"Something you wouldn't understand," Tom answered. "I'm helping someone in need."

"You're a fool."

"Why?"

"Just look at him, Tom. He's no older than twenty-five, with no disability except for some drug habit. And look at his feet. He's wearing better sneakers than I am." As soon as he said it, he regretted it. *But it's the truth.*

As the kid approached the car, Tom quickly looked him over and rolled the window back up.

"Always look at the shoes," Jason said, "and not just mine."

They pulled up to Gibsons and got out of the taxi. Jason extended some cash his brother's way, but Tom refused to accept it—shaking his head. "The tour was on me," he said, pushing the cash away again.

What the hell? Jason thought, confused. *He insults me one minute and then treats me to a tour of the city the next? He's one messed up dude.* "This is starting to feel more like a vacation than . . ."

Tom waved him off.

From the moment they walked into Gibsons, Jason realized it was a pretty high-end place. *Now Tom's trying to spend away my retirement too*, he thought, turning to his brother. "I thought we were going to a Japanese steakhouse to sit at the hibachi?"

"You said you wanted steak. Gibsons serves one of the best steaks in the city."

Jason looked around. "I have no doubt," he said. This classic American steakhouse was dimly lit with chestnut-paneled walls and a vaulted ceiling—elegant but comfortable. As they were being seated, Jason took note of some of the dishes being devoured at neighboring tables. *They have seafood*, he thought, surprised, *and huge portions.* He also noticed that while a few of the patrons wore jeans, most men were either decked out in suits or slacks and jackets—just like Tom. *Damn it*, he thought, feeling embarrassed and instinctively sucking in his gut. Although food had become one of the few remaining joys in his life, he always cursed himself for his waning willpower toward junk food when faced with social situations like this.

Their final destination was a booth against the wall; beneath a small lamp, a linen tablecloth covered the table situated between two high mahogany leather bench seats.

Continuing his city tour, Tom said, "They have great appetizers here; oysters on the half shell and . . ." His eyes lit up. ". . . and the tomato and goat cheese with pan-seared mushrooms in a walnut vinaigrette is amazing."

"Goat cheese?" Jason repeated, feeling repulsed.

Tom laughed. "Then try the spicy lobster cocktail in steamed artichoke."

"I think I'll play it safe and go with the Alaskan king crab claw," Jason said, shaking his head.

"Safe?" Tom said, "That's no fun."

"Says Mr. Spontaneity," Jason replied, snickering. As he read the menu, his eyes bulged out of his head. *A twenty-ounce T-Bone is fifty bucks and the fifty-ounce porterhouse is a hundred.* "A hundred bucks for a steak?" he blurted.

"It's the best money you'll ever spend," Tom said. "And it's a much better investment than handing it over to some casino or buying those stupid scratch tickets every time we stop to gas up."

Jason watched as a waiter crossed past their table carrying an order of frog legs. *Oh my God*, he thought, *the only thing the chef did is chop the poor thing in half and lay it spread-eagle on the plate.* The dish was nothing more than the bottom half of a frog. He looked at Tom. "If you order those, I'm going to eat at the bar—alone."

"I hate frog legs," Tom said. "But you've just made it a very tough decision for me."

They both chuckled.

Jason felt so torn. He was completely out of his comfort zone in the place, but another part of him was grateful to Tom for introducing him to this strange, new world. He shook his head. *I'm getting a tall draft beer,* he thought, *bucket-sized, if they have it.*

After finishing the last bite of the best appetizer Jason had ever tasted, the waiter returned. "I'll have the T-bone, medium rare, with a loaded sweet potato." He handed back the closed menu.

"Why don't you try the blue cheese scalloped potatoes for your side?" Tom suggested.

The waiter looked at Jason, hopefully. "I have to agree," he said.

"Hell no," Jason said, feeling another wave of self-consciousness roll over him. "It's a baked sweet potato for me."

The waiter nodded. "Fine," he said, adopting Tom's same look of judgment.

Bringing his shaking head to a halt, Tom told the snobbish waiter, "Let me start with the walnut and cranberry salad with goat cheese." He scanned the menu one last time. "And I'll try the miso-marinated Chilean sea bass for my entrée." He closed the menu and handed it to the smiling man. "And another glass of Chardonnay, please."

"Very good, sir." With a nod of approval, the waiter scurried away.

Jason smiled. "What the hell? Goat cheese? Chardonnay?" he said, his tone thick with judgment.

"That's right," Tom said defensively. "Sorry if I've evolved and you . . ."

"Oh, you've evolved all right," Jason interrupted, feeling a little more than defensive in this unfamiliar atmosphere. "I'm surprised you haven't sprouted butterfly wings on your back and fluttered out of here."

Tom's face burned red. "Do you even realize how ignorant you are?" he hissed, delivering the final few words through gritted teeth—as the waiter returned with their drinks.

"No more ignorant than you are pretentious," Jason fired back. "You didn't think I knew that word, did you?" He shook his head. "Dad really did twist you up sideways."

Tom nearly streamed white wine out of his nose. "He twisted me up?" he said, his voice reaching a new octave that drew attention from several surrounding tables. "You must live in a world without mirrors, brother." He intentionally surveyed Jason and snickered. "Your brain was like soft putty in that asshole's hands, and what he created is the hideous monster that sits before me today."

"Fuck you," Jason roared, his entire body enflamed with an old rage that burned right from his soul.

One of the neighboring patrons cleared his throat in an obvious attempt to stop the argument from escalating any further. Jason nearly stared the poor stranger out of his skin.

The brothers ate in silence for the remainder of the decadent meal. Though he'd never admit it, Jason thought he'd found heaven in the piece of steak he'd ordered. Through the grunts and groans, he washed his medium-rare slab of meat down with three more "cold ones," while Tom took his time with a small dish of crème brûlée. Jason's slice of carrot cake was big enough to feed a village in the Philippines for a month.

As they walked out of the place, the restaurant manager caught them at the door. "I hope you gentlemen enjoyed your dinner," he said.

Jason placed a toothpick into his mouth—adjusting it a few times with his tongue until it was seated where he wanted it—before replying, "The food was top-notch, boss, but the company sucked something terrible."

The manager opened his mouth to reply, but no words followed.

"It really did," Tom confirmed, walking past the confused man to hail another cab.

As they drove through the blues bar section in the Hyde Park area, the new taxi—reeking of orange-infused incense—stopped at a red light. Jason looked around; there wasn't a single car or truck to be seen. Yet, he heard something rumbling—really loud. *What the hell?* he thought, scanning all around them. The loud rumbling began to shake the car. While Tom grinned beside him, Jason looked behind them. *Nothing there*, he told himself before scanning up and down the streets. *Nothing*, he confirmed, *but something's definitely heading our way.* Although he was tempted to scream out and tell the taxi driver to run the red light, he waited. The rumbling got so loud he swore a Mack truck was going to slam right into the side of them. Now laughing, Tom pointed skyward. Jason saw several sparks fly overhead and realized they were stopped beneath the elevated train.

"It's the L," Tom confirmed.

Feeling a mix of relief and newfound embarrassment, Jason nodded. *Of course*, he thought.

"So besides the atmosphere, did you enjoy dinner?" Tom asked in an obvious attempt to make him feel better.

Jason chuckled. "Are you kidding me? It was one of the best meals I've ever eaten."

"It's true, you know," Tom said.

"What's that?"

"You get what you pay for," he said, grinning. "It's a long way from the cucumber sandwiches Pop used to make us."

With their recent argument already behind them, Jason smiled. "My favorite was his fried bologna sandwiches. I still can't get enough of those."

Once he'd stopped laughing, Tom said, "If we'd had an earlier dinner, we could have headed over to the Goodman Theatre to catch a show."

"A show?"

"The opera."

Are you shitting me? Jason thought, happy he was able to keep the thought in his head.

"Do you enjoy the theater?" Tom asked.

"You mean the movies?" Jason said, messing with him. "Sure, I like the epics . . . *Braveheart, Dances with Wolves, Gladiator* . . ."

"So all the historically inaccurate films then?" Tom said.

"Exactly."

"I wasn't talking about films. I was referring to live theater."

"It's not my thing," Jason said, still scanning skyward for any new surprises.

"Have you ever been?" Tom asked.

He thought about it. "Sure, I saw *Grease* years ago."

"I'm not talking about high school," Tom interrupted.

"Thanks, but no theater for me," Jason said matter-of-factly.

"That figures," Tom muttered.

"What the hell does that mean?" Jason said. "I can't get into the snooty tooty club if I don't enjoy theater?"

"Snooty tooty?" Tom repeated, snickering. "I think you mean *hoity toity*."

"When's the last time you watched a hockey game?" Jason asked, ignoring the comment and turning the tables on his brother.

"I don't remember," Tom admitted.

"You loved the Boston Bruins when we were kids."

"I loved climbing trees when we were kids, too," Tom said. "But I grew up."

"That's too bad."

"It's not, actually," Tom said, "considering where we came from."

Still looking out his window, Jason nodded. "I can't argue that," he said and suddenly longed for a hot shower and his soft hotel bed.

chapter 6

YOU ONLY LIVE ONCE, Tom repeated in his head, afraid of its true meaning. He snickered, thinking, *We'd better be back for my weekly tune-up with Dr. Baxter.*

After enjoying a lone nightcap at a local bar, he returned to the hotel feeling as empty as the homeless man's cup he'd just dropped a few bucks into. Sitting alone in the hotel room, he thought, *It feels like my life's playing out like someone else's iPod on shuffle.* His whole world was unraveling while he was stuck on some godforsaken cross-country road trip, and they were only as far as Chicago.

He suddenly pictured the brown wooden box and his father's smirking face. It didn't take much of an imagination to picture a young and rugged man with a face that could easily attract the opposite sex. But time, hard labor, and even harder drinking had worn down those sharp edges. From early Friday night until late Sunday night, Stu Prendergast had embarked on his weekly benders, somehow finding the salt to rise each Monday morning and report to the steel foundry, woodworking factory, school janitorial office, or any of the backbreaking jobs he was forced to take. Stu had nearly no schooling and carried the curse of menial labor. For that alone, his words and actions resembled that of a frustrated man who knew nothing of culture, wealth, or prominence. He was a blue-collar stiff who found his pleasure in staying comfortably numb whenever he could. Outside of the house, many found him to be crude, rash, and ignorant. Inside the house, he was a heavy-handed dictator whose words cut deeper than his flying fists.

It was insane, the power his father held over him—*still.* Phrases like "I'm ashamed," or "you've disappointed me" cut deeper than any knife, and his dad had never been shy about wielding that blade.

For years, Tom wore his rage like a worn pair of suspenders, barely holding everything together. *Just let it go,* he thought, giving himself a hard mental slap. *Forget the vile prick,* he pleaded with himself, trying desperately to slam the door closed in his mind.

His thoughts immediately traveled to Carmen and the kids. *Oh, my children,* he thought, picturing them. Grabbing a pen and a pad of paper, Tom took a seat at the small desk to try to capture the sea of feelings that stormed inside of him. He stared at the paper for a long while, without once raising his pen. A sound, although quite rhythmic, called for his wandering attention. He stepped up to the window and sighed, as blank sheets of rain reflected the cruelty of a dreaded writer's block.

Driven by a nagging sweet tooth, he ventured out again into the dreary night, alone with the fears of an unknown future. Downtrodden with the suspicions of a betrayed husband, one coffee roll hardly replaced the comfort of marital security. Hoping for instant gratification, he was disappointed once again. Suddenly, a glimpse of many yesterdays appeared out of the corner of his eye.

In one of the back booths, a young couple made love through penetrating stares, both unaware of Tom's curious presence. Envious, almost saddened, he headed back to a blank pad of paper—his mind still threatened by instability.

Evidently, a normal life was always too much for my wife to bear, he thought. "It's been a long road," he muttered to himself, "but in the end, it takes two to make it work."

Staring at the lined paper, Tom decided to start at the place that meant the most to him; he thought about his children. At his laptop, he fought to capture his feelings and explain his truths to Caleb and Caroline. He labored to find some way of letting them both know that although life could sometimes be cruel, no matter what lay ahead some things would never change. *I want them to always believe in happily ever after*, he thought. *I need them to know I'll always be there for them, that they'll never be alone—just like Jason said.*

He wrote the poem "Higher."

> *A pair of wide eyes search the unfamiliar play-*
> *ground,*
> *as the giggle of captivating innocence turns to a*
> *squeal.*
> *Seated upon a swing, a young girl looks back,*
> *begging,*
> *"Push me higher, Daddy!"*
> *With only a few pumps of her legs and a set of*
> *strong,*
> *but gentle hands behind her, her fears are con-*
> *quered*
> *and she steps into the sky.*
>
> *A pair of eager legs march into adolescence,*
> *tripping on the discovery that the world can be*
> *unkind.*
> *Again, looking back, those same eyes betray her*
> *silent plea,*
> *"Push me higher, Dad!"*
> *The labored hands of love take her desperate grip*
> *and lead her on her chosen path.*
> *Still, the sky is within reach.*
>
> *A pair of old, tired arms long for a hug that has*
> *died,*

as two feeble legs buckle at the knees.
With weary eyes, she looks toward heaven and
whispers,
"Push me higher, Father!"
A pair of stronger, more loving hands lift her up
and carry her home.
For eternity, that sky shall be her carpet.

With a heavy heart, Tom read his poem again and again. It was accurate and honest, capturing his truest feelings. And then it hit him, the answer that would help him survive the inevitable. *Peace will never be found in concentrating on my own feelings*, he thought. *I'll find my serenity tending to my children's feelings.* It was simple. *If they're happy, then I have a shot at the same.*

He grabbed for an amber-colored bottle of pills and snickered. *With my luck*, he thought, *these'll end up making me grow breasts.* Palming two pills, he swallowed them down without a drop of water. He then closed his eyes and waited—patiently—to fall asleep.

Tom was no more than a toddler. Startled from a nightmare, he awakened in a room filled with daylight. *It must have been a nap*, he thought. Yawning, he rolled off the couch in search of his mother. She was in the kitchen, stirring a pot on the stove. She had curly auburn hair—*just like Jason remembered.* The kitchen floor was yellow and his mother seemed so tall. She turned toward him when she heard him cry. "I had a bad dream, Mama," he said. Hurrying to him, she bent down and scooped him up into her arms. Taking a seat at the kitchen table—with him in her lap—she stroked his cheeks and hummed a soft song, soothing him.

Tom opened his eyes and lay in the hotel bed, trying to reconcile whether he'd just experienced an actual memory; a factual glimpse of the past, or just some scene he'd conjured up in his own mind long ago, trying to make his mother real. It was always the same—in daydreams or his sleep—recalling his mother in vague bits and pieces, everything confused in detail and context. He placed his hands behind his head and sighed. *We really needed you, Mom*, he thought, *but had to suffer the old man instead.* Even now, being middle-aged, his soul still ached for a mother's love he'd barely known and had all but forgotten.

Breakfast at The Florentine, inside the hotel, consisted of an egg white frittata with spinach and goat cheese for Tom, and a mushroom and cheese omelet for Jason. *Another wonderful meal*, Tom thought, enhanced by a cup of the richest coffee and a pulpy glass of fresh-squeezed orange juice.

Jason was still huffing and puffing in complaint. "The butter's freezing cold. I can't even spread it with this silver butter knife."

"If you have to find something wrong," Tom said, "I guess that would be it." He watched his brother fumble through breakfast and felt sorry for the way he'd treated him. *He's obviously outside of his element here in Chicago*, he thought. "I ended up going out last night," he admitted, "after we got dropped off."

"Oh yeah, where'd you go?"

"I took a walk—a few walks, actually—the first one for a drink and the second one for some pastry." He shrugged. "I would rather have gone to the opera."

Jason nodded. "I went out, myself. I ended up walking to some local pub—The Penalty Box, I think it's called. I had a few beers and watched the last period of a hockey game on the tube."

"You missed a mediocre coffee roll," Tom said.

"And you missed a pretty anticlimactic hockey game," Jason countered.

Tom nodded. "How much of an impact do you think not having a mother has had on both our lives?" he blurted.

Jason looked at him for a long moment. "Night and day, I suppose," he said.

"What do you mean?"

"With the old man, we grew up in the darkness," he explained. "But I think if we'd had a mother, we might have been raised in the light."

Oh my God, Tom thought, taken aback by his brother's surprising insight. Wiping his mouth with the cloth napkin, he stood. "Are you ready to hit the road?"

"I am," Jason said, "but Dad and I aren't leaving this city until I get a deep-dish pizza."

"You're kidding me, right?" *Please tell me you're kidding.*

"Nope, I'm not."

"I'm not even sure we can get a pizza this early in the day."

"Oh, I'm sure we can find one if we look hard enough."

Tom felt perturbed. "It had better be takeout," he said.

"Of course," Jason said. "Is there anything better than takeout pizza?"

Choosing to access the parking garage from the street, Tom watched as Jason approached a homeless beggar; the filthy man was sitting on the cold sidewalk holding a cardboard sign. Jason threw a few bucks into his coffee can.

Do as I say and not as I do, Tom recited in his head, recounting his father's despised quote. *Jason's such a hypocrite!* As they entered the garage, he told Jason, "I saw what you just did."

"You have no idea what you saw," Jason said.

"Do as I say and not as . . ."

"I hate that saying," Jason said. "To me, it's the epitome of hypocrisy and the creed our jackass father lived by."

"So why is it okay for you to give money to drunks then?"

Jason stopped and turned. "If you took a closer look, Tom, you would have seen that the *drunk* is actually a disabled vet." He nodded. "And besides, his shoes have holes in them."

Whatever, Tom thought, making a beeline to the SUV.

"For such a smart man," Jason said, "you're absolutely oblivious to your surroundings and everyone in it."

"So is that an insult or a compliment?" Tom asked, preparing to engage in a new verbal joust.

"Yes," Jason said, before popping open the rear of the SUV and throwing the old man in. "Consider this a timeout," he told the box. "Now let's see how you like it."

Forgetting their recent exchange, Tom laughed aloud.

Leaving Chicago—Jason's deep-dish pizza filling the SUV with aromas much too early for the day—they took the on-ramp for I-294. Tom nodded. *According to the map,* he thought, *we'll pick up I-90 and then grab I-39 from there.*

Easing back into his seat, Tom watched as Jason searched for a country and western channel. *Maybe I was trying to show off a bit in Chicago,* he thought, still feeling bad about it. "So you still enjoy fried bologna sandwiches, huh?" he said.

Jason looked at him. "Are you shitting me? I'd starve to death before I ever ate that crap again." He shrugged. "But I'll still make the occasional English muffin pizza when there's nothing else in the fridge."

"I still can't do it," Tom said. "Born with silver spoons in our mouths, weren't we?"

"Not quite." Jason nodded proudly. "Nope, we got the wooden ones."

". . . loaded with splinters," Tom said, thinking back for a few moments. "At 525 Maple Avenue," he said; it was their childhood home. He could still picture every nook and cranny of the place. It was a two-story tenement, with a realty office on the bottom floor. It had two bedrooms, their ceilings pitched to the roof. The hallway leading up to the apartment was made of horsehair plaster, crumbling into dust on the worn wooden stairs. Stained linoleum covered both the kitchen and bathroom floors—with a claw-foot tub for bathing. Stu Prendergast had erected a steel frame and hung a shower curtain that sagged, spilling water onto the old yellowed linoleum. Cast-iron radiators, sprayed in silver leaded paint, kept the place warm enough to keep them alive. In the outdated kitchen, there was a gas cookstove and a kitchenette table surrounded by six faux leather chairs, two of them mended with black electrical tape. Half of the doorknobs were missing from the dark-stained pine cabinets. A new refrigerator, which looked completely out of place in the room, sat beside a microwave that took up half the faded counter. Although everyone looked forward to the day it broke for good, it never did. Whether it was pizza, popcorn, or day-old dishes from Roger's Spa Restaurant—each dish was heated perfectly, and the microwave continued taking up the room where new, more attractive appliances could have found a home. The living room was furnished with a recliner chair, couch, and love seat atop an area rug that had seen better days a decade before. Framed pictures of deceased relatives—like a museum capturing their history—hung askew on the ugly papered walls. Tom could still remember how the cheap old man begrudgingly threw out the floor model twenty-five-inch TV when he discovered it was cheaper to go out and buy a new one than to keep repairing the old relic.

Jason put on his directional and slowed to take the next exit.

As he was pulled from his thick haze, Tom asked, "Why are we getting off the highway?"

Jason gestured toward the dashboard. "We didn't fill up yesterday before we hit Chicago. We need gas."

Tom nodded and stared out the windshield again—at nothing. "Remember when you dismembered my G.I. Joe doll and he spent the rest of his life dressed in some ridiculous duct tape astronaut suit?"

"And that's coming from the only kid who ever padlocked his toy box and charged interest when he loaned out his allowance," Jason replied.

Tom tried to conceal it, but he couldn't help laughing. "You were an animal."

"And you were a shylock," Jason countered, as they reached the gas station and steered into the parking lot. Jason pulled up alongside the pump—its neon sign buzzing like a mosquito meeting its maker—and got out. Before heading for the pump, he leaned into the window. "Can I borrow a few bucks?" he teased.

"Sure," Tom said. "But there'll be interest."

They both chuckled.

After topping off, Jason was no sooner back behind the wheel—with a handful of scratch tickets and two cold drinks—before he took the next step down memory lane. "Remember when we had our paper routes?" he asked, handing over a bottle of water to his brother.

Tom laughed. "Whoever didn't tip us good during the year got hit pretty hard on Halloween."

The boys had collected dozens of eggs weeks before the big night, hiding them so they'd be just rotten enough to throw on the scariest night of the year. They also used soap, lipstick, and shaving cream to leave their mark. They thought they were real bad boys until they saw Roland Benoit, the neighborhood maniac, throwing gourds off the overpass highway bridge—aiming them at car windshields.

"And the cops thought we'd lit that dumpster on fire," Jason said.

Tom nodded. "I still say it was Roland who did it."

"No doubt," Jason said, shaking his head. "Those were crazy times."

"What about the night Pete Martin bit into his own finger thinking it was a cheese puff?" Tom said.

"I thought it was Bob Caron who did that?" Jason said, laughing harder.

Was it? Tom asked himself, searching his memory. "Yeah, I think you're right. It was Bob."

It had been dark, their friend Bob was tired and, with the orange powder completely covering his fingers, it was easy to mistake his finger for a cheese puff. One chomp later, he let out a howl that made Jason and Tom feel bad enough to conceal their laughter.

"I guess there are some good memories?" Jason suggested. "Like that old minibike Pop got us for Christmas."

"It was a Honda CT-70, used," Tom said.

"Yup, but not as used as the full face helmet that went with it," Jason added.

They both laughed.

"I'll never forget that Christmas morning. It was snowing hard . . ."

". . . when the old man had us throw on our coats and brought us out to the shed."

"And there it was, the blue Honda," Tom said.

"Blue and rust, as I remember it," Jason recalled. "Even still, I'd never seen anything so beautiful in my life."

They nodded in synch.

"The old man wheeled it out of the shed," Jason went on, "put the kickstand down, and looked at us both. 'Merry Christmas,' he said in that rough smoker's voice."

"And as the oldest," Tom said, "you got to take the first ride."

"Best ride ever!" Jason said. "The bike turned over on the first kick. I jumped on, opened the throttle as wide as it would go, and lay flat on the gas tank . . ."

". . . and drove it right into the woods, where you twisted the handlebars and mangled the bike so bad that it could no longer be ridden," Tom recalled. "After calling you a punk, Pop turned to me and grunted, 'You should have jumped on first, dummy.'"

"Yeah, that sucked. I don't think Pop got that bike fixed for six months."

". . . which is when I got to take my first ride on it."

Jason looked at him and grinned. "But was it worth the wait?"

"Mangler," Tom said, resorting to an old nickname Jason once hated.

Jason laughed. "Dummy," he mumbled.

Tom laughed along with him.

They covered miles of highway, the radio replaced by shared nostalgia. Although most memories were recalled quite differently, they all ended in some humiliating experience or a beating from their father.

"The old man was a cruel prick, though," Tom said, shaking his head. "I'll never forget it; I was maybe seven or eight years old. We were running an errand to Chase Grain. I had to go to the bathroom really bad and kept asking him to pull over so I could go. 'You should have gone before we left the house,' he screamed at me. 'Now you can hold it!'"

Jason shook his head at the terrible memory.

"When we finally got to the grain store, I got out of the car and pissed my pants right there in the parking lot."

Jason was still shaking his head when he said, "I remember."

"I begged the grinning bastard to let me stay in the car," Tom said, "but he wouldn't hear of it. Nope, it was another opportunity to traumatize one of his boys." As Tom peered out into the distance, he gritted his teeth. "He dragged me into that fucking store where he humiliated me in front of every person in the place."

"Yeah, he was a mean bastard," Jason confirmed.

"That's the day I realized I didn't only fear him, I hated him too." Tom remembered the wooden box in the back. "Come to think of it, I need to empty my bladder right now." He looked back at his brother, grinning a devilish grin. "Do you think there's enough room in the timeout box for a few cups of piss?"

Jason shook his head and hit the right directional. "Probably not," he said, shrugging. "Besides, if you turn the old man into a paste it might be a little harder to dump him for good."

Tom thought about it for a moment before laughing so hard that he nearly pissed his pants—again. *Oh shit*, he thought, *we need to stop*. "Pull over at the next exit," he told Jason.

"Are you serious?" Jason said. "You should have gone when we stopped to fill up. Now you can hold it."

"Screw you!" Tom said, trying not to laugh anymore. Crossing his legs, he tried to slow his breathing. "Please find a bathroom."

"Well, if you put it that way," Jason said, speeding up for the next exit. Pressing the GPS screen, he shook his head. "Squeeze it tight," he said. "I hate to tell you this, but the next exit isn't for another six miles."

"We could always scoop him out of the box," Tom suggested, referring back to the idea of pissing on his father's ashes.

Jason shook his head. "You never once stooped to his level. You should be proud of that."

"Just pull over," Tom said, feeling like his bladder was going to explode.

"Okay, but you're better off pissing in one of the empty bottles. If the cops drive by . . ."

"Pull over now!" Tom barked, his legs dancing to hold it in.

Jason swooped into the breakdown lane like a diving hawk. Tom jumped out and hobbled toward the tree line. *Ahhhh* . . . After relieving himself, Tom walked back to the SUV to discover a police cruiser's flashing blue-and-red lights pulsating behind it. Jason had his badge out and was talking to the young patrolman. "Listen," he said above the whoosh of passing cars, "I've been on the job for almost thirty years." He pointed toward Tom and grinned. "He's no deviant, trust me. He definitely has some bladder control issues he needs to get looked at, but that's about the worst of it. Trust me, he wasn't in the woods trying to expose himself to traffic or anything like that."

The cop looked at Tom. "You're lucky I don't arrest you right here. I have no idea how you boys do things in Massachusetts, but in Illinois we use a bathroom when we have to urinate."

"Yes sir," Tom said, feeling torn. He'd just been saved by his brother, but he'd also been humiliated for the sport of it. *Asshole*, he thought.

The cop jumped back into his cruiser, shut off his light bar, and pulled out into traffic—throttling away.

"You're welcome," Jason said, as they jumped back into the SUV.

"Yeah, thanks," Tom muttered—*asshole*.

They were many miles from the near arrest when Tom turned to Jason. "How can you not hate him as much as I do?" he asked.

"Who?" Jason asked, confused.

"Who else?" Tom said, looking behind him toward the rear of the SUV. "The ghost in the wooden box."

Jason grinned. "I figured out long ago that whether I loved him or hated him made no difference at all—at least not to him. He never knew whether I held a grudge or was so mad at him that my stomach was all torn up, like I'd drunk a gallon of lava. And if he did, it didn't bother him in the least. I was the one who was being tormented; I was the only one doing the suffering. Once I figured that out, I gave the old man exactly what he deserved—apathy."

Tom was taken aback by his brother's simple wisdom.

Jason went on. "The moment I decided I couldn't care less about anything that bastard thought was the moment I broke free from his bullshit." He looked at his brother and nodded. "That's when I was free." They rode on for a while. "You know, if I've learned anything it's this: when someone tries to cause you misery, the best retaliation is to be happy." Jason added,

"Let it go, little brother. He was never worth all the trouble in the first place."

Tom sat back in shock. *Little brother?* It had been years since he'd been called that. He smiled to himself, still trying to reconcile Jason's rudimentary wisdom. *He's right, though. The big oaf's right.*

They drove listening to country music for a long while—with Jason being entertained and Tom being equally tormented—until they reached Wisconsin, the Badger State. *Maybe I should check in with the kids?* Tom wondered, letting the thought blend together with other thoughts, like the yellow lines that separated them from oncoming traffic.

They picked up I-94 and were just past Madison when Jason suddenly slowed the car. He was perched at the edge of his seat, scanning the side of the road like a bird of prey.

"What is it?" Tom asked, his heart rate on the rise.

"I think someone just skidded off the road and drove down the embankment up ahead of us," Jason said, never taking his eyes off the road.

A rush of adrenaline—or fear—shot into Tom's extremities, making his body tingle. "So why do *we* have to stop?" he asked, feeling panicked.

As Jason slowed the car to a crawl, he glanced sideways at him. "Because someone might be bleeding to death in a ditch right now and we're the only ones who can help save them." He drove slowly in the breakdown lane.

Tom could see the smoke billowing from the wood line a couple hundred yards ahead of them. "Do we have time for this?" he thought aloud, the panic now spreading throughout his body.

"It doesn't fit into our itinerary, no," Jason growled contemptuously. "Why don't you try being a man for once?"

"Okay, Dad," Tom answered instinctively.

Jason glared at him again. It was obvious; he could have either backhanded him into the next county, or let the comment go. It didn't look like he cared either way. Fortunately, while Tom's heart pounded away in his throat, Jason's eyes went back to the windshield and the side of the road. "Just call 911," he said before bringing the SUV to a jerky stop, then jumping out and sprinting down the embankment toward the black plume of smoke.

After providing the female dispatcher with their location, Tom got out of the vehicle and—like he was a kid again, willing himself to return to the cemetery—he hustled down to the accident scene. Before he saw anything, he could hear the panicked whimpers of a teenage girl begging for help—followed by his brother's baritone promises that she'd "be okay." *Oh God*, Tom thought, picking up the pace and dreading the gruesome scene he was sure to witness.

The flipped vehicle was literally resting on its passenger side door in the ditch, its motor hissing angrily. The windshield was so smashed, it was difficult to make out the girl's terrified face at first. Somehow, she was suspended by her seat belt, her cries getting louder and more frantic with each moment that passed. Tom thought he was going to vomit. *Oh no . . .* As his legs wobbled, threatening to take him to the ground, he heard his brother's calm voice.

"It's going to be okay," Jason told the girl. "I'm right here with you and I'm not going anywhere, I promise." He looked up and made eye contact with Tom, offering just enough strength for Tom to move closer to the heap of metal that was once a car. "We're going to get you out," Jason told the sobbing girl, without a hint of doubt in his voice.

If anyone can save her, Tom thought, *it's my brother*. A new wave of terror struck his heart. His nose—once filled with the nauseating smell of deep-dish pizza—caught the first whiff of leaking gasoline, rocking him back on his heels. "Gas!" he screamed.

With a nod, Jason acknowledged that he smelled the same. The truth of it, however, didn't stop him from going right to work and ignoring his own safety. His massive hands grabbed a corner of the shattered windshield and started pulling. The

frame that held the glass shards together moaned like the final complaints of a capsized ship. Jason pulled again and again. Finally, his bloody hands peeled it away enough to reach the girl. Somehow, he was able to unstrap her and, with one grunt, pull her out—carrying her a safe distance from the smoking wreck.

Oh my God, Tom thought, in complete awe of his brother. Up until that point, he hadn't realized he'd been frozen in place while his brother worked alone.

Sirens wailed in the distance as Jason pulled off his button-down shirt and balled it up for the girl to use as a pillow. He huffed and puffed, trying to catch his breath, while elevating her feet to treat her for shock. "The ambulance is on its way, sweetheart," he gasped her way, spitting a few times into the grass. "You've been through the worst of it, okay?"

After the girl was placed on a stretcher and loaded into the back of the ambulance, the paramedics tended to Jason's bloodied hands.

"You're lucky that car didn't catch fire," a middle-aged patrolman told Jason, gesturing toward the wreck. "She would have gone up like a Roman candle."

"I know," Jason said.

The cop patted his back. "Nice work, fellas," he said, looking back at Tom.

Don't look at me, Tom thought, *I didn't do anything.* But he only nodded and never said a word, feeling like a complete fraud.

When Jason's eyes met his again, the big man shrugged. "Maybe I do need to lose a few pounds," he said, grinning.

"I don't know," Tom said. "I'd say you did a pretty damned good job."

Jason nodded again before looking down at his bandaged hand. "I need to get a fresh shirt out of my luggage."

Tom nodded and hustled off to retrieve it, thinking, *It's the least I can do.*

They were quite a stretch down the road when Tom couldn't take the silence anymore. "I apologize, Jason," he said. "I get pretty nerved up at the sight of blood so . . ."

". . . so you'd drive past someone in trouble just to avoid a little discomfort in your perfect life?" Jason asked, his eyes focused on the windshield.

"Perfect?" Tom snickered. "It's hardly perfect."

"The way I see it," Jason said, his tone less angry, "if it was Miranda or Caroline bleeding out in that ditch, I'd want someone to stop and help. Wouldn't you?"

"Of course," Tom admitted.

"Well, there it is then," Jason said, meeting his brother's gaze again. "You're not a bad guy, Tom, but I hope I'm not around when karma shows up to give you a colonoscopy with a cheese grater."

Just when we were starting to get along, Tom thought, disappointed in himself.

They drove in silence for a very long time—right into Eau Claire, Wisconsin, where Jason decided they were going to stop for lunch.

After a couple rich meals in a row, they agreed to get something quick at a drive-thru. Jason pointed straight at the golden arches beckoning on Craig Road.

"Fine," Tom said. "But we'll be looking for a bathroom soon, and not because of my bladder."

Jason nodded. "I can live with that."

I guess I deserve that, Tom thought.

At the drive-thru window, Jason ordered three burgers, adding, "No seeds on my bun."

"Why not?"

"I can't have seeds," Jason said. "I had diverticulitis."

"So do I," Tom said, shocked. *It's obviously a genetic issue,* he thought, but couldn't recall their father ever having the same issue. *It must be from our mother's side.*

After they received two bags of food and two enormous drinks, they parked to eat.

"I had to have a colon resection," Jason added, yanking the first seedless burger out of the bag. "They took out a third of my radiator hose. Any more and it's a colostomy bag for me."

"No more swimsuit modeling if that happens," Tom said. "What about you?"

"Not yet for me," Tom said, thinking, *I have more pressing health concerns at the moment.* "I'm just watching what I eat right now. No nuts or seeds."

"Me either, but some doctors say that's bullshit," Jason interrupted, tearing off a quarter of his burger with one bite.

"I guess it depends on who you talk to, but I'm not taking any chances." Tom shook his head. "The doctor said if I have another bad flare up, I'm going to see the surgeon because it's already borderline."

"Ulcerated?" Jason asked, gulping from his small jug of soda.

Tom nodded. "When it's bad, it's real bad. The last thing I want is to go under the knife."

"You're right, you don't want that," Jason interrupted. "It's a rough patch of road, believe me."

"It hurts like hell when it flares up," Tom said. "I can't even imagine the surgery."

Jason nodded. "I had an abscess, an ulcerated colon, and couldn't even walk because of the pain. I was frozen in a pharmacy parking lot and couldn't take another step. Miranda had to pull her car up alongside me, open the door, and watch as I collapsed in. The doctor put me on a Z-Pak, but once the infection had cleared up, I was off to the butcher shop."

"Nice," Tom said.

"They gutted me like a fish," he said, recounting the experience. "The intake nurse took blood, but was having trouble finding the vein, so I asked her if she was trying to harvest bone marrow." He laughed. "After signing a stack of waivers, the anesthesiologist gave me a sedative, rolled me onto a moving gurney, and took me on the back lot tour of the surgical floor. Everything was getting fuzzy when he wheeled me into some wide elevator. There was a Red Cross poster tacked to the elevator wall, with a giant pepperoni pizza on it. It advertised a coupon for a free pizza if you gave a pint of blood. I was feeling loopy and found the whole thing funny, so I asked the guy, "What do I get for a pint of piss, bread sticks?' The guy laughed harder than he should have, making me wonder whether he was the right man to be putting me to sleep."

Tom laughed.

"They rolled me into the operating room, transferred me to the table, and threw a rubber mask over my mouth." He shook his head. "I was supposed to count backwards from ten, but I don't think I made it to seven when I woke up with a belly full of staples." He looked at Tom. "No bullshit, it looked like they gave me a zipper without the pain. It was my first taste of morphine, and that's when I understood how people can get addicted."

Tom nodded.

"They starved me for three days before starting me on Jell-O. I begged Rhonda, my girlfriend of the year, to smuggle me in some food. 'Just get me a tuna pocket,' I told her. 'I'd do it for you.' She refused, saying it could put an end to me." He grinned. "*Just like this relationship*, I thought."

Tom laughed again.

"Six days into the nine-day hospital retreat," Jason continued, "the head nurse—who had the girth of a defensive tackle—marched into the room like she was on a mission from God. 'The catheter needs to come out,' she said, pulling the sheets off me. Without any sweet talk or even a warning, she grabbed lil' Jason by the neck and pulled the tube out of him like she was trying to fire up a three-and-a-half-horse Briggs and Stratton lawn mower motor."

Tom was rolling now. *Lil' Jason?* he thought.

"'You have two hours to provide a urine sample,' she told me. 'If not, the catheter goes back in.' I was still recovering from the trauma, but told her, 'I'm as weak as a house cat right now, but you still don't have enough people on this floor to shove that thing back into me.' She actually grinned, like she was looking forward to the challenge. 'Let's see how it goes,' she said."

Tom waited to hear more. "And?" he asked impatiently.

"Are you kidding me?" he said. "I pushed and pushed until lil' Jason did his thing." He handed Tom one of his burgers.

"I don't want it," Tom said, reluctantly accepting the burger.

Jason shrugged. "Possession is nine-tenths of the law," he said. "It's yours now." He nodded. "Maybe we should both avoid the nuts and seeds to be on the safe side."

On their way back to the highway, Jason discovered a Dairy Maid Ice Cream shop on Birch Street. "We have to stop," he announced excitedly.

He's like an eating machine, Tom thought. *I've never seen anything like it.*

While Tom lapped at a small cone of vanilla, Jason tore through a concoction known as the hurricane—a mix of ice creams with various sauces and toppings stirred in.

They weren't one block down the road when Jason's belly started rumbling, his internal blender churning loud enough for Tom to hear.

"Now I know why they named it the hurricane," Jason said, "because it's ripping right through me." The giant frozen treat had settled in like some nasty coastal storm, preparing to leave some real destruction in its wake. Jason lifted his backside off the passenger's seat and gritted his teeth. "We'd better find a bathroom soon," he told Tom, grimacing in real pain.

Tom laughed so hard, he thought he was going to shit his own pants. *I just hope this helps us get beyond my shameful behavior at the accident scene back there.*

chapter 7

I STILL CAN'T BELIEVE IT, Jason thought, *if I wasn't there, Tom would have driven right past that accident scene.* Learning long ago that true nobility is simply doing the right thing when no one else is watching, Jason shook his head in disappointment. *Even now, my brother has no sense of honor,* he thought. *In fact, he has some real character defects.* He felt his stomach rumble again, the hurricane threatening to attack from one end or the other. *I just hope I got it all out.*

As Tom barreled down I-94 toward Minnesota, he called each of his kids. "Call me back when you get this," he told them both. Within seconds, his cell phone rang. "Hi Caleb," he said, answering the call.

Jason smiled. *Good boy,* he thought, *that's progress.* While Tom spoke to his son, Jason relaxed in the passenger seat, his eyelids shut. *But still no call from Carmen,* he thought. *Something's definitely up there.*

Once Tom finished the call, he rolled through the radio stations until he found a talk show that came in clearly. Jason could feel his head buzz.

"Police profiling is a legalized criminal activity," the female caller claimed. "Even after the tragedies of nine-eleven, it's one hundred percent criminal."

"Oh, here we go," Jason said, already aggravated.

"So you're in favor of police profiling?" Tom asked, lowering the radio.

"Of course," Jason said, nodding. "It's now necessary for the safety of the police and the security of this nation. With so many fundamentalists creeping around out there, I'd say it's better to be politically incorrect than dead." Jason opened one eye. "And I'm guessing you disagree with me?"

Tom nodded. "I do," he said. "In my opinion, too much power corrupts."

Jason chuckled. "So I imagine you're opposed to the death penalty too, right?"

"Of course," Tom said. "I think the entire practice is inhumane and barbaric. If one innocent human being can be put to death as a result of another human's error, we shouldn't even entertain it."

"Really?" *Innocent human being?* Jason thought. *Do those really exist?*

"Besides," Tom said, still on a roll, "it's more expensive than what it's worth." He half-shrugged. "Maybe a lifetime of incarceration is worse than death?"

"You only feel that way because you've never met Vince Rakowski, the cold-blooded killer," Jason said. "Trust me, Tom, some people are just wired wrong."

"So you're in favor of the death penalty?"

Jason nodded. "Absolutely," he said. "It's simple: you take a life, be prepared to offer your own in return."

Tom's face filled with disgust.

"And if we're following your financial reasoning, the average inmate costs taxpayers thirty-five thousand dollars per year, while the average death row inmate costs one and a half million dollars in exhausting the appellate process."

Tom's face grew red. "So the whole world is black and white, huh?" he said. "The bad guys should sit in Sparky's lap? Kill 'em all and let God sort it out, right?"

Jason grinned. "Well, I do know that the world's not all gray like you see it," he said, intentionally maintaining a calmer voice than his flustered brother. "Maybe I should get you a visitor's pass to come inside and spend an afternoon with big Vince?"

"The way I see it, the entire justice system is one big, ineffective, corrupt business that shows mercy only to those who can afford it," Tom said, unwilling to concede.

"I can't argue with you there," Jason said, finding pleasure in crawling under his brother's paper-thin skin once again. "The basic concept is noble and just. But you're absolutely right; the practice is corrupt and ineffective." He nodded. "The law works. It's those who interpret and practice it that screw everything up."

Tom was clearly taken aback.

"And I should know," Jason added. "I've devoted my entire life to a system that only works in theory."

They were just past Minneapolis, the state's capital, when a tractor-trailer cut them off and began hogging two lanes, pushing Tom onto the shoulder of the road. "Son of a bitch," he grumbled. "I swear, trucks should be banned from major highways during the day."

"Are you crazy? Those trucks are the main supply line for Main Street America."

"That's fine, but they should only be allowed to make their runs at night," Tom said.

"If you say so."

"Why don't we follow him so you can spank him when he stops?"

"There are two reasons," Jason said, grinning.

"And what are those?"

"Because that'll just take us off course, which, in turn, will make you pout for hours."

"I don't pout," Tom said.

"Sure you don't."

"And the second reason?"

"Because most truck drivers carry shotguns," Jason said.

Tom nodded. "We should probably stay on course then."

"It's your call," Jason said, his grin turning into a full smile. A moment later, his cell phone rang. He looked at the caller ID and cringed. As if it was a virus, he threw the phone onto the dashboard.

"You're not going to answer it?" Tom asked.

Jason shook his head. "It's Janice again. She either wants to shit on me for something or spend more of my money. Either way, I don't want anything to do with it."

Tom nodded. "That must have been a friendly divorce, huh?"

Jason chuckled, closing his eyes again. "The friendliest," he joked, but it was anything but funny. "I admit I could be tough on the old lady back in the day, with my drinking and all, but she made me pay in spades." He shook off Miranda's face and concentrated on Janice. "When me and Janice split, I moved into my buddy's cellar. That was the bottom for me. For the longest time, I believed that Janice had betrayed me. But as the months went by, I realized it was actually youth that did me wrong."

"How do you mean?" Tom asked.

"When we'd met, I was too young and blind to see who she really was . . . what she really is. A few months after we'd tied the knot, Janice became the typical neurotic housewife who'd sacrificed her looks for her daughter and wasn't pleased with the price of motherhood. The ex prom queen spent most of her time reminiscing about her days in the sun, either sulking in the mirror or sleeping on the couch. To most of the world, we were a traditional family. But behind closed doors, we were miserable." Although the harsh memories were still there, Jason could no longer feel the pain. Time had taken care of that. "Janice is the most selfish person I've ever known." Miranda's little face popped into his head again. He quickly shook off the image.

Tom nodded.

As they reached road signs for St. Cloud, Jason's cell phone rang again. He reached up and plucked the phone off the dashboard. *It's Miranda*, he thought, immediately answering it. "Hi, sweetheart. I've been thinking about you. How's everything going?"

"Great," she said. "How about you?"

He looked at his brother behind the wheel. "Could be worse, I guess," he said, shrugging.

"That's good," she said, but was already focused on her next thought. "Mom's been trying to call you."

"I know."

"You do?"

"Yup."

"Oh, okay," she stammered. "We were thinking . . ."

"What is it?" he asked, thinking, *And how much will it cost me this time?*

"We were thinking that it might be a nice touch to have two ice sculptures of angels kissing at the reception." She paused. "Like it's me and Mario," she finished in the same voice she used as a little girl to bend and twist him around her little finger.

"Ice sculptures? Really?"

"Please, Dad. It'll be so beautiful."

"You're the one who's going to be beautiful," he said, well aware that he could never deny her anything. "If that's what you want, then . . ."

"Oh, Daddy," she said, "thank you so much. I really appreciate it."

"You're welcome," he said, feeling a pang of joy for making her happy.

"Be safe, Dad," she said. "I can't wait until you're home."

"Me either, baby girl, believe me." He looked back at Tom and grinned. "And don't you worry about your old man. It's the rest of the world that should be careful."

She laughed. "Bye, Dad."

146

"Bye, sweetheart." As he hung up, he caught Tom's judgmental grin. "What?" he asked.

"Couldn't say no to her, huh?" Tom said.

Jason shook his head. "Nope. Will you be able to when it's Caroline asking?"

"Nope."

They both laughed.

"After all these years, they still have us wrapped tight," Tom said.

"Ain't that the truth."

"It sounds like you raised a great kid," Tom said, being sincere.

Instantly, Jason's chest swelled with pride. "I did," he said. "Although I don't know how much credit I can take for it. When Miranda was in the sixth grade, she won the Kendall Vars Memorial Award for being a remarkable kid." He smiled wide. "I knew she was remarkable long before that."

"I'm sure you had something to do with it," Tom said.

Jason was taken aback. "It hasn't been the easiest road, that's for sure," he said, sidestepping the praise.

Tom looked at him, but said nothing—waiting to hear the details.

Jason took a deep breath. "It can be hell, being a single dad," he said, already feeling himself getting choked up. He quickly collected himself. "I've lost many things in my life, but to not tuck my little girl in every night was inhuman. Since she could speak, Miranda's called me her 'bestest friend.' Even at eight years old, she still believed I was the strongest, smartest, most handsome man in the whole world." He sighed heavily. "And that's when 'irreconcilable differences' kicked me out of my comfortable recliner and into a living hell.

"At first, Janice and I decided to act like real adults and 'do what was in the best interest of our child.' But I quickly learned this would be impossible because 'the best interest of our child' was as different in our minds as our ideas for saving the marriage. Right away, Janice considered our daughter her closest ally and decided that she and the girl were a package deal. She couldn't see the separation. My daughter was hers and if I wasn't with Janice, then I was nothing but an outsider. In other words, if she and I were going to be separated, then so were Miranda and I."

"I get it," Tom said, his face flushed with fear.

"Janice and I went to court, a place designed to bring criminals to justice, not reconcile family differences. Both lawyers muttered half-truths while a stranger dressed in a black robe allowed us no more than fifteen minutes to decide our family's future. I panicked and cleared my throat to speak, but the judge quickly threatened me into silence."

Tom swallowed hard.

"Before it started, it was over. As a man, I was screwed. With nothing for me to do but watch, my entire world was destroyed. The judge issued a punishment harsher than any prison term I'd ever seen: I could take my daughter on loan, two nights a week for a few hours and every other weekend. I was in shock. I'd heard the rumors, read the stories, but I still couldn't believe it."

"A father who was no more than one-half of a marriage that no longer worked," Tom added, recapping the story. "That's so unfair."

Jason nodded. "The judge suggested Janice and I work together with regards to Miranda's education, religious aspirations, and activities, but it was all bullshit. Not long after we left court, reality set in: I'd take Miranda for our court-ordered visits, only to drop her off a couple hours later." He stopped and looked at Tom. "Just imagine that the person who hates you most controls the person you love most."

Tom nodded. "Unfortunately, I can," he mumbled.

Jason sighed heavily. "The playing field is so damned uneven!" *Fucking bitch*, he thought, a tidal wave of old, painful feelings rising to the surface. He took a moment to compose himself. "Back then, everything I'd ever been taught—everything that makes me who I am—raged inside of me to lash out. I wanted to go to war with Janice, I really did, but the same question always stopped me: *Do I pull on Miranda until she breaks in half?*" He shook his head. "Of course not," he said. "The only thing I could do was become the best dad I could be and hope that, in time, Miranda would know how much I love her."

"Amen to that," Tom said.

Jason took a few deep breaths before softening his tone. "Through the years, I've had to remind myself that I can only find happiness in my life through forgiveness. Although I still believe that fathers are at a terrible disadvantage when it comes to child custody laws, I also know that the child *must* come first."

"Good for you," Tom said, his pale face betraying his worry.

He's afraid to travel down the same broken road, Jason realized. *That's what it is.* "And do you want to know the damndest thing?" he asked.

Tom nodded.

"Through it all, even on the worst days, there was a part of me that was grateful Miranda had her mom . . . something we'd been cheated out of."

Tom nodded. "I get it," he whispered.

Jason sighed heavily. "Recently, Miranda and I had dinner at our favorite Mexican restaurant," he said. "During the conversation, I was teasing her and said, 'You were raised better than that.' She looked at me and smiled. 'I know, Dad,' she said, 'and I thank you for that.' It took all I had not to break down crying right there and then."

Tom nodded one last time, but looked away to conceal the tears that were swelling up in his frightened eyes.

They rolled into Fergus Falls, Minnesota—nothing but some indiscriminate dot on Tom's map—where they agreed to spend the night. AmericInn on Western Avenue was a typical motor lodge, with a cozy fireplace in the common room off the lobby. While Tom took a seat on a brown leather couch and checked his phone—balancing the lackluster box of ashes on top of his luggage—Jason decided to have fun at the check-in counter. "They have free Wi-Fi," he yelled back to Tom, too excitedly.

"Wow, that's big," Tom called back, playing along.

Kelly—the girl behind the counter—grinned proudly, like she really had something to offer them.

"What's there to do around here?" Jason asked, drawing a heavy sigh from his brother behind him.

"The Fergus Falls State Hospital is beautiful. It looks like a castle."

"It's a hospital?" Jason asked.

"A psychiatric hospital."

"Good. I'll swing by and see if I can drop my brother off." Tom chuckled.

"Other than that, we have the Central Lakes Trail you can hike on," Kelly said, "or a horseback riding ranch just up the road."

"We'll stick with the asylum, I think," Jason said.

Kelly looked over at Tom, nodding as if she understood.

The room was clean, but hardly the palace Jason had stayed in the night before. After getting showered and dressed for dinner, he swung by the fitness center to peek his head in—even though he had no intentions of using any of the equipment. The room was the size of a walk-in closet. He laughed. Across the hall, he noticed that the motor lodge had a decent-sized indoor pool, with red cedar planking covering the high ceiling. As he took his first step onto the slick tiles, the sauna-like heat hit him right away, making his eyes burn from the heavy chlorine that hung in the thick air. *To hell with this*, he thought but, as he was about to leave, he eyed a young couple wading in the shallow end of the pool, teaching a little girl how to swim. *She looks like Miranda,* he thought, his mind immediately returning to the glorious days when he'd taught his daughter how to keep her head above water. *All that screaming and whining,* he thought. *I remember thinking that I couldn't wait until those days were over.* He smiled at the young family, who smiled back. *What I wouldn't do to get those moments back.* Before turning to leave, he waved at the child's father. *It feels like only months ago when Miranda took off her inflatable vest and paddled around like some proud guppy.* His eyes stung with tears. *Damned chlorine.*

Dressed as dapper as ever, Tom was already waiting in the lobby—empty-handed.

"Where's Pop?" Jason asked, trying not to laugh. "He's not coming to dinner with us tonight?"

Tom shook his head. "I put him in the closet." He grinned. "You were right. If someone does take him, it won't be long before they bring him back."

Jason chuckled. "So you don't think he'd fetch a handsome ransom?"

"Not one red cent," Tom said.

They both laughed.

Illuminated by multiple spotlights on the sprawling grounds, the Fergus Falls State Hospital did look like a castle. *Screw that place,* Jason thought, less interested in visiting a locked facility than anything he could think of.

"Do you miss work?" Tom asked, as if reading his mind.

"Not at all. You?"

Tom shook his head. "Not even a little bit." He pointed toward the scar over Jason's eye. "No one's ever tried to maim me, though. The worse I have to deal with is some hungover student nodding off during class."

Jason laughed. "I got this souvenir from some nut who tried to pick my nose with a prison shiv that looked a lot like an ice pick." He shook his head. "And I'm pretty sure he was trying to kill me, not just maim me."

"I can't even imagine experiencing something like that. It must have been scary as hell."

Jason nodded. "It's odd, but when things go down you don't think about the possible outcomes. You just react and meet violence with even more violence."

"Damn."

Jason shrugged. "Lots of bleeding on this one, though," he said, pointing to his scar, ". . . for both of us." He could remember the fight as vividly as the night it had happened. "After getting slapped around all those years by the old man, I have a serious intolerance towards people putting their hands on me. It's amazing how the slightest aggressive touch is still a real trigger for me."

Tom nodded. "I can understand that."

"Believe it or not, I got suspended for how I reacted to getting stabbed," he explained, recalling how he was two or three solid punches away from taking his aggressor's life. "They sent me to see the department's shrink, where I was forced to lie for two weeks straight until I could get back on the job."

Tom was clearly taken aback. "Is there any satisfaction in punishing inmates?" he asked, innocently.

"Punishing?"

"Beating up on prisoners," Tom qualified.

Jason shook his head. "In that fight, I was attacked by some maniac with a weapon and had to fight for my life. It was as easy as that. For the most part, though, officers don't beat on inmates," he said. "Inmates beat on inmates."

"I don't get it."

"You probably don't want to," Jason said before drifting off to a recent memory.

Although Sergeant Jason Prendergast had started his new block assignment on a Monday, by Wednesday he was already having a problem with one of the younger Hispanic inmates. "When I tell you to do something, it needs to get done," he told the kid, rotating the unlit cigar in his mouth.

"You can kiss my brown ass," the kid spit out of the side of his face.

Jason grinned, thinking, *And the game has begun.*

The following morning, Jason released the block for chow—late. This made everyone shuffle their feet uneasily. Even Pauli Patricio—an old mobster who maintained a "leader" status among his fellow inmates—appeared antsy. Being institutionalized, the slightest delay in scheduling rocked them really hard. Everyone shrugged off the major change as just something the "new Screw" needed to get used to. That afternoon, however, after the mail had arrived late, Patricio sent one of his mice down the tier to get some answers.

Jason ensured that the dispatched messenger would report back that he was withholding a stack of letters. After receiving word, Patricio stepped out of his room, stared down every one of his neighbors, and then returned to his confined suite—enraged. Jason smiled. *Perfect*, he thought. *The entire prison experience, and it doesn't matter which side you play on, is designed around time. Good officers always get their man. They have to. Reputation dictates survival and, for whatever he didn't give me, Pop raised me to be a survivor.*

The following day, when it was time to turn on the showers, Jason waited fifteen minutes longer than usual. This was no accident and Patricio knew it. Jason might have been new to the block, but he was a veteran officer and knew better. By this point, everyone understood that Sergeant Prendergast was intentionally rocking the boat.

When Patricio approached the desk, all the other cons scattered. It was going to be a private conversation. "What's

153

the deal with this week's movie?" the mobster asked Jason, smirking.

"Haven't decided whether I'm going to run it yet," Jason said with a shrug.

Patricio grinned. "Is there gonna be a ball game on Saturday?" he asked.

Jason returned the grin. "According to the extended forecast, the weather doesn't look promising, does it?"

Now there was no denying it. The block was being informally punished. Patricio asked one last question. "What's the problem?"

"The block's dirty," Jason said, simply, "and someone needs to clean it up."

Patricio nodded, turned on his heels, and strutted away—whistling.

Within the hour, the young, disrespectful Hispanic inmate stumbled up to Jason's desk. Both eyes—now a mix of purple and yellow—had been nearly closed shut. His face was so swollen it looked like it had been plunged into a hornet's nest. He was bleeding profusely from his mouth, while bruises were beginning to appear over much of his exposed skin. *Someone's worked him over pretty badly*, Jason thought, immediately getting on his radio. "144 to Southeast Control, we need an escort for one to the HSU." He clipped the radio mic back onto his uniform epaulette. "Tell me what happened," he told the prisoner with the beehive face.

"I tripped and fell in the shower," the man said, grimacing. "I tripped on a . . . on a bar of soap."

"It looks like you tripped on a few bars of soap," Jason said, nodding. "That's a real shame."

The inmate shrugged, but he wasn't about to rat anyone out. The wolves that lined the tiers were carefully watching. Before long, the silenced wiseass was carted off to the Health Services Unit.

Jason stood. "Line up for chow!" he barked, his announcement right on time.

On his way past Jason's desk, Patricio asked, "How's the weather looking for Saturday's ball game, Sarge?"

"They say it'll be nice and clear now," Jason said, nodding. And that was the game. It wasn't nice. It wasn't fair. But that's the way things went down behind the wall. Officers didn't beat on inmates. Inmates beat on inmates and kept their own house clean.

Patricio chuckled. "You boys in uniform might be a little less organized, working for the government and all, but don't kid yourselves. In this place, you're all *made men*."

And then it hit Jason. His occupation as a correction officer wasn't all that different from being a thug keeping order on the street. He realized that the traits he despised in the inmates were the same things he disliked in himself. *Maybe me and Pauli Patricio aren't so different after all?* he wondered. Thinking on it some more, he finally shrugged. *No matter what it takes, it's my job to keep 'em behind the wall. And maintaining order in this shit hole is the only way to do it.*

Emerging from his daydream, Jason shrugged. "It's easy," he told Tom. "Let's just suppose I'm having a problem with one of the younger inmates. For the sake of argument, we'll say that he disrespects me, challenging my authority in front of the whole block."

"Yes," Tom said, completely enthralled.

"Well, in order to maintain law and order, I can't have anyone questioning my authority, right? We're talking about an environment of survival here."

Tom nodded. "I understand."

"All I have to do is play with the entire block; mess with their chow times or hold back their mail." He nodded. "Believe me, it doesn't take long before they figure out there's a problem and that they need to come up with a solution."

"So they punish the young prisoner for disrespecting you?"

Jason nodded again. "You got it and you can't imagine how vicious that punishment can be." He looked at Tom. "So tell me, how fucked up is that?"

Tom thought about it for a few moments.

Here comes my penance, he thought.

"It sounds to me like you're only doing your job."

Jason was surprised, never expecting these words to roll off his brother's forked tongue. *But his words are genuine,* he decided, disarmed.

"I wouldn't punish myself over it, if I were you," Tom added. "In fact, it sounds like you're really good at your job."

"So I've saved a few pedophiles' lives, big deal," Jason snapped.

"Serving your community *is* a big deal, if you ask me," Tom said.

Jason suddenly felt incensed—not at his brother, but at the career he'd devoted his entire adult life to—and was unable to contain his deep emotions. "You have no idea the pieces of shit that are still drawing breath because of yours truly!" After a long while, he nodded. "But if I'm being honest, there are times when it does feel good to slap around a predator."

Tom nodded. "I bet," he muttered, his tone melancholy.

Something's wrong, Jason thought, his head whipping sideways. "What about you? Have you ever been so pissed at someone you wanted to beat the snot out of them?"

Tom shrugged. "I don't know . . ."

"Bullshit," Jason said. "That's bullshit." He slowed the car until it seemed they were going to pull over. "You're telling me you've never wanted to beat the hell out of some asshole?"

Tom took a deep breath and sighed. "Well, there is this one guy . . ."

"Is?" Jason asked, surprised. *Tom's speaking in the present.* "Is someone giving you a hard time right now?" he asked, feeling the age-old obligations of an overly protective big brother. After all these years, as much as he disliked many of Tom's ways, he couldn't help but still feel defensive of him; it was almost at a molecular level, part of his DNA that he could neither understand nor control.

"Not really," Tom said.

That's a lie, Jason thought, considering whether he should dig deeper.

"There must be something that's taken place in the last thirty years that you feel good about?" Tom said, deflecting the focus away from himself.

"Actually, I've been volunteering my time over the past few years, working with kids in DYS lockup." Jason shrugged. "Trying to scare them into staying out of the big house, you know?"

Tom gawked at him, his clever tongue at a standstill.

"What is it?" Jason asked.

"I'm surprised, that's all."

"And why would you be surprised?" Jason asked.

"No reason," Tom said. "I guess I shouldn't be."

"You can't believe what the payoff's like," Jason said, feeling a real sense of accomplishment warm his chest.

Tom chuckled. "Yeah, I know. I teach for a living, remember?"

"Nope, you get paid to deliver information to people who are only concerned with getting three credits, that's what you do for a living. I'm talking about working with kids who are still young enough to give a shit. You should consider volunteering."

Tom started to respond but stopped.

"I'm not suggesting this because of what they'll gain," Jason quickly explained. "I'm saying that you're the one who will receive the most from the exchange." He nodded. "Volunteering to teach youths and pass on our knowledge," he said, shrugging again, "sometimes I think it's one of the few purposes we have left to fulfill."

Tom half-nodded.

"Do you still enjoy teaching?" Jason asked.

"At this point, I'm just feeding my kids, you know? It wouldn't make any real difference if I did something else for a living, as long as I made the same money." He shook his head. "I'm not sure I enjoy anything anymore," he added, being honest.

Jason snickered. "It looks like we both need to work on that," he said, as they pulled in front of the Viking Café.

There was no real street appeal. The Viking Café looked like a brick-faced barroom, an illuminated two-sided Coke sign hanging over the curved wooden door. Tom parked under an ornate green lamppost across the street. The restaurant's round windows—like portholes on a grounded ship—made Jason wonder, *Seafood joint?*

It was dark inside, taking Jason's eyes a few moments to adjust. At the hostess station, he said, "Can I pull up a seat to the buffet? You know, just to save time."

"Sorry, sir. That's not allowed."

He shook his head. "So many rules," he sighed.

Ignoring the comment, she asked, "Two for dinner?"

Jason nodded. "Our dad's out in the car, but he's not hungry."

"Ummm . . . what?" she asked, confused.

Tom laughed aloud. "You're brutal," he whispered, clearly enjoying the harmless banter.

"Pop hasn't been on his best behavior," Jason said with a straight face, "so he's . . ."

"That's terrible!" she interrupted, mortified.

"He'll be fine," Tom said, trying to conceal his grin. "He's as snug as a bug in his crate."

With a huff, she grabbed two menus and scurried off into the shadows of the place. Beyond the bar, they were seated at a small table—the kind you would expect to find in a bar turned restaurant. While Tom made a beeline for the men's room, Jason took the seat against the wall and checked the specials board. *Roast turkey dinner with all the fixin's sounds perfect*, he thought.

Jason scanned the fairly crowded restaurant. He'd become such an expert at human behavior that he could read any situation in an instant. There was a young couple leaning in toward each other, hanging on to one another's every word. Another couple, much older, was dining in silence; by their body language and ages, Jason surmised, *They're most likely waiting for their children to finish college before putting the house up on the market and a merciful end to their miserable marriage.* A guy, seated alone, was talking too loudly on his cell phone. Jason glared long enough to soften his volume but not so long that the loudmouth ended the call. There was a waitress with a neck tattoo and enough facial lines to paint a story of a checkered and challenging past. Finally, there was an elderly woman dining alone in the corner, clinging to her diminishing place in society. *Poor thing*, Jason thought and, with a smile, nodded her way. She returned the kind gesture. When Jason had confirmed there was no danger, he sat back, opened the menu, and relaxed. *Turkey with all the fixin's*, he confirmed.

Tom returned to the table, still wiping his hands on his pants. "Why do you always take the seat with your back against the wall?"

"Never gave it much thought," Jason said, shrugging. "Self-preservation, I guess. Just another souvenir from my years in . . ." His words came to a screeching halt. One of the waitresses took the floor and made Jason's heart plummet into his shoes. For a moment, he couldn't peel his eyes away. She was young, a few years older than Miranda. *But she's not my daughter*, he quickly reminded himself. Her hair was strawberry blonde, naturally curly, and pulled back away from her face. Jason couldn't decide whether she was drop-dead gorgeous or cute—the kind of cute that stole your breath away.

He finally decided, *It's both.* By her body language, she was clearly a self-confident young woman. She caught him looking and locked on to his gaze, holding it long enough to make him catch his breath and feel thirty years younger—all in one magical moment. She smiled at him with her eyes, finishing it with a subtle wink and mischievous grin. She then turned, as if to give him a 360-degree view of everything she had to offer. Her protruding ass, which gravity had not yet claimed, sat tall and proud just beneath the small of her back. As she brushed past, she smelled good—not perfumed, but the clean scent of a moisturizing body lotion. Her perky breasts were on the smaller side but ample. She had a flat midsection, which featured a diamond-studded belly button. There were dimples at her hipbones, which were also exposed. There was a black tattoo, some foreign script, on the inside of her wrist. She was maybe twenty-five, definitely old enough to be legal but still young enough to make his moral compass spin out of control. Cutting his age in half and adding seven years, he figured, *She's still too young.* He shook his head. *Toys that are shiny and new are a lot of fun*, he thought, *but driving a Ferrari down a dead end street can be a really dangerous trip.*

When their waitress—an older woman dressed in a stained smock and comfortable shoes—arrived with two glasses of water, Jason ordered the chicken dumpling soup, while Tom got the old-fashioned tomato. Even while ordering, Jason craned his neck in search of his newest infatuation.

"What are you looking for?" Tom asked.

My youth, Jason thought, but merely shook his head. "Nothing," he said. "One of the waitresses looks like someone I used to know."

Tom said nothing.

After slurping down the bowl of soup, Jason told their waitress, "Just give me the steak, please. No veggies. My body will reject them anyway." He took a deep breath and exhaled. "I should have just started with dessert."

Tom was nearly shaking his head off his shoulders when the strawberry blonde reappeared and shot another smile Jason's way. As he winked at her, his heart skipped again. She brought back a warm rush of long-forgotten memories of hot summer nights in the bed of his first pickup truck, an old, rusted Ford F-150: a white Styrofoam cooler filled with ice and cans of beer; a sky full of stars; music playing; glimpses of his first love lying on a pile of tattered blankets, naked and moaning—as hungry for him as he was for her. Needing to relieve their aching bodies, they pulled each other into themselves until they became a gaggle of entwined arms and legs. Their lovemaking was awkward and rough—hard, vigorous thrusts that ended in some hyperventilating and a broken condom. *Oh shit . . .*

Jason also recalled the fear that followed—all the while wondering whether sex was even worth the trouble—until she called and announced, "I got my period." And then they were at it again, like two hyperactive bunny rabbits, testing dozens of more condoms and the terrifying thrills of adolescence.

Jason returned to the present to find her wiggling her cute little index finger at him—gesturing for him to come talk to her.

Me? he thought, looking behind him to see if she was summoning another person. There was no one behind him. *What would a young, gorgeous girl want with an overweight guy in his fifties?* he wondered.

She wiggled her finger again.

"I think we're going to need a safe word," he said, starting to stand.

"What's that?" Tom asked, looking behind him for a clue about what he was missing.

"Just give me a minute," he told Tom, and got up to meet the flirtatious girl out near the bar—his heart trying to beat out of his chest. With one simple wink, the hook was baited. *Boy, is it baited,* Jason thought, *and the line cast. But I shouldn't bite*, he told himself, *not even a nibble. Although her sexy act is intentional and mature*, he thought, *she has no idea what she'd be in for.*

She was leaning on the jukebox, waiting for him.

"Hi there," he said.

"You're not from around here, are you?" she said.

He shook his head. "Just passing through," he answered, knowing it would only add to his intrigue.

"I get off in three hours, if you want to get together for a drink. I could show you around."

I bet you could, he thought and couldn't remember the last time he'd felt so elated—or grateful. His skin tingled while a swarm of butterflies danced in his gut. If only for a moment, he felt young again, desirable, filled with testosterone. *And anything but invisible*, he thought. "I'm flattered, beautiful, I really am . . . but I can't."

"Are you sure?" she asked, giving him his wink back. "It could be fun."

"Oh, I have no doubt about that," he said. "But I can't."

"Can't or won't?"

"Does it matter?" He placed his hand on her arm, which was even softer than he expected. "Listen, you're absolutely stunning, the sexiest woman I've met in a very long time, but I can't." He slid his hand down her smooth forearm. "But thank you, sweetheart. You've given me a gift I didn't realize I needed."

She pulled her hand away. "It's your loss," she said under her breath; she was still too young to handle any type of rejection.

"Don't I know it," he said before starting to walk back to his table with a little more swagger in his step.

"It was just a bet anyway," the young waitress blurted.

Jason stopped and turned.

"She bet me that I couldn't get you into bed," the girl said, pointing to her blushing friend standing near the bar.

Nodding, Jason considered this. *It was a wager*, he thought and shook his head. *Now that makes more sense.* Even still, the feelings it stirred in him were as real and thrilling as any he'd ever felt, and he decided to savor them. "It looks like you just lost your bet, beautiful," he told her before finishing that strut back to his table.

"What was that all about?" Tom asked, writing something down on a napkin.

Even if Jason tried to conceal his smile, he couldn't. "That strawberry blonde just told me that I'm not invisible."

Tom searched his face and smiled. "Good for you," he said, a hint of jealousy in all three words.

"What's that?" Jason asked, pointing at the napkin.

"The start of a new poem for my kids," Tom said, stuffing it into his pocket.

After dinner, they returned to the rented SUV with Jason's feet barely touching the ground. It was dark.

"I wonder if that waitress is Irish," Tom said. "She looks Irish."

"She could be," Jason said, grinning, "by injection." He jumped in behind the steering wheel and fired it up. Tom never even pointed out that it was still his turn to drive. "I've decided that I love Minnesota," Jason said.

Tom laughed.

Jason punched the accelerator and, as they reached the motel, he yelled, "Hold on to your shorts, we're coming in hot!" Just then, he struck a curb in the dark parking lot. The SUV caught some air, smacked down on the left front tire and hopped—making Jason laugh hard.

Tom laughed too. "Stop," he said, "or I'm going to piss myself."

"What else is new?"

Jason got out of the SUV and hurried for his room, thinking, *I need a cold shower.*

chapter 8

SANDI WAS LYING NAKED ON THE BED, pretending to be asleep, when Tom tiptoed into the hotel suite. Giggling, he thought, *Oh, the things I'm going to do to this woman.* In record time, his clothes were lying in a pile on the floor, and he was mounting his playful lover. The heat between them made his loins ache. He kissed her neck, stopping long enough at her ears to make her return his giggle. Without opening her eyes, she flicked her tongue across his chest, causing his manhood to convulse. "I want you more than I've ever wanted anyone," he whispered.

"Actions speak louder than words," she said, pulling him into her.

His thrusts were slow and even. *I need to make this last,* he thought. *I need to make her . . .*

Tom awakened from his dream. His eyes struggled to open. *Where the hell . . . ?* he thought, scanning the strange room for answers. *It's a motel room,* he told himself, needing to focus harder . . . *in Montana, I think.* The only thing that looked familiar was the erection that pitched his sheets in the shape of an army tent. Placing both hands behind his head, he sighed heavily. *Oh Sandi*, he muttered, *why can't we ever finish?*

Whenever possible, Tom's head floated among the stars where kinder, safer, and much more exciting places could be found. Whether dabbling in the past or future, the present bored him to no end and, as a result, he spent little time there. Fantasy proved the only remedy, and he overdosed on it. Where else could a man—destined to live a mundane life— discover great treasures, explore strange worlds, and make love to an enthusiastic woman. At a young age, Tom had discovered that real or imaginary made no real difference to him. As a result, he'd always lived one of the finest, cultured, and most enriched lives a man could hope for. He only needed to close his eyes and a new journey would begin.

Following a pathetic breakfast of burnt bagels and frozen cream cheese, Tom told Jason, "I know. I know. We need to stop and get you an egg and cheese sandwich, or three."

"You're starting to learn," Jason said, looking around. "You know, my whole life, I've been told to dance like nobody's watching me. And the last time I tried it, they asked me to leave the mall." He shrugged. "But this looks like a much friendlier place."

"Please don't," Tom said. *Please don't!*

It was raining hard, like when they'd left Salem, only fifteen degrees colder and raw. After tossing their luggage into the SUV, Jason took the wheel and immediately changed the radio station to a country music channel.

"Did you end up going back to the restaurant last night to see that cute girl?" Tom asked, breathing easily, his belly rising and falling like a baby, carefree and relaxed.

Jason shook his head. "She was too young," he said. "But I definitely considered it a couple dozen times."

Tom laughed.

"In the end, I didn't want to spoil her for some young buck that's in shape and has enough stamina to go more than seven minutes."

Tom laughed louder. "The time did go fast, didn't it?"

"Now there's an understatement," Jason said, shaking his head. "I sometimes think about the road ahead and realize it's much shorter than what I've already traveled in the rearview mirror."

"Oh shit!" Tom blurted, popping up in the passenger seat and sitting erect.

"What is it?" Jason asked, his face ready for battle.

"We need to go back," Tom said. "Dad's still in the hotel closet."

Laughing, Jason slowed the SUV to make a U-turn. "Wow, this is the second time you've forgotten that poor man. I think something deep in your psyche is trying to get rid of him."

"You don't have to be a shrink to figure that one out," Tom said.

Jason laughed.

After retrieving the box of ashes, Tom handed it to Jason. "He's all yours now."

Jason lobbed the box over his shoulder. It bounced once, then twice, before resting upside down on the backseat. "Safe and sound," he said, smiling at Tom.

"Damn, you're more abusive than he was."

"Are you kidding me?" Jason said, his brow nearly folded in half. "Not even close."

As they pulled into another fast-food drive-thru lane, Tom picked up the conversation where they'd left off. "When you're young, you think you're going to hit the cosmic lottery; get the perfect job, perfect marriage, all if it. When you realize there's no such thing as perfect—except for intentions—it can be disheartening." He thought about it. "For me, the glory of life has been found in the grind; getting up every morning at five o'clock, busting my ass to get ahead—broken up by weekends that are too short and vacations that are usually more fun in the planning." He shrugged. "But when I look back, that's where I feel the most sense of accomplishment, the most pride." He nodded once. "In the grind, where I earned every bit of what I have and who I've become."

"Well said," Jason said sincerely, before ordering his second breakfast.

Tom pondered his life and felt torn. *How can I be so proud and ashamed at the same time?* he wondered.

"Hey, do you remember the McCaskie's cornfield races?" Jason asked, diving into the bag of food.

"Remember them?" Tom said, chuckling. "You almost died in one of those cornfields."

As he recalled, Jason's need for speed found him, Tom, and some guy named Randy out in the cornfield one freezing November afternoon. It was a 1979 Chevy Monte Carlo and Jason was perfecting the art of the "Jim Rockford." He'd drive the car as fast as he could in reverse then, just before he lost control, he'd spin the wheel hard and go for the ride. Tom and Randy had squealed in delight, watching the trees whip by their windows, as they rode the amusement park ride for the price of a gallon of gas. It was all about the thrill of being out of control.

On their last spin down the field, Jason had put his foot to the floor. The car had swayed to and fro, threatening to unhand the reins from him before he made the decision to give them up. At the last second, Jason had turned the wheel, whipping the car into a violent spin. Just then, the driver's side door had flown open. *It had actually looked like something invisible snatched Jason from his seat and yanked him out of the speeding car,* Tom remembered. Terrified for his brother's safety, Tom had looked over the front seat to see Jason's foot wedged beneath the dashboard. As gravity summoned them in the opposite direction, Tom had hurried to the rear window on the driver's side. He was just in time to see Jason's body being dragged, the front wheel missing his head by no more than a few inches. Jason's eyes had been open and he hadn't appeared to be enjoying the ride. *Holy shit*, Tom had thought, the shock starting to paralyze him. Randy had grabbed the wheel from the passenger seat and straightened out the car, struggling to place his foot on the brake. Afraid to see the damage, Tom had paused to hear his brother's groan. *He's still alive.* Only then did he and Randy burst out laughing.

Jason had wiggled his foot free and gradually gotten to his feet. His face had been white. Without a word, he'd reclaimed the driver's seat, slammed the door, and turned the car around. "Let's try that again, boys," he'd said through gritted teeth, stomping his foot on the gas pedal. Tom and Randy held on. *Jason's making peace with his demons*, Tom had thought, *a back on the horse kind of thing*. It didn't matter why. And besides, it had still been less dangerous than being home with the old man and his unpredictable temper.

Returning from the past, Tom looked at Jason. "You've always been crazy," he said, complimenting his brazen brother. "It was like you enjoyed being hurt back then."

Jason laughed. "And what about you? What about when you took that vicious beating from Holly Pearlman?"

"That was just a bad breakup," Tom explained. "And Holly was a lot bigger than me."

They were both laughing when they entered North Dakota, the Roughrider State. *We're halfway there*, Tom thought. *Now if we can just survive the second half of America together.*

As they passed the sign for Fargo on I-94, Tom asked, "Did you ever see the movie?"

Jason grinned. "Let's just say that if renting a wood chipper didn't require two forms of positive ID, I'd be serving time myself right now."

"Janice?" he asked.

Jason nodded.

Tom laughed. "How was the sex at the end?" he asked.

"What sex?" Jason said, "Janice nearly cured me of a normal healthy sex drive."

"The sex was never any good?"

"Sure it was, in the beginning when we were having audition sex."

"Audition sex?"

Jason grinned. "The sex we had when she was auditioning to be Mrs. Prendergast. But once she landed the role, the audition was over."

Tom nodded. *I know exactly what you mean,* he thought sadly. *Getting close to Carmen has always been like placing a matchstick to a block of ice.* He shrugged to himself. *She was impossible to thaw.*

"These days, I mostly just have sex with myself," Jason said, his face serious. "Sometimes, I sit on my hand until it falls asleep." He shrugged. "I think it's probably why I have carpal tunnel syndrome now."

"You're really messed up, you know that, right?"

Jason laughed. "No more messed up than you are, I'm sure." He looked at Tom. "I used to think about sex every seven seconds. Now it may dawn on me every few hours, and that's if a food commercial isn't playing on TV."

"I hear you there," Tom said, laughing. "Those cooking shows are like porn for the middle-aged."

"I used to drink, smoke, fight, and screw like a bull," Jason said, "really live, you know?"

Tom nodded.

"Now all I have is food."

Looking down at his feet, where all of his brother's snack wrappers had accumulated on the passenger side floor, Tom said, "I hate to tell you this, but I really doubt you'll make it to fifty-four."

"Sure, and you'll be the best-looking skeleton in the graveyard," Jason replied, glancing down at the snack wrappers. "Tasty cakes, wasn't that your nickname in high school?"

"Be honest, how much did you weigh when you first started in the prison?" Tom asked.

"One ninety-five even," Jason said. "But the next time I expect to be at that weight, I'll be decomposing."

Tom laughed.

"What I wouldn't do to be as fat as the first time I thought I was fat," Jason said, smiling. "There's always exercise," he added, thinking aloud. "But the motivation is getting harder and harder to find." He stopped and peered hard into Tom's eyes for a few long moments, making him feel uncomfortable. "So all bullshitting aside, what's really going on with you and Carmen?"

"I really don't want to talk to you about Carmen," Tom quickly countered.

"And why's that?"

"Because you slept with her, remember?" Tom said.

Jason chuckled, amused by the comment.

Feeling a volcano of fury erupt from his core, Tom barked, "Why in the fuck would I ever . . ."

"Because I never slept with your wife," Jason interrupted.

"That's bullshit!"

"I never slept with Carmen," Jason repeated calmly.

Tom studied his brother's face. *He's telling the truth*, he realized. "But I thought you and Carmen . . ."

Jason shook his head. "A few weeks after I got caught with that bag of weed and my future was flushed down the toilet, I was getting drunk every day."

Tom swallowed hard, preferring to avoid the topic altogether.

"As I vaguely remember, I was hammered at some party when your girlfriend came on to me." He stopped.

"And?"

"And I know Carmen and I didn't actually sleep together because I passed out before anything could happen."

Tom studied his face again. *It's the truth*, he decided. "So you're saying you would have had sex with her if you hadn't passed out?"

Jason gave it some thought and shrugged. "I honestly don't know, Tom," he said. "You cost me everything back then, you know?"

Ashamed, Tom nodded. "I always thought you got back at me by sleeping with Carmen," he muttered, still trying to wrap his head around the fact that he'd never been betrayed by his older brother. He looked at Jason. "For all these years, you let me believe it happened."

"If I'm being honest with you, I was so pissed for so long that I didn't care what you believed." He shrugged again. "Besides, you suffered for it as though it actually happened, so what's the difference whether it did or not? You were tormented and I was good with that."

There was silence for a while, Tom taking the time to contemplate this new truth.

"So what's really going on with you and Carmen?" Jason asked again.

Screw you! Tom screamed in his head, but the need to get the weight off his chest felt so much more critical than worrying about being judged by his brother. "When Carmen joined the single wives' club . . ."

"Single wives' club?" Jason repeated.

"Carmen and I used to hang out with a few couples—dinners, long weekends away, you know. And then slowly but surely, the men were squeezed out while the girls were living it up all by themselves—the guys staying at home to watch the kids." He shook his head. "That was the start of it. And before long, resentment and anger took hold with the husbands blaming one woman or another—anyone but his own wife."

"Isn't that great," Jason said, "exactly what you signed up for when you got married."

"Yeah, sure."

"That sucks."

"It was the beginning of the end for Carmen and me. I was never a jealous husband, someone who felt the need to suffocate his wife. But this got ridiculous."

Jason shook his head.

"The girls were off gallivanting two weekends a month, drinking, dancing, who knows what else—whatever they wanted."

"The single wives' club," Jason repeated, finally understanding the title.

"Exactly."

"Before long, Carmen's sex drive didn't come close to matching mine, nor did her sense of marital obligation. That's when we entered the *Ice Age*, as I like to call it." He took a deep breath, shaking his head at the absurdity of it. "I started wondering whether it could even be considered cheating if your wife refused to meet your basic human needs."

"And?"

"And that's when I found out she was meeting some other guy's needs instead," Tom confessed, immediately turning his head to stare out the passenger window. "The dirty bitch betrayed me."

"Carmen's cheating on you?" Jason asked, the pitch in his voice changing. "Are you sure?"

"Carmen's been cheating on me for months, Jason . . . maybe even years," Tom confirmed, still unable to make eye contact with his brother.

"But are you sure?" Jason asked again.

"I saw it with my own eyes," Tom said, filled with shame.

"Oh man . . ."

"The asshole was humping the shit out of her when I walked into the bedroom . . ."

Jason looked away, his face crimson red.

"I remember feeling so enraged, but I didn't know what to do," Tom said, before taking a few moments to go on. "I really wanted to hit him, but I wasn't sure it would help anything."

The air escaped Jason's lungs in a disgusted sigh.

"I figured what good would it do, you know?" Tom continued. "Would it actually solve anything?" He shook his head. "The answer always came back to no."

Jason looked back at him, his face sick with disgust.

Tom smirked. "So I punched him anyway," he said, feeling a tiny sense of pride. "And wouldn't you know it, I was right. I didn't feel better at all, except for those few moments when he screamed like a girl, his eyes wild with fear when he realized he was at my mercy." Tom shrugged. "I guess I didn't look like I was in a merciful mood because he begged me not to hurt him." He looked at his brother. "Imagine that, someone begging *me* not to hurt them?"

"Good for you, you stud," Jason said, respect returning to his eyes. "And I'm sorry to hear about Carmen stepping out on you. That's really screwed up." He patted Tom's arm in a show of support.

On the brink of tears, Tom looked back out the passenger window. *At least Jason's not judging me*, he thought. *That's something, I guess.*

They drove in silence for a stretch. *I thought it would make me feel better to come clean about Carmen*, Tom thought, *but I don't feel any better at all.*

As they entered Bismarck, North Dakota, Jason said, "I'm starving. Are you ready for lunch?" He was already tapping the GPS screen, searching out restaurants.

Tom nodded. *Whatever*, he thought. *I don't care whether we eat or not.*

"Okay, you have a choice," Jason said, grinning, "China Garden, Hong Kong China Restaurant, or Grand China Restaurant's buffet?" He was clearly trying to lighten the mood.

"Whatever," Tom said, surrendering to his brother's simple whims. *I hope we consume enough MSG to put us both out of our misery.*

They weren't back on the road for five minutes when Jason asked, "Please tell me you're not still with Carmen, are you?"

And it begins, Tom thought. *Jason's never had any problem picking at scabs until they bleed good, leaving them alone long enough to start picking again.* He reluctantly nodded. "But there's more to it than that," he quickly explained. "The house, our life together." He shrugged weakly. "I mean, what will the kids think?"

"The real question is, what will they think when they realize their father's a mouse?"

A mouse? Tom thought, his breathing picking up in depth and pace.

"It's kind of hard to raise adults when you can't be one yourself," Jason added.

"That's easy for you to say," Tom said, his self-pity dissipating into a growing anger.

"No, not easy. Not easy at all," Jason said. "I've had more shit piled onto my plate than you can imagine, and life would have been much easier on me had I bowed my head and surrendered to it. But I hate the taste of shit, the lies, and I refuse to eat more than my share. The truth is the truth, Tom. You're living a lie, period."

"What about the kids?" Tom asked, sounding pathetic— even to his own ears.

"They'll survive," Jason promised. "Besides, they'd be deaf, dumb, and blind not to know their mother is humiliating their old man."

He's right, Tom thought, *but . . .*

"There's a price to pay for everything, brother," Jason said. "Be honest, when's the last time you felt like a man?"

Tom opened his mouth, but the words got tangled up somewhere behind his tongue.

"We all have choices," Jason said. "For me, I'd pick dignity over a savings account any day of the week . . . honor over material wealth."

"So you would sacrifice your daughter's stability, her happiness?" Tom asked, defensively—pleased that some of his vocabulary had returned.

Jason took a deep breath and lowered his tone. "I've never lied to my kid, so there's no way I'd allow my life to become the biggest lie of all." He shrugged. "I'm sure Caroline and Caleb know anyway, Tom, and I'm guessing they're not too proud of you for sitting this one out on the sidelines." He shook his head. "You need to dump that dirty whore once and for all."

"You don't know anything!" Tom roared, sounding like his brother now. *But the kids have to know*, he thought, and couldn't make sense of this conversation. *For someone who isn't supposed to know anything about me, Jason still knows me better than anyone. He always has.* They grew up together in a survival camp, where there was no place for pretenses, where strengths were honed and weaknesses were revealed only to be preyed upon. *He's right*, Tom decided, chewing on his tongue. *The cold-hearted bastard's right. Carmen is a dirty whore and I need to put an end to this joke of a marriage.*

They drove down a long stretch of road—over the border of Big Sky Country, Montana—listening to dozens of country love songs. A few times Tom was tempted to ask his brother to pull over so he could vomit, but he was able to breathe through each panic attack and beat back the bile that bubbled in the back of his throat.

They pulled into the Days Inn on Parkway Lane in Billings, Montana. It was a typical motel, located right off Interstate 90, near the Red Lodge Mountain Resort and Golf Course. *This is getting so old*, Tom thought.

"It must be nice," Jason commented, referring to the resort next door.

"We can stay there, if you want to spend the money," Tom said angrily. "I'm more than happy to switch hotels."

"I can't," Jason said, snatching up the box of ashes from the backseat. "I'm paying for a wedding and we already chewed through most of my travel budget in Chicago."

"Of course we did," Tom said, feeling more aggravated than he had since leaving Salem.

During the usual check-in, the young man behind the counter suggested, "The Montana Sky Restaurant in the Crowne Plaza Hotel has an amazing menu."

"You're sending us to a different hotel to eat?" Tom asked.

"It beats our vending machines," the kid said, shrugging.

I'm so done with this friggin' trip, Tom thought.

The Montana Sky Restaurant was located on the twentieth floor, overlooking Billings.

Jason was dressed unusually nice for dinner. He wore khakis, an oversized polo shirt, and comfortable shoes—the kind worn by someone who'd suffered enough aches and pains to stop caring about appearances.

"Did you buy a new shirt?" Tom asked.

"Nope," he said, obviously lying. "I've been saving my best outfits for you."

The restaurant's interior was painted yellow with red accents. Walls of glass overlooking views of four mountain ranges and downtown Billings brought the slightest grin to Tom's face. *Finally*, he thought, *a decent place to eat.*

He and Jason were seated at a table near the window. Crystal water glasses sat atop a linen tablecloth.

"I know why they call this Big Sky Country," Jason said.

"Oh yeah, and why's that?" Tom asked.

"Because most of the buildings are short," he said, laughing—alone. When the waiter arrived, Jason ordered steak and potatoes.

"That's original," Tom said, before looking toward the waiter. "I'll get the chef salad with the dressing on the side, and let me try a side of your sweet corn tamales."

"And for your entrée?" the waiter asked.

"The salad and tamales should be enough for me," Tom said.

Jason grunted and groaned through the entire meal.

Disgusting, Tom thought, watching his massive brother devour everything but his own hands. "It's like you're on death row, eating your final meal," Tom said.

Jason laughed. "That reminds me of a funny story I recently heard," he said, his mouth full of food. "On death row, inmates are allowed to spend sixty dollars on their final meal before sitting in the chair."

Tom shook his head. *Barbaric*, he thought.

"One dude from Texas just ordered sixty bucks worth of chili and orange juice. He said he wanted everyone to smell him for a week after they fried him." Jason laughed. "Now that's what you call a cold man right to the end."

"That's great," Tom said. "You chose quite the profession."

Jason stopped laughing.

"It would be nice to get an after-dinner drink in Montana's Lounge," Tom suggested, hoping alcohol might help his outlook. "But it looks like they close at ten o'clock."

Jason's smile returned. "I agree," he said. "The last thing I want to do is go back to the room and surf another hundred channels that have nothing to watch. Do you want to go out and find a place that serves real drinks?"

Tom nodded.

"Do you think you're ready to sit at the big kids' table?"

Tom offered his middle finger in response. *Screw you*, he thought.

It was a typical honky-tonk located in a vast, darkened parking lot, somewhere a honky-tonk should not have been found. The hissing neon lured them in like two large-mouthed bass. Tom opened the door, and a fog of cigarette smoke engulfed them. It took a few long moments for his squinted eyes to see anything beyond shadows.

"Wow, this looks like an AA meeting gone wrong," Jason said.

There was a small, L-shaped bar, most of the wooden stools occupied by truckers or men in one blue-collar outfit or another—farmers, mechanics, even a few fake cowboys. Tom spotted a high-top table in an empty corner. He made a bee-line, with Jason in tow.

"I'd rather sit at the end of the bar," Jason said.

"Where?" Tom asked. "In someone's lap?"

Tom took a seat, scanned the place, and immediately relaxed—until he saw his brother sitting upright. He watched as Jason's eyes moved over the place like a prison searchlight, occasionally lingering on a man covered in tattoos, seated at the middle of the bar.

"What's the matter with the tattooed guy?" he asked.

Without interrupting his surveillance, Jason said, "Tattoos read like résumés in my industry, and our friend at the bar is a gang member who would be considered quite accomplished in his field."

Tom's heart quickened. "Are you serious? What can you tell about him?"

"The two teardrops indicate the lives he's taken. He's at least a lieutenant who's worked his way up in his organization." He looked at Tom. "Trust me, he's a pretty bad dude."

"In Montana?"

"My guess is he's just passing through, like we are."

"Should we leave?" Tom asked.

"Do you owe him money?"

"No."

"Well, as long as you don't piss on his shoes in the bathroom," Jason said, "then we should be fine."

"Does he know you from the prison?" Tom whispered.

Jason shook his head. "No, but he knows I'm on the job. And he's as aware of my presence as I am of his." Jason's brow furrowed; he looked like he was ready for combat.

A cute barmaid—in her early twenties—approached, wearing a tight T-shirt sliced at the collar to reveal some ample cleavage. Her jean shorts were also cut too short, leaving little to the imagination. Tom tried not to gawk at her. *She's a kid, for God's sake*, he scolded himself. But he couldn't help it. She was clearly dressed to rake in as many tips as she could.

"What can I get you handsome gentlemen?" she asked, wearing the kind of smile that suggested anything was possible.

Damn, she's good, Tom thought. *I'm already at the age where I've become invisible to most women, never mind someone who could have anyone she wants.* He glanced over at his brother, who looked like he'd also fallen in love.

Before Jason could open his mouth, Tom told her, "Let us have two draft beers in the tallest glasses you have."

"For you boys, I'll find the biggest we got," she said in a flirtatious tone.

Smiling, Tom looked toward his brother when he noticed Jason's attention was already diverted back to the bar. He quickly looked in the same direction to discover one of the young bucks at the bar glaring over at them. He didn't need any prison experience to realize the muscular kid was confused about his ownership over the pretty waitress and was taking some serious offense to their harmless exchange. The stud downed his beer, stood, and began his approach—strutting over to their table like a little banty rooster, his arms spread wide enough to be carrying two full pails of sand. *Oh, here we go,* Tom thought, his heart thumping hard in his chest.

"Hey asshole," the kid yelled out, ten steps from their table.

Tom's heart was now in his throat, making it feel like he was breathing through a coffee stirrer. He was able to maintain eye contact but could not yet respond.

The muscle-head took five more steps. "That's right, I'm talking to you, asshole," he said, looking Tom straight in the eye.

"Asshole?" Tom said, fighting to maintain an even voice. "What the hell did I do?"

"You flirted with my girlfriend, that's what the hell you did," he barked.

"Listen," Tom said, struggling to speak. "I ordered two drinks. If . . . if you can't handle watching your girlfriend flirt with other men, then you should probably hang out at a different bar." He then waved his hand, trying to dismiss the angry man like he was some whiney college student.

But the guy didn't budge. Instead, his eyes went wild and he took a fighting posture.

Panic filled Tom's body; he suddenly felt cornered and didn't know what to do. *I can't cower*, he was thinking when Jason stood and half-shoved him out of the way, the same way he'd done when they were kids.

Jason lashed out like a cobra, grabbing the kid's shirt and balling it up into his fist. A split second later, he brought the loudmouth a half-inch from his face. "Listen, you little pissant," he hissed, spraying spittle on the kid's shocked face. "If you don't return to the hole you just crawled out of, I'm going to beat you like I'm getting paid good money to do it. Do you understand me?" It sounded like he'd asked the question in a low growl.

While the young buck stood frozen, his eyes glassing over in terror, Tom was filled with mixed emotions; he was furious that—as a middle-aged man—he still needed his big brother to fight his battles. But he was also relieved that he no longer faced a humiliating beating.

Jason shoved the kid once, releasing his grip. "If I have to talk to you again, you little fuck, there'll be hell to pay," he said, the words spoken in the tone of a disappointed and angry father—their father—just before doling out a terrible beating.

Tom watched as the kid swallowed hard, his eyes darting around. Wiping Jason's saliva from his face, his mind undoubtedly raced about what to do next. "Whatever," he finally muttered and, in the end, he wisely elected to backpedal—even if he was getting louder with each step.

Jason took his seat, letting the red-faced guy salvage what little dignity he could. As they accepted their giant beers, Jason said, "There might be a little too much chlorine in that boy's gene pool." He laughed—alone.

What the fuck, Tom thought, needing to get more alcohol into his system.

"Not all his oars are in the water," Jason added, still referring to the kid.

"Yeah, I get it," Tom said, trying to conceal his trembling hands. *There's no question about it*, he thought. *Jason's definitely a badass.*

The brothers drank in silence for a while.

At the arrival of their second round, Jason pointed out an older man sitting at the bar who resembled their high school baseball coach. "Doesn't that man look just like Coach Murphy?" he asked, clearly trying to take Tom's mind off of the fear the muscle-bound bully had instilled in him.

Tom looked at the man. "A little, I guess," he said, shrugging. He couldn't stop himself from looking over at the kid at the bar. *He's still staring over here*, he thought, his heart thumping somewhere between his chest and the wad of cotton in his mouth.

"The only thing I wanted in high school was to make all-conference MVP, and it broke my heart when I didn't," Jason said. "Three years later, I was having lunch at a local pub when Coach Murphy walked in. I told him who I was and we started reminiscing. Then, all of a sudden, he says, 'Hey, I got something for you in the trunk of my car.' He leaves the place but comes back a few minutes later, and hands me a plaque. 'What's this?' I asked him. 'It's for the all-conference MVP,' he says. 'You won.' I thought he was playing with me. 'But that was three years ago, Coach,' I told him. 'Yeah, I know,' he says. 'I've been meaning to get it to you.'" Jason took another long draw off his beer. "I stared at the plaque for the longest time, but it didn't mean a damn thing to me anymore," he said, shaking his head. "I was amazed at how the thing I wanted most just a few years before now meant absolutely nothing to me." Taking another drink, he shrugged. "Time has a funny way of changing priorities, I suppose."

As Jason finished his story, Coach Murphy's look-alike rose from his stool and stumbled, nearly falling to the filthy floor. The man was staggering drunk. "It looks like someone's going to get kicked out of here," Jason said, laughing. He looked at Tom. "Hey, remember that party when the old man got legless drunk and the bartender shut him off?"

For a moment, Tom forgot about the sneering kid at the bar and chuckled. "I do," he said. "After Pop got shut off, he leaned into the bartender and slurred, 'Have you ever heard the word *inscrimination?*'"

"And the bartender shook his head. 'No . . . no, I haven't, sir,'" Jason said. "I thought I was going to piss my pants laughing."

Tom lost his breath in laughter. When he came up for air, he jumped off his seat. "Stop," he said between convulsions, "or I'm going to piss my pants."

After Tom scurried off to the bathroom—avoiding eye contact with anyone at the bar—they decided it was best to leave. On their way out, Jason made it a point to pass by the bar and slap the muscle-headed loudmouth on the shoulder. "You've had a few more to drink so, if your decision-making has become clouded, let me make something clear for you: If you take one step into that fucking parking lot before we drive out of here, I'm going to throw you over my knee and spank you like a child in front of every dude in this place. You got it?"

"Whatever," the kid repeated, staring straight ahead and taking another long swig of his beer.

The gang member with the two teardrops looked their way and grinned.

Tom and Jason stepped out of the cigarette fog and into the buzzing neon that illuminated the starless night.

"That was a little harsh just now," Tom said. "Do you really think it was necessary?"

Jason stopped to face him. "Listen, I'm sure you're good at what you do, Tom," he said, looking back at the bar. "But confrontation is what I do. Trust me, if we hadn't swung by the bar to deliver that gentle reminder on our way out, that stupid kid would be out here right now—with a few of his drunken friends and just as many broken bottles—dancing with the two of us."

Tom felt both ashamed and angry. "You didn't have to butt in, you know," he blurted. "I could have handled it."

"No, you couldn't have," Jason said, sliding into the SUV's passenger seat.

He's right again, Tom thought, *the son of a bitch*. A few miles into the dark night, he turned to his dozing brother and chuckled. "He would have whooped the shit out of me, wouldn't he have?"

Jason laughed. "Oh, he would have beaten you like a drum."

Tom nodded. *Don't I know it*, he thought.

His eyes still closed, Jason shrugged. "My theory's always been: unless you have a dog in the fight, don't get involved." He opened one eye. "But I had a dog in the fight," he added, grinning. "A small, nippy dog, but a dog nonetheless."

Tom punched his arm, surprised that it felt like a cinder block. "Well, for whatever it's worth, thanks for what you did for me back there," he said, surprised the words didn't have the bitter aftertaste he'd expected.

Jason leaned back in his seat and closed his eyes again. "No worries," he said. "Years ago, I made a promise to myself that only I could beat on you."

Tom laughed.

Jason didn't.

At the motel parking lot, Tom asked, "Do you think you could have taken that young punk, one-on-one?"

"I would have destroyed him," Jason said. "Unfortunately, I only have one good fight left in me . . ."

"That's it?"

"It's enough," Jason said. "And whoever it is, he'd better have a solid ground game, because we're going to the floor right away. I'm too damned old and slow to stand toe-to-toe, exchanging punches."

Tom laughed but considered his brother's demeanor. Jason was matter-of-fact, with no hint of emotion in his voice.

Thank God he's on my side, he told himself, never expecting to have such a thought on this trip.

The sun had already risen when the brothers met outside their motel rooms in front of the SUV. "Let's go grab some breakfast and then hit the road," Jason said.

"Right after mass," Tom said.

"Mass?" Jason repeated, surprised.

"That's right. It's Sunday."

"And?"

Tom paused just in front of the SUV. "You don't go to church anymore?" he asked.

"Last night at the bar shook you up pretty bad, didn't it?" Jason said.

"Not exactly. You don't go to church?"

"I'm not a religious man," Jason said. "I'm more what you'd call *relational*."

"So the prison's turned you into an atheist too?"

"Just the opposite," Jason said. "I've never met a man behind the wall who didn't believe in God—or at least begged for his help—when the shit hits the fan, myself included."

Tom shook his head. "What the hell does 'I'm more relational' mean?"

"It means I'm more interested in having a relationship with God and trying to live in the grace of the day." Jason opened the driver's side door and jumped in. "Religion is different from faith. In my opinion, it's nothing more than a big business."

Taken aback, Tom slid into the passenger's side. "Just take me to church," he said.

On the ride, Jason looked at him. "So you're still buying into all that dogma, huh?"

"I am," Tom said. "But not you, huh?"

Jason half-shrugged. "I practice my religion, my faith, on the street—in everyday life—not in some church where folks are screaming the Lord's name loud enough for everyone to hear them, and then—when no one's watching—treat their brothers and sisters like dogs."

"Wow," Tom said. "That's pretty cynical."

As though he'd never heard a word, Jason went on. "I can understand most behavior and forgive most people for their stupidity . . . or moments of poor decision making. We're all sinners, every one of us, and I think most of us are just trying to do the best we can with what we have." He shook his head. "But from my experience, the self-righteous are the greatest sinners of all and, while they're disrespecting the Lord by judging the rest of us, I don't want to spend a minute in their false company." He snickered. "I couldn't give a damn about any of them." He looked at Tom and gritted his teeth. "I friggin' hate hypocrites who spin clever double standards to serve their own purposes. I *hate* them. They live their lives in a perpetual lie and you never know where you stand with a liar."

"Wow," Tom repeated, as they pulled into the church parking lot. "Your dark side is even darker than I thought."

Jason grinned. "I also believe the Lord has a very twisted sense of humor," he added.

"And how's that?"

"He sent Pop to raise us, didn't he?"

Tom chuckled as he climbed out of the SUV. "Last call," he said. "You going in?"

Jason turned off the ignition, leaned back in his seat, and closed his eyes. "Nope. God, Pop, and I are good right here, thanks."

"I'll say a prayer for you," Tom said sarcastically.

"Please do," Jason said seriously. "And keep the old man in mind while you're in there. I'm pretty sure he can use all the help he can get."

Shaking his head, Tom joined the white-haired parade filing into the massive Catholic church.

The priceless stained glass windows filtered in colors of warmth and joy. The convex ceiling stretched forty feet to an exquisite portrait of plump cherubs battling demonic figures. Statues carved from marble kept vigil over centuries of tradition. A giant wooden crucifix hung above the altar. Tom genuflected before taking his seat in the narrow pew.

On bended knee, Tom prayed, *Father, forgive me for not attending church these last few months. As you know, things have been rough at home, with Carmen cheating on me and me getting sick.* He stopped and shook his head. *To be honest, I don't know what to pray for anymore. Part of me wants my family back, but I'm also smart enough to know that's not going to happen—at least not in a way I can live with. I suppose I should leave it to faith at this point.* He took a few deep breaths and looked up at the altar. *Please bless Caroline and Caleb and keep them safe from any harm. And please help me to find peace in my heart.* He began to bless himself and conclude his prayer when another thought surfaced. *Oh, and please stop me and my brother from killing each other during the rest of the trip. We need to take our dad to his final resting place and I can't remember a more trying experience.* He blessed himself again. *Give us the patience and strength to get to where we need to go.*

After speaking silently to the Lord, Tom slid onto the hard seat, skimmed through the weekly handout, and scanned the crowd. *It's not like years ago*, he thought, *when Sunday mass was standing room only.* Today, most communicants were elderly folks, those nearing the gates of heaven. Appropriately enough, they sat up front, while the younger families claimed the rear of the church.

With the help of an ancient organ, the first notes of a small choir rang out, calling the congregation to its feet. On the first note, families surrendered their children to a teacher who waited in the rear. *It looks like the kids are considered an interruption.* Yet, not so long ago, both young and old alike—

entire families—worshipped together. Somewhere along the way, the little unpredictable people were deemed nuisances and rounded up prior to mass. *It's sad,* Tom thought. Worshipping alongside children always made him feel closer to God. *I'm betting the Lord would be more prone to listen to a tiny voice than the rest of us who do nothing but complain.*

The procession started at the rear of the church, with an altar boy guiding the way. A crucifix, fixed atop a long wooden pole, bobbed along, while the second boy steadied the oversized Holy Bible. Dressed in white and purple, the young priest nodded into aisle after aisle as he made his way toward the front. Tom snickered. *Everything the Catholic church does is ceremonial,* he thought, *even the priest's entrance.* Before the thought even left his mind, Tom recognized that he was viewing the experience through his brother's cynical perspective.

Father Bousquet commenced the Sunday mass and went through his perfected routine. Although it had been a long time since Tom had attended, he could have mimicked every word. People rose, stood, and knelt without being directed. It was always the same—safe, predictable, and controlled. Tom now noticed all the subtleties during the service. *Damn you, Jason,* he thought.

The first reading was brief. The second was not much longer. People checked their watches and grinned. And then the time arrived for the Gospel, the Word of the Lord. Tom knelt and listened hard. Father Bousquet repeated the words of Saint John, and Tom's soul bathed in each syllable. Miraculously, the Gospel always found a way of applying itself toward any one of life's situations at hand. Saint John conveyed the warnings of Jesus for His church and Tom pondered them all. He looked around. It appeared that most others were barely listening.

Everyone blessed him or herself and sat to endure the sermon. Tom hardly thought it a test of endurance. To him, it was the most rewarding segment of the Sunday service.

Father Bousquet repeated the Lord's warnings in layman's terms, then went on to speak about the shortage of men called to God's service in the priesthood; about the dwindling numbers of attendants each week, along with some of the more probable reasons for this. Tom thought it courageous of the young pastor. For as long as he could recall, priests didn't dare acknowledge problems within the church, never mind suggest potential solutions. The congregation yawned. Tragically, the years had made some of the faithful so numb they'd stopped listening altogether. *Many of them have become deaf,* Tom thought, *and it's sad.* Father Bousquet was doing everything he could to make a difference. *He's clearly arrived too late for some,* Tom thought.

Tom reached for his thin wallet and fed the collection plate that slowly made its way down the long center aisle. During the lull, muffled complaints drifted through the pews. Obviously, some people who showed up to church, week-in and week-out, did so because they felt they had no choice. Most others, however, truly embraced the message of God. *It's the church, the messenger, they have a problem with.* Tom completely understood.

Upon blessing the offerings to the Lord, the enthusiastic priest asked that everyone offer each other a sign of peace. This was always Tom's favorite, being able to shake hands with people he might never lay eyes on again. Once done, the Holy Eucharist; the sacred body of Christ was brought to the altar. It was blessed and then offered to the Shepherd's flock. Lifting the white, circular wafer into the air, Father Bousquet announced, "All Catholics are welcome at the Lord's table." Tom cringed before peering down the long pew at those who sat alongside him. Some shifted in their seats, while others closed their eyes. No one stood. *Divorced, Jewish, gay—who knows?* The many different possibilities made Tom feel like the church was cheating its starving flock.

After receiving communion, Tom returned to the pew and spoke to God again. *Please Lord; please keep me strong in my faith . . . whether I worship within the church or outside of it.* After the priest's final blessing, Tom stood and marched out the door into the morning sunlight. He could hear Jason's snoring before he even reached the parking lot. He looked skyward. *Patience and strength, Lord,* he repeated in his head, *please!*

chapter 9

EVEN WITH THE OPTION OF RETURNING TO THE MOTEL for a free continental breakfast and the morning newspaper, Tom folded and agreed to go to Grains of Montana on Grand Avenue.

With Tom now at the helm, something in the hum of the early morning talk radio show caught Jason's attention.

"It's my Constitutional right to burn the American flag anytime I want," the caller said.

"Oh, fuck you," Jason said, turning the radio off. He looked at Tom. "I'm sorry, but I can't listen to that shit."

Tom nodded. "No worries," he said. Three miles down the road, they arrived at the breakfast nook. The parking lot was packed.

"It must be really good here," Jason said, his mood immediately changing to happy for the little joys in life. He jumped out of the SUV like he hadn't eaten in days.

"Easy, Big Boy," Tom said, locking their father in the vehicle. "You don't want to pull a hamstring before you get a shot at winning the pancake challenge."

Smartass, Jason thought, laughing. "You're a lot smarter than you look," he said.

Ashes

As they walked into the restaurant, Old Glory crackled and popped in the freezing wind, making both brothers look skyward and acknowledge the great symbol of freedom.

Jason shook his head. "Can you imagine all the knuckle-heads in this country who actually think it's okay to burn our flag?"

"Freedom of spee . . ." Tom started to say but stopped.

"I'd love to see just one flag-burning ceremony in prog-ress," Jason said, his chest aflame. "While they invoked their freedom of speech, I'd be doing the same."

"And giving someone a pummeling, right?"

"Unlike anything you've ever seen," Jason said. "These stu-pid kids have no idea about the thousands and thousands of heroes who had to die for that flag to fly." He grinned. "The least I could do is honor their memories by handing out a good, old-fashioned ass whoopin'."

"That's one way to deal with it, I guess," Tom said.

"Do you have a better way?" Jason asked, thinking, *I can't wait to hear this one.*

Tom smiled. "Nope. I don't," he said, not hesitating with his answer.

Grains of Montana was a bustling place, waitresses dart-ing around, slinging hash. There was a buzz of separate conver-sations taking place all over the restaurant, while the smell of freshly brewed coffee and pancakes filled the air. *Ahhh,* Jason thought, inhaling deeply, *we've made it to the Promised Land.*

When ordering, Jason leaned in to the waitress, as if he were about to share a secret. "Poor guy," he whispered, gestur-ing toward Tom with a jerk of his head. "Tom and I just got back from a long ride to Sterling."

"On your bikes?" she asked, still writing in her pad.

He nodded. "It was a rough trip. Tom hit some sand and totaled his moped. I went down right behind him and cracked my bug shield. And that's when it happened." He stopped long enough to put on his most frightened face. "We started getting slapped around by some Harley guys." He shook his

191

head dramatically. "Sorry, but I don't want to talk about it anymore . . ."

"Oh man," Tom said.

"Oh no," the waitress said, playing along. She obviously tried to hold it in, but when she looked at Tom, she began to laugh.

Tom couldn't help himself and laughed along with her.

"How did you guys meet?" she asked. "In school?"

Jason shook his head. "Business partners," he said. "We raised hamsters for a while together. To be honest, they're tough to herd and they kind of freak me out." He leaned in even closer. "Did you know that the harder you squeeze their bellies, the more their eyes bulge?" he whispered. "It's crazy."

She studied his face for a moment. "You're a little bit crazy, am I right?"

Tom nodded. "You have no idea," he confirmed.

Jason smiled. "A little," he admitted.

Tom appeared to enjoy his French toast while Jason tore through the scrambled egg platter covered in melted cheese, as well as a South of the Border breakfast sandwich that oozed with salsa and green chilies.

"Do you win a T-shirt if you finish everything?" Tom asked.

Jason shook his head. "Nope, but I may need to buy a bigger T-shirt the next time I get to Walmart," he said, wiping a wad of cheese off his chin.

"I need to take you shopping," Tom said.

"No, you really don't."

As they ate, an elderly woman at the next table began giving the young waitress a hard time. "It's not like you have a tough job, dear," the hag said condescendingly. "You should be able to handle a simple order like decaffeinated coffee."

The waitress nodded. "I'm so sorry, ma'am, I'll get you your decaf," she said, hurrying off to fetch the coffee.

"You do that," the woman said disrespectfully.

As the waitress came back their way—with a new pot of coffee in hand—Jason grabbed her arm. "It must be a lot of fun dealing with the public," he said, loud enough for everyone in the restaurant to hear.

The waitress smiled gratefully, while the old woman shot him a nasty glare.

He returned it, holding it long enough to make her turn away. *Screw you, you old witch*, he thought.

Tom laughed.

"What is it?" Jason asked. "I should have minded my own business, right?"

"Not at all," Tom said before raising his voice to also be heard. "That old biddy just left church with me. And if I remember correctly, she was sitting in the front row."

"Of course she was," Jason said sarcastically. "She needs all the hell insurance she can buy," he added, chuckling.

The woman looked back over, her eyes glazed over with venom. This time, Jason leaned in toward her as he stared back. She tried to hang in there but eventually looked away.

After paying the bill—and leaving a generous tip—the brothers stood to leave. On their way out of the place, Tom stopped at the elderly woman's table and looked her in the eye. "Peace be with you," he said, echoing the same words they'd just exchanged in church.

That a boy, Jason thought, proud of his brother.

As if Jesus was nowhere to be found, she remained silent and looked at Tom like she wanted to peel his face off.

Being even less subtle, Jason winked at the woman. "God is always watching," he told her.

The hag's breathing became heavier, and Jason could tell she was working herself up into a tizzy. "Maybe I should call the cops?" she huffed.

Jason nodded. "Maybe you should," he said sincerely. "I'm sure they'll appreciate it when you start shitting on them, too."

The woman sat snarling, looking like a bulldog chewing on a wasp.

As the brothers walked out, they shared a hearty laugh. The dark sky was spitting a mix of rain and frozen slush.

"Kind of early for snow, isn't it?" Tom said.

Jason shrugged. "Who knows? This is my first time, and probably last time through here." He chuckled. "Too bad Dad was too tired for breakfast. I think him and the old witch would have really hit it off."

Tom laughed all the way to the SUV.

Beyond the slashing windshield wipers, fighting off the frozen precipitation, Tom took it slow on the slippery road. He turned the radio back on and rolled through the static until finding some monotone news anchor.

"I-90 west should take us the rest of the way into Seattle," Tom said, just as they accessed the highway.

Jason nodded. *Thank God.*

The light snow began turning into a heavier downfall.

"Have you ever met a serial killer?" Tom blurted.

"A few," Jason said, amused by his brother's enthusiasm.

"Really?" Tom said, looking like a little kid again.

"Sure. Come to think of it, I've killed a few bowls of cereal myself." He chuckled. "I love those frosted corn flakes the best, I think."

"You're such an idiot."

"I thought that was your nickname?"

"Nope, I'm dummy—punk."

They both laughed. They were at the next road sign when Tom asked, "You really hate your job, don't you?"

"Yup."

"Then why don't you just leave?"

"I told you already, I'm two years from retirement."

"You can't collect if you go early?"

"It isn't worth the money I'd lose," Jason said, thinking, *though I wish it was!*

"What about finding a different job to make up the difference?" Tom suggested, trying to be helpful.

Even though Jason despised his chosen career, he was still having trouble reconciling the fact that he was facing retirement. "For almost thirty years, I've had great authority," he explained. "Once I leave the joint, then what? I'm either going to become a mall cop or work some security gig for twenty hours a week." He shook his head. "It's pathetic just thinking about it."

"Then why do it?"

"So I don't burn through my retirement."

"Then why does it have to be a security job?"

"Because it's what I know."

"So you can't learn something new?"

Jason opened his mouth to reply but said nothing. *I hadn't even considered that,* he thought, strangely intrigued by the new idea. *After all these years, I've become institutionalized too,* he thought. *It's been so long since I've felt free.* Even on the open road, he was still behind bars in his mind.

"You can do anything now," Tom added, trying to change his brother's stifled thinking. "You can go anywhere." He smiled. "You've wrapped up your bid, Jason. You're free now, if that's what you want."

Wrapped up my bid? Jason repeated in his head, grinning. His baby brother was finally using language he could relate to.

The sky was dark now, dumping a surprising amount of downy flakes. Tom slowed the SUV to a safe speed. They were just past Bozeman, Montana, when Jason's cell phone rang. "It's Miranda," he said aloud, answering it. "Hi, babe," he said. "What are we looking at now for the wedding?"

She sighed. "Believe it or not, I just called to say hi."

"Sorry, sweetheart. It's this trip. It's worn me down."

Tom glanced over at him.

Jason shrugged. "I'm glad you called," he said. "And please don't take me the wrong way. I don't mind at all when you call for—"

"I know, Dad," she interrupted. "I get it." She laughed. "I just wanted to check in to make sure you and Uncle Tom haven't killed each other."

"Not yet," he said, smiling at Tom. "But if things end up going that way, you might want to put your money on me."

She laughed again.

"Whatever you're referring to, I know it's not a spelling contest," Tom said loud enough for his niece to hear.

Miranda laughed.

"Hey, have you made a decision on getting a band or a DJ?" Jason asked his daughter. "I told you, I don't mind paying the extra money for the band."

"I appreciate that, Dad, but I think we're going to stick with the DJ. My friends love to dance and—"

"They can't dance to a band?" he interrupted.

"Not really," she said, chuckling. "Things are different from when you used to dance," she teased.

"Don't I know it," Jason admitted before saying goodbye to the only pure and innocent thing in his life—Miranda. *I love that kid*, he thought, as he felt the SUV sliding sideways. He looked up to see the vehicle in front of them spinning out of control.

"Oh shit," Tom said, fighting the steering wheel and doing all he could to avoid smashing into the back of the car.

Within seconds, they were spun out in a ditch just beyond the breakdown lane, while the vehicle that had caused it regained control and was safely back on course.

"Oh shit," Tom said again, while the sound of the whining motor and spinning tires dragged them deeper down the embankment.

"Stop," Jason yelled, "and get off the gas before we dig in so deep we can't get out."

Doing as he was told, Tom looked over at Jason. "I couldn't help it," he said. "By the time I saw their brake lights, it was too late to slow down. All I could do was hit the brakes."

"Relax," Jason said. "You're not in any trouble." He looked toward the backseat. The box of ashes had fallen onto the floor but remained closed. He reached back and threw it onto the seat. "Although Dad doesn't look too happy right now," he said. Chuckling, he got out of the warm SUV. The cold snow immediately hit his face. It felt good, refreshing. He took a few deep breaths before walking to the rear of the vehicle. *Oh man*, he thought, surveying their predicament, *we're in trouble.* He looked up to find Tom standing beside him. "Dad's gonna be really pissed about this one," he told his worried brother.

They rifled through the rear of the SUV for anything that could be used as a shovel.

"Nothing," Tom said. "I wish we had some salt."

"I have an idea," Jason said, retrieving the box of ashes. "We only need to get a little traction. Do you think Dad would mind?"

"Are you nuts?"

"He'd want to help us if he was here, right?"

Tom shrugged. "I guess."

"Well, here he is," Jason said, extending the box. He couldn't help it and began to laugh.

"I thought you were serious," Tom said.

Jason shrugged. "Trust me, if you were okay with it, the old man would be under the rear wheels right now." He grabbed the floor mats, hoping they would provide enough traction to get the vehicle moving—but to no avail. *Now what?* he thought.

"I could call AAA," Tom suggested when a pickup truck stopped in the breakdown lane beside them.

"That was quick," Jason joked, as he watched the driver of the pickup get out—holding a steel chain. Within seconds, Jason had already sized him up. *Wiry but strong*, he thought, studying the man's face from a distance. The approaching stranger had steel blue eyes beneath a worn John Deere hat; his black hair, peppered with streaks of gray, was creeping out on both sides. His face was wrinkled from some harsh roads and brutal weather. *Some hard miles on this ol' boy*, Jason decided. *If he gets stupid with us, we're going right to the ground. I've got plenty of weight on him.* He turned to Tom. "If you've never met karma, then pay close attention. She's just arrived." He smiled. "And you might want to watch your backside."

The man approached Jason first. "Name's Hank McCarthy," he said, extending his hand for a shake. "Looks like you boys got yourself into quite a pinch." He surveyed the situation for a few moments, before starting to hook one end of the chain around the SUV's rear bumper. "Let's see if we can get her to budge," he said, shrugging. "Worse case, I'll fetch my boy, George. He's got a winch on his rig."

"Early snow?" Tom asked, as the man worked to secure the chain.

"Not too early for these parts, I reckon," Hank said.

Fifteen minutes and three attempts later, Hank pulled them back onto the road.

"We're grateful," Jason said, shaking Hank's hand again.

"It ain't nothin' you wouldn't do for me or mine," Hank said, before driving away.

Jason turned to Tom and nodded. "Like I said, karma."

"I get it," Tom said. "I get it."

They were back on course when Jason's cell phone rang again. He looked at the caller ID and didn't recognize the number. *It might be Janice calling from a different number*, he thought and let it ring. *Or it might be Miranda.* He answered the call.

"Hey, are you around today?" It was Eric Denson from DYS.

"Nope. I'm actually on the road for a few more days," Jason said. "Why, what's up, Eric?"

"I have something for you, but it's nothing that can't wait."

"Oh yeah, and what's that—a beating from the kids?"

"Not quite," Eric said, laughing. "I'll just throw it into the mail. You'll have it when you get home. No big deal."

"That's it?" Jason asked, "No clues?"

"Just this . . . it's not a beating from the kids," he said and hung up.

Jason laughed.

"Who was that?" Tom asked.

"Some guy who works at DYS. He says he has something for me."

"Maybe it's a child. Did you get him pregnant?" Tom asked. "Maybe you're going to be a dad again." He laughed.

Jason peered hard at him. "Keep running your mouth and I might decide to get you pregnant."

Tom's brow creased.

"And even with all the screaming you're sure to do, there isn't a damned thing you can do about it." This time, only Jason was doing the laughing.

They stopped for lunch in Missoula, Montana, pulling into the parking lot of Ruby's Diner on Regent Street. The neon beckoned them to come inside and lick a greasy spoon or two. "This is right up your alley," Tom said.

It sure is, Jason thought, hoping they served breakfast all day.

As they bellied up to the counter, an older man—dressed in a postal carrier's uniform—greeted them with a friendly nod.

Jason returned the gesture. "Good afternoon," he said.

"Afternoon," the mailman replied, grinning. "Do I detect a different accent?" he said. "East Coast, maybe?"

"Right on the money," Jason told him.

"Name's Eddy Howard," the friendly stranger said, shaking both their hands. "What's brought you fellas all the way out here?"

"We're on our way to spread our father's ashes," Jason answered honestly.

"Oh, I'm sorry for your loss," Eddy said solemnly.

"No need for condolences," Tom said, leaning over his brother to look the stranger in the eye. "We appreciate it, but our old man was a no-good son of a bitch."

Eddy's left eyebrow stood at attention. He grabbed for his coffee, giving it a quick sip. "You know," he said, "at some level, even terrible parents did their best."

"How do you figure that?" Tom asked.

"He kept you alive, didn't he?" Eddy offered a single wink before returning to his half-eaten meal.

Jason turned to his brother. "Would you say Pop did his best?" he whispered.

"If you ever hear me admit to that, you have my permission to rip my lips off," Tom replied in more than a whisper.

"Gladly," Jason said, smiling.

They both laughed again—like they did when they were kids.

Twenty minutes later, Jason was tearing into the French toast combo; it was a sliced cinnamon roll, served with two eggs and thick-cut bacon.

Tom started with a cup of chili, topped with shredded cheese and green onions. For his main dish, he ordered the turkey club sandwich.

While Jason finished eating, Tom watched him like he was visiting the zoo. "Are you going to finish off with a sundae?" he asked.

Jason shook his head. "I'm not sure my system could survive that type of trauma again," he said, knocking the syrup bottle off the table where it began pooling on the floor. *Oh shit* . . .

Before hitting the road again, Jason and Tom stood side-by-side at a pair of urinals, relieving themselves. Jason looked at Tom and grinned. "Browsing?" he asked, loud enough to draw the attention of two other men standing behind them, waiting to go next.

"What?" Tom asked, glancing sideways.

"Eyes straight ahead, please!" Jason barked, trying not to laugh.

"You're such an asshole," Tom said through gritted teeth.

Jason finished up, flushed, and, as he started to walk away, he leaned into Tom's ear. "That may be true," he said. "But you're never going to treat me like some piece of meat again." After washing his big mitts, he hurried out of the bathroom, leaving Tom alone with a couple disturbed men—who were now trying to hurry up their own business and leave.

Back at the SUV, Tom asked him, "What the hell's wrong with you?"

"The list is long," Jason said, laughing. "Just be happy I didn't pull the Angry Andy on you."

"Angry Andy?"

"Our senior year, just weeks before prom," Jason explained. "My buddy Andy and I were the only two in the boys' room between classes. I finished first, hurried out, and began screaming. 'Oh my God, that was so gross!' A hundred students stopped in the hallway. 'What is it?' they asked. I pointed to the bathroom door. 'I just caught a perv in there playing with himself.'"

"Oh my God," Tom muttered, laughing. "You are brutal."

"Not three seconds later, the door opens and out walks Andy, fixing his belt." Jason shook his head. "I don't think he got laid until after he graduated from college and ended up serving time."

Back on the road, Jason grabbed the steering wheel with one hand and his bulging midsection with the other. *What the hell*, he thought, wincing from the sharp pains that shot through his gut.

"What is it?" Tom asked.

"Just heartburn," Jason said. "It's nothing."

"Heartburn in your stomach?" Tom said. "You probably have ulcers. You need to go see a doctor and get that checked. Who knows what else they'll find wrong with you."

"In my body or my mind?" Jason joked.

"What's your cholesterol?" Tom asked, not finding any of it comical. "Around four thousand?"

"Not quite, but my heart rate has to have been hovering close to that since we left Salem."

Jason changed the channel to a country music station. Another sharp pain shot across his abdomen, fizzling out somewhere in his intestines. *Between the stress and my terrible eating habits*, he thought, *I need to make some changes if I'm ever going to meet my grandchildren.*

"So what's the worse fight you've ever been in?" Tom asked, his eyes filled with the curiosity of a child.

Jason grinned. "I remember this one afternoon when the old man pitted us against each other . . ."

"No seriously," Tom interrupted.

Jason took a deep breath and exhaled. "I once fought a guy by the name of Vince Rakowski and, according to anyone who knows him, fighting Vince is a once-in-a-lifetime experience."

Tom looked confused.

"Vince's killed more people than cancer," Jason explained.

Tom nodded, eager to hear more. "A real bad guy, huh?"

"About ten years ago, I was at the sports club with a few brother officers when Vince Rakowski walked in with his wife. By all accounts, Vince was a ruthless enforcer who killed for the sport of it. Anyway, some young thug came into the place, stepped up to the bar, and asked Vince, 'Who's the tramp?'"

"Oh shit," Tom blurted.

Jason nodded. "Everyone expected Vince to slit the kid's throat with a broken beer bottle right there and then, but he didn't. Instead, he turned to the baby brain and said, 'She's my wife.'" Jason shrugged. "While the kid froze, Vince finished his drink, tipped the barkeep, and marched out of the place with his butt-ugly wife hanging on his arm."

"That's it?" Tom asked.

"Nope. Two years later, almost to the day, Vince Rakowski waited in the pouring rain for that same kid to come home. By this time, the loudmouth was married with a baby on the way. Vince waited, hunkered down in the bushes with a cinder block. The kid came home and made it up two steps when Vince called out, 'Remember me?' before smashing the concrete block over his head, caving in the boy's derby."

"Oh shit," Tom repeated.

"Vince had waited two years to get the kid and, knowing him, he was thinking about it the whole time," Jason said. "Once the coast was clear and he figured no one would suspect him, he paralyzed the kid for life."

"And you fought him?" Tom asked.

Jason nodded. "A couple years after that, he arrived at my prison, and we ended up locking horns."

"And you beat him?"

"It's the only reason I'm here today, believe me."

"Sounds like a fun place," Tom quipped.

"Picture an interactive petting zoo," Jason joked.

"Interactive petting zoo?"

Jason nodded. ". . . where the animals pet you back."

"I hate the zoo," Tom said.

"I'm not too fond of it either."

As they passed the sign that read *Welcome to Idaho*, Jason yelled out, "Loaded baked potatoes."

"Is food all you think about?" Tom asked.

Jason nodded. "What else is there?" he said. "Like I said, I used to smoke, drink, fight, and fuck. Now all I have is food." He looked at his brother. "And you want to take that away from me, too?"

Tom shook his head. "It'll be a miracle if you make it to the end of this trip, never mind fifty-four."

Jason looked at him and kept looking. "Are you feeling okay?" he asked, being serious.

"I'm fine. Why?"

"You look pretty worn down today, that's all. Your skin's more pasty than usual."

"I'm fine," Tom repeated.

With all of the road construction and traffic slowing them down—with Jason occasionally yelling out, "Friggin' rubber-neckers"—it was already dark by the time they arrived in Spokane, Washington. On cramped legs, Jason got out of the SUV and looked around. *I'm so done with this bullshit,* he thought. *I'm sick of spending this much time with myself, never mind Poindexter.* He looked over at Tom and shook his head.

"Are you okay?" Tom asked, retrieving their dad.

Jason sighed heavily. "Just getting cagey," he said. "Tired of all the traveling, you know?"

"I know."

Jason's phone rang. He looked at the number and cringed. "It's the prison," he said, reluctantly answering. "Hello."

"Sergeant Prendergast?"

"Speaking."

"It's Captain Eklund. I wanted to give you a heads-up before Boston got a hold of you."

"What's up, Cap?"

There was a heavy sigh on the line. "It seems they're sending an investigator down to take a look at the Pires hanging."

"Take a look?" Jason repeated. "Take a look at what?"

"They want to make sure it wasn't an assisted suicide."

"Are you shitting me?" Jason asked, his blood throbbing in every extremity. "Do you know who they assigned?"

"Lieutenant Robinson."

"Robinson?" Jason repeated, his free hand instinctively balling into a fist. "He's a friggin' headhunter."

"Which is why I called you," the captain said.

"When does the hunt begin?" Jason asked.

"I'm told he'll be down next week to conduct some interviews. You're the first on the list."

"Well, that's just great," Jason said. "Thanks for the heads-up, Cap." He hung up.

Tom was staring at him. "What's the matter?" he asked.

Jason shook his head, trying to quell his adrenaline buzz. "Just before we left for the road, I responded to an inmate suicide . . . a hanger."

"And?"

"And now it's under investigation."

"Why would a suicide be under investigation?" Tom asked, looking for clarity.

Jason shook his head. "They want to make sure we didn't string him up and then pull down on his waist for good measure."

Tom stared at him for a moment, his eyebrow standing at attention.

"Don't you dare even ask if I did it," Jason said. "Or I'll be assisting you into the afterlife."

"Are you kidding me?" Tom said, heading for the motel. "I wouldn't even think of it." He nodded. "If you were going to end someone's life, I doubt you'd put in that much thought or effort."

In spite of himself, Jason chuckled.

The Quality Inn on Fourth Avenue in downtown Spokane cost a hundred bucks a room for the night. After Tom worked his anal-retentive magic, they only had to pay eighty dollars each.

"We're located in the heart of Spokane, just a short walk from Riverfront Park," the motel clerk said.

"Good," Jason said. "I can use a long walk." He looked at his brother. "Do you mind if we go our separate ways tonight? I need some time alone and . . ."

"I get it," Tom said. "Trust me, it'll be good for us both. We've become worse than a married couple."

"I'll look after the old man."

Tom grinned. "He's in good hands then."

The clerk looked behind them, searching for a third person.

Intent on enjoying the gift of individual dining, Jason grabbed the SUV and hit a Sonic Drive-In. *We don't have these back home, and they serve tater tots. I love tater tots.* Without anyone looking over his shoulder or providing judgmental commentary, he ate—all by himself, in peace—a tray of fried, melty, cheesy delights. And when he'd finished, he went back up and ordered a thick vanilla shake. *Worse comes to worst,* he thought, *the motel is close by.*

Ignoring his throbbing abdomen, Jason parked the SUV in the motel lot and took off on foot toward Riverfront Park. It was a little too cold to be outdoors without a jacket, but he never considered going back to retrieve one from his room. *Screw it,* he thought, *I'll be sweating my fat ass off in a few minutes anyway.*

As he walked alone, he took an inventory of his and Tom's odd trip out west. *Maybe Tom's not as bad as I thought. And I could use a different perspective of the world. Lord knows I've been sheltered, hidden behind a damned wall for too long.*

And then he tallied his life. *Thank God for Miranda. She's the only good thing in my pathetic life. Come to think of it, I don't care how much this friggin' wedding costs me. She should have everything she wants. She deserves it.* He then thought about the future. *After this friggin' witch-hunt is over at work, I have two more years to serve and I'm a free man. And then what? Tom's right. I've never really been anywhere or done anything.* He felt a rush of sorrow course through him. *According to the statistics, I'm only a couple years away from hanging out with my asshole father again.* He kept walking. *I wonder how Lou is,* he thought, picturing his prison mentor and friend for the first time in much too long. Jason walked late into the chilly night, long after his swollen belly felt normal again.

Back in the motel room, on bended knee, Jason prayed for the people he'd lost, as well as those who were still with him on earth and needed the prayers even more. *You know you're getting older when the first list is longer than the second*, he thought, climbing into another strange bed.

He closed his eyes and lay still for a few minutes, until the tossing and turning commenced. *Here we go again*, he thought.

Deep into the silent night, he saw every single number on the alarm clock, glowing red and rolling through again and again. He continued to close his eyes and open them, dissecting the numbers by how the lines were arranged to define the time. This dragged into the early morning. His thoughts were random and disconnected, as if his conscious mind was trying to do the illogical job of the subconscious. Without sleep, the data files of the day still needed to be processed and put away.

Folding his hands behind his head, he dwelled on his chosen profession and the bizarre human warehouse he spent his every workday locked within. He couldn't help it. It was that consuming. "It's just another day at work," most said, but he didn't want to hear it anymore. He knew better. *I'm so sick and tired of that dungeon*, he thought, his eyes starting to grow heavy . . .

It was a living nightmare, with Sergeant Jason Prendergast's blood pressure threatening to punch out the crest of his skull.

Drip. Drip. Drip . . .

Two more years of stink, the smell of piss and shit so bad you can taste it. Two more years of punks trying to test my gut. Watching the strong, no matter how, take anything they wanted. And the weak take even more from the weaker. Each day surrounded by con men, hit men, pimps, and the queens who fill their pockets. Men so unpredictable, they'd just as soon jam a pen in your eye as give you the time of day. And in this pit, everybody can spare a little time. But it's the ones with AIDS who scare the shit out of me. Of course, nobody can know who they are. That has to stay confidential.

Nope, it's not like years ago when you could bleed on the floor with a guy and not have to worry you were just handed a death sentence. Friggin' junkies! They should house 'em in their own pen. Let 'em tuck the drugs up their assholes somewhere else. God knows they have no problem getting the shit in here, no matter how hard we try to stop it. I guess that's the wonder of the human will. Where there's that will, some ingenious bastard will always concoct some harebrained scheme to get the drugs in.

And the way I see it, there are only two ways out of this house of horrors: escape or suicide. I've witnessed both. But not me. No, I'll walk out the same way I walked in.

Yup, twenty-eight down and two more to go.

Drip. Drip. Drip . . .

Two more Thanksgivings, just sitting and counting the cock-roaches—most of which should outlive me. Two more Christmases hidden behind a wall. Almost there . . .

A portable radio squelched once, calling Jason's attention back to reality. Bobby Couture, a much younger correction officer, stood over him. For a moment, the sight startled him.

"What's your problem?" the smaller man asked. "Everything okay?"

Jason stood, unhooked his radio, and handed it over to his second-shift relief. "The boys were quiet today. You might want to keep an eye on Patricio, though. It looks like he's getting ready to strong-arm the new guy, Thompson. The nut just got admitted yesterday and, from what I can tell, he doesn't look like he's going to do too well in his new home." He chuckled and added, "Other than that, the count's the same—sixty living, breathing convicts."

Bobby Couture laughed before turning to face the block.

"Oh, and Bobby," Jason said, as he opened the heavy steel door to step out of the block. "If you get a chance, call mainte-

Jason awoke from his recurring dream, sweaty and panting. *Oh God*, he thought, trying to shake off the nightmare. But he couldn't. *My life is the nightmare, at least while I'm at work.*

For him, concealed behind tons of concrete, bricks, and steel, reality took on a horrifying appearance. Time stood silently still within the hidden jungle, while the desperate cries of men fell upon deaf walls. Shunned by a self-sedated world, yesterday knew no memories, today was blind, and tomorrow tasted of broken glass. Like the caches of lethal weapons and plentiful drugs, these truths were also hidden well. Somewhere along the way, razor wire had replaced a once-blue horizon, while a single gun tower became the only beacon of hope.

Jason solemnly shook his head. His future was one where getting the edge could mean certain death, and staying on top equaled another day in hell. Even in the warmth of a motel room, it chilled his bones.

Before trying to fall asleep again, he experienced one final sobering thought. *I wonder what other people think about when they finish an honest day's work.*

After chugging half a bottle of Nyquil, he put on the radio—a country and western channel—and folded his hands behind his head again, waiting for the chemically induced slumber to begin.

chapter 10

Tom awoke feeling like a wet dishrag. Still exhausted and now nauseous, his muscles felt like over-stretched rubber bands. *We need to get this trip over with,* he thought, grabbing for his hormone pills. Swallowing both pills—without water—he headed for the shower. *I need to see Dr. Baxter soon.*

There was no drive-thru at the Satellite Diner. "Let's just get breakfast to go," Tom suggested. Besides feeling like shit, they were getting close and he was feeling antsy.

"Sounds like a plan," Jason said, ordering two breakfast sandwiches constructed of a couple eggs, ham, and melted cheddar cheese on focaccia bread. "And let me get the hash browns on the side for the extra buck."

Tom was content with a medium hot tea. *I just want to get to Seattle,* he thought, glaring back at the menacing wooden box, *and be rid of the old man for good.*

"Are you sure you're okay?" Jason asked. "You look like death warmed over."

"I told you, I'm fine," Tom lied.

"Are you sure?" Jason asked, concerned. "You're as pale as a ghost and your eyes look . . ."

"I'm fine," Tom repeated, his volume raised three levels.

Shrugging it off, Jason ate his breakfast—but his eyes never left Tom's face.

Before getting back on the highway, they pulled into a gas station to top off the gas tank. Jason returned to the SUV with his usual handful of lottery tickets. As he began to scratch away, Tom said, "Do you realize your chances of winning?"

"So you're saying I have a chance to win?" Jason asked, sarcastically. He shook his head at the first loss.

Tom was not amused. "Why even play if the odds are that stacked against you?"

"To win money . . ."

"But you already have money, right?"

"Listen, the state lottery is an integral part of my redneck retirement plan."

"I love that you used the word *integral* in the right context, but your long-term strategy leaves a lot to be desired."

Jason looked at him, dumbfounded.

"You need some serious help."

"Then maybe you should help me," Jason suggested, scratching the next losing ticket.

"I plan to."

Jason stopped scratching and looked up at him, speechless.

Suddenly, Tom's stomach felt like it was being wrung out; he dry heaved twice before jumping out of the SUV, bending at the waist, and vomiting a mix of tea and bile onto the oilstained asphalt.

"What's the matter?" Jason asked, hurrying to his side.

I can't hide this anymore, he thought, looking up at his brother through hazy eyes. "I'm sick," he confessed, heaving whatever was left in his belly.

"Was it something you ate at the diner last night?"

Shaking his head, Tom stood erect to face his brother. "I have prostate cancer," he explained.

Jason's face bleached white. "P-prostate cancer?" he stuttered.

Tom nodded. "I need to get to a hospital, Jason," he said.

Jason helped him back into the SUV—nearly lifting him like a child—and sped off to the local Emergency Room. "You're going to be okay," he said, obviously trying to convince himself as much as Tom. "You're going to be just fine."

Dr. Baxter phoned in Tom's temporary protocol. Tom was relaxing on a gurney with a full IV bag of saline draining into his thirsty arm when Jason walked in, his face showing the fears of an older brother.

"I'm sorry. I should have told you," Tom said, as Jason took a seat beside him. "I have the same type of cancer that took Pop and . . ." His eyes started to fill.

"If it's detected early, isn't prostate cancer one of the most controllable cancers?" Jason asked.

Tom nodded.

"When did they find it?" Jason asked, like he was conducting an interview.

"My doctor claims he found it early enough, but . . ." He shook his head. "This is some scary shit, Jason. My kids are so young and . . ." He stopped, fighting off the emotions that thundered inside of him.

Jason clamped his large hand onto Tom's forearm. "The old man never took care of himself, so of course he wouldn't have found out until it was too late." He gave Tom's arm a good squeeze. "But you listen to me right now, Tommy. You're going to fight this and be around to play with your kid's kids. Do you hear me?" Jason's eyes were now swollen with tears. He squeezed again. "I've got your back, brother, and I'm right here for whatever . . ." He stopped and looked away before the tears had a chance to break free and escape down his cheeks. "What's your treatment look like?" he managed, giving Tom's arm another strong squeeze.

"Dr. Baxter, my oncologist, has me on a protocol of chemotherapy treatments that I'll resume when we get home. I'm also on a cocktail of medications."

"What kind of medications?"

"Believe it or not," Tom said reluctantly, "he put me on estrogen pills." He waited for a smartass reply.

Jason turned and faced him again. "Whatever heals your body, brother," he said. "And as far as this crazy-ass trip, we can put an end to it right here and . . ."

"No," Tom said firmly. "We need to finish this trip."

"But, Tommy," Jason said. "Knowing the old man, there ain't anything worth anything in that damned envelope."

Tom shook his head. "I don't care about the envelope anymore," he said. "Something tells me we need to finish this thing."

"But are you sure you're up to it?"

Tom nodded. "I feel better already," he fibbed. "And I'll be as right as rain in another hour or so."

"Are you sure?" Jason asked.

"I'm positive," he said, gesturing toward his IV. "Just let me finish my breakfast and we can hit the road."

Jason gave his arm one last squeeze. "You *are* going to be as right as rain. I know it." He nodded. "You just need to stop worrying so much and have a little faith. If you're going to heal, you need to . . ."

"Do you have any regrets?" Tom blurted.

"Regrets?" Jason said, surprised.

"Yeah, life's regrets . . . big ones."

"Of course I have regrets," Jason admitted.

"What are they?" Tom asked.

"What is this, confession time?"

Tom shook his head. "Nope, just two middle-aged men taking an inventory of the things they should have done and didn't, or might still have the chance to do."

"Might?" Jason said. "Of course we have the chance."

"Then what are they?" Tom prodded. "Your regrets?"

Nodding, Jason exhaled heavily. "I regret putting up with the old man for as long as I did."

"For me," Tom said, "it was not killing him any of the times I had the chance."

They both laughed.

"I regret not knowing our mother, or really anyone in our family," Jason said solemnly.

Tom nodded. "I have that one too," he said, "as well as marrying an ice queen."

"Ice queen?" Jason repeated, laughing.

"I shouldn't say I regret marrying her, though, because she did give me two beautiful kids." He shrugged. "But man, has there been a price to pay."

Jason nodded. "Trust me, I also regret wasting time on relationships I knew were doomed," he said.

"I regret not being there more for my kids," Tom admitted.

Jason looked surprised. "But I thought you were always there for them."

"I was, as much as I could be, anyway. But there were events I missed because of work obligations—or whatever—and now I'm sorry that I did."

"We're all guilty of that," Jason said. "I know I am."

"Sure," Tom said. "But there were times when I put work before family, telling myself it was all for them." He shook his head. "Times when they needed me more than they needed the money I could bring home."

"I regret the same thing," Jason admitted. "You can't imagine the overtime shifts I took when I should have been watching Miranda at dance rehearsal or pitching on a softball mound."

As they continued to cite their regrets, Tom recognized that neither listed the fact that they—he and Jason—had been estranged for years. *And that needs to change right now*, he decided. "What about you and me?" he asked.

"What do you mean?"

"You know what I mean," Tom said.

Jason half-shrugged. "I remember you threw some hissy fit over something stupid I said, and you and Carmen stormed off with the kids," Jason said. "And then I didn't see you for fifteen years."

Tom shook his head. *And the old man called me dummy?* he thought. "That's not the reason why and we both know it."

Jason opened his mouth but nothing came out.

"It's because I was too weak and pathetic not to protect you when I should have," he said. "It's because I betrayed you, Jason." His guilty mind instantly traveled back to survival camp on Maple Avenue, so he could finally share the dark details of that terrible afternoon with Jason.

Tom returned home from school to the sweet, pungent smell of marijuana lingering in his and Jason's bedroom. *Jason must have just left,* Tom thought. He lay on his twin-size bed and had just placed a set of headphones onto his ears when his bedroom door flew open, making him spring up to a seated position.

"You smoking reefer in here?" the old man roared.

Panicked by the wild, drunken look in his father's scanning eyes, Tom struggled to get the headphones off his head. "Wha . . . what's that?"

"You heard me!" he screamed. "I smell pot in this room. Where you hiding it?"

"I . . . I . . ." Tom stuttered.

His dad backhanded him, returning him to the prone position on the bed.

While Tom lay on his back, his brain registered the blow, sending a sharp pain to his mouth. Sliding the back of his hand across to his lips, he came away with a smear of fresh blood. "It . . . it wasn't me," he squeaked, his mind racing for a believable explanation. There was none.

"Don't you lie to me, dummy," Pop screamed, lunging for the bed with his clenched fists at the ready.

"I don't smoke pot," Tom screamed back, as wave after wave of fear ran through every cell in his body.

"Then it must be your punk brother," he said, his squinted eyes searching the room again. "Where does he keep it?"

"I . . . I don't . . ."

Another backhand landed square on Tom's face, this time on the cheek—nearly stunning him into silence. He wished it had.

"Tell me now or I'm going to rip this entire room apart until I find it. And then . . ." He leaned in close until Tom could smell the whiskey on the trembling man's breath.

As if the movement was involuntary, Tom's index finger pointed toward the bedroom closet door.

"In the closet, huh?" his dad said, already tossing out anything he came into contact with. As his breathing became labored and angry, he turned to face Tom again. His eyes were on fire now, flickering with some demonic rage. "Where?" he yelled louder than Tom had ever heard him.

Shriveling inside, Tom muttered, "The ceiling tile." After spouting the three words, he couldn't remember feeling more disloyal in his whole life. *Traitor*, he screamed in his head, already feeling every dark emotion that accompanied the self-imposed, well-deserved title. And while his mind spiraled, his body remained on the bed, paralyzed with fear.

Pop rummaged frantically for a few more minutes before he found the plastic baggie containing a small amount of oregano-like substance and a square of rolling papers. "You're damned lucky it wasn't you," he hissed, leaving the room a mess and Tom weeping sorrowfully on the bed.

A moment later, Tom could make out his father's muffled voice talking to someone. *Oh no*, he thought, *it's Jason*. He hurried to the door and cracked it open to listen. Right away, he could tell his father was on the telephone. *Thank God*, he thought, relieved. His mind then jumped to trying to figure out how he could warn his brother, and even help with the alibi. *We'll just say a friend was over the house and the pot's his.*

"Can you send a patrol car to 525 Maple Avenue," Pop said. "My delinquent son's been smoking pot in my house and I want him arrested for it."

Oh no, Tom thought, more panicked than ever. *Jason's so screwed and it's all my fault.*

Tom returned to the present, shaking his head. "I'm still amazed we survived that asshole," he said, even now feeling the weight of the anchor he'd carried since adolescence.

"Ain't that the truth," Jason muttered.

"It's because we had each other," Tom said. "And I screwed that up."

Jason's Adam's apple bounced a few times in discomfort. "I spotted the police car parked on the curb outside the house when I pulled into the driveway," he said. "I remember sprinting toward the house, afraid that something had happened to you."

Tom cringed.

"I opened the front door to find the old man standing side by side with some cop in the living room—and the no-good bastard was grinning." Jason shook his head. "And that's when the cop lifted a plastic bag of marijuana into the air for me to see. I knew right away I was all done."

Tears flooded Tom's eyes. As he fought to keep them at bay, he played out the rest of the terrible scene in his mind.

Although the conversation was muffled, Tom listened carefully as the nightmare unfolded.

"Is the pot yours, son?" the policeman asked Jason.

But before he could answer, Pop yelled, "Of course it's his, and I want him locked up for it right now."

"Well, I . . . I . . ." the policeman stammered.

"His brother told me exactly where to find it," the old man said.

In the brief silence, Tom could already picture the pain in his big brother's eyes.

"Tommy," the old man screamed. "Get your ass out here right now!"

With his head hung low, Tom entered the living room—unable to look Jason in the eye.

"Did this bag of pot come from your bedroom?" he asked.

Tom nodded.

"And it's your brother's, right?"

Tom stood still.

"Tommy?" the old man screamed, making him nod again.

The old man turned to the cop. "I want him arrested," he demanded, gesturing toward Jason.

"No, Dad," Jason said, his dreams of being a policeman hanging in the balance. "Please . . . not that."

Shaking his head, the cop turned to Jason. "Son, you do realize that the possession and use of marijuana is against the law, right?"

Jason nodded. "Yes, sir."

The lawman turned to the old man and lowered his tone. "I don't actually have to arrest him," he said. "If you'd rather, I could . . ."

"I want him locked up!" Pop roared. "He brought drugs into my house, and he needs to learn a lesson from it."

Tom glanced at Jason and couldn't ever remember seeing such fear in his brother's eyes.

"Please, Dad," Jason begged. "I made a mistake. But . . . but if I get arrested, I won't be able to . . ."

"Lock him up," he told the cop. "And use the cuffs."

"No!" Tom screamed, while a piece of him died inside.

The cop shook his head again before getting on his portable radio. Pressing the button, the radio squelched once. "Dispatch, I'm coming in with one for the possession of a Class C substance." He removed his handcuffs and faced Jason. "Place your hands behind your back, son."

"Please no," Jason begged, his voice quivering. "Not this." But he did as he was told.

The cop clamped the cold steel onto both of his wrists. "You have the right to remain silent . . ."

Through his haze of tears, Tom saw his father grinning at him. *Jason's done with me now*, he thought. *He'll never forgive this.*

". . . and whatever you say," the cop continued, "can and will be used against you in a court of law."

Jason finally looked at Tom, who was now pleading for his brother's forgiveness with his eyes. "You little rat," he hissed before looking away.

"Jason," Tommy screamed out as his brother was being escorted out the front door. "Dad made me tell him. I'm sorry . . ." He was crying so heavily now that he could hardly speak.

But Jason never looked back. He kept marching toward the patrol car—with his hands restrained behind his back—toward an unknown future.

They'll never let Jason be a cop now, Tom realized, feeling another piece of himself wither away and die, *and it's all my fault.*

Tom emerged from the past again. "I've never been more sorry or ashamed of anything in my life," he confessed, before looking straight at Jason. "I'm sorry, brother," he said. "I let you down in the worst way possible and I'm sorry."

"Forget it," Jason said, shaking his head. "It's in the past."

"No," Tom said. "I've thought a lot about this, and the older I've gotten, the more I've realized that the old man was so pissed at you for challenging him on our way home from the dog track that he was looking for any way to drive a wedge between us." He shook his head. "And I gave him that opportunity. I let him destroy your chance at being a policeman, as well as our relationship in the process."

Jason stared at him but said nothing.

"But you got me back and evened the score," Tom said.

"Because you thought I slept with Carmen?" Jason said.

"No," Tom corrected him. "Because you left me alone with that monster." Even now, Tom could still feel the sting of his brother's abandonment. They'd taken terrible beatings as kids and, in Tom's mind, they'd only survived because they were a team, forever having each other's backs. There were many times when Jason would confess to something he didn't do, just to save Tom the beating. Tom remembered being in awe at how his brother never screamed out, never giving the old man the satisfaction of hearing his pain. Instead, Jason had turned his fear into fury, exactly what their father had wanted. To do his piece, Tom had covered for Jason by making up the most elaborate alibis. Even as a kid, he knew he was smarter than their father and he was pretty sure the old man knew it too. And so, together, they played their twisted charade for years. In a way, childhood was a sort of gladiator training camp. *That is, until Jason moved out and left me to suffer Pop's cruelty all by myself,* he thought, *and the old man was no less relentless.* In fact, Tom began experiencing the pain for the both of them. *Unforgivable,* he thought, recalling how he'd hated himself for begging for his father's mercy, only to learn the curse of self-loathing in the process. But he couldn't help himself. *The fear was so intense.* Even now, at fifty years old, Jason's abandonment felt like such deep betrayal that it still haunted his soul.

A silent resentment had hung between them for years, with long-simmering hostilities that never obtained any real outlet to bring everything to a head. Time took care of the rest, with each passing year creating even more distance— until they were essentially strangers. To top it off, neither one wanted anything to do with the old man or anything that reminded them of him. *He was poison and everything he touched became poison.* All it took was one final push, one simple argument, for Jason and Tom to be exiled from each other's lives for nearly fifteen years.

"I know you wanted to leave the old man's torment as soon as you were able to, but you left me there alone," Tom said. "Alone with that monster," he repeated, sounding much younger than his age.

"I know," Jason said, his quiet tone revealing a hint of shame. "And I'm sorry about that."

"Sorry?" Tom squeaked.

They sat in silence for a while, with Tom staring down the hospital corridor. He didn't know what to think or feel, never mind know how to express it.

Jason shrugged. "Like I said, it's all in the past."

"Is it?" Tom asked, filled with more hope than he'd known in a long time.

"It is," Jason promised. "It has to be."

"Good," Tom said, gesturing toward the empty IV bag. "Because it looks like I'm done with my breakfast and we still have a few more miles to travel together."

Jason extended his hand for a shake. "That, we do," he said.

Just as the trees were turning into picket fences again, they stopped at a Subway sandwich shop right off the highway in Ellensburg, Washington. Jason got the cold cut combo with lettuce, tomato, and mayo. Tom got the veggie delight with Italian dressing. With large fountain drinks in hand, they were back on the highway—their father resting comfortably in the backseat—in less than twenty minutes. "Let's go get this done already," Jason said.

Abandoning his maps, Tom looked at the GPS. "We're exactly a hundred and ten miles from Seattle," he said, a bolt of excitement ripping through him. "Two hours away." He looked to his side to see his brother wearing the same smile. *Six days and five nights from Salem to Seattle*, Tom thought. *We actually friggin' made it!*

An hour and forty-five minutes later, Tom could feel a wave of excitement—and relief—roll over him, rocking his entire body. His breathing became shallow, his palms got sweaty, and his extremities began to tingle. In similar situations, he'd be bracing himself to fight off a panic attack. *But not this time*, he thought. *Nope, this is a good thing.* According to the GPS, they were only blocks away from the address their father had given them, his final resting place.

"I've been thinking that we should get the families together some time," Jason said. This was clearly not meant as small talk but a sincere gesture.

"We should," Tom agreed. "Though I doubt my kids would be up for it at this point. They hardly have the time to see me."

"Maybe you're right," Jason said. "Maybe that ship's already sailed."

Tom thought about it. "Although, you could invite me to Miranda's wedding."

"I'll tell her to put you on the list."

"Good," Tom said. "She's missed a lot of Christmas and birthday gifts from me. I'll be sure to make it up in the card."

"She won't care about that, Tom," Jason said, looking at him. "She'll just be happy, and surprised, to see you there."

"I'll be there."

He grinned. "If you say so."

"I won't miss my niece's wedding," Tom confirmed, breaking the awkward silence.

Jason nodded.

Tom noted that his brother's demeanor toward him had significantly softened since the start of their trip. *I guess we have made some progress*, he thought.

They traveled another block. "Do you think Pop sent us on this wild goose chase to—" Tom began to ask.

"Whatever the cold prick's reasons," Jason interrupted, "you can rest assured it was to ease his own conscience and make himself feel better." He looked at Tom. "My guess is that the closer he got to death, the more worried he became."

"And rightly so," Tom said.

"He never gave a shit about us or anyone else," Jason said. "That man was just plain wired wrong."

"True, but it still doesn't add up," Tom said.

Jason shrugged. "I wouldn't give it much thought, brother. We survived the trip together and we're almost here. Whatever the old man's motives were will be spread out soon enough by the wind, right along with him."

"I guess," Tom said, but his wheels were still spinning at full steam. *It just doesn't add up.*

Within minutes, they reached their final destination; it was a housing project, with a sign that read *Seattle Housing Authority.* Jason looked at Tom and shook his head. "Un-fucking real!"

Tom checked the address three times—1165 Milford Road, Seattle, Washington. "This can't be right," he said. "Something's wrong." He looked back at the box of ashes, as if he expected some explanation for the confusion. But it was a housing project; redbrick units—four per building—with postage stamp-sized front yards behind chain-link fences. Each front stoop had two concrete stairs and a black steel railing leading to its front door.

"Who's shitting who?" Jason said. "Dad couldn't give a rat's ass where we spread his ashes." He paused for a moment, surveying the housing project. "Which makes me even more pissed off about this fool's errand."

They got out of the SUV and, with their manipulative father in hand, stepped up to the address. Tom knocked on the door. There was no answer. Jason pushed by him and pounded away on the chipped paint. Still, there was no answer. The brothers looked at each other in disbelief. "Un-fucking real," Jason repeated, stomping back for the SUV.

An elderly black man sitting on the stoop next door called out, "You fellas looking for someone?"

Jason stopped. As they approached the old-timer, Tom extended his hand. "Name's Tom Prendergast," he said, introducing himself. "And this is my brother, Jason. We've come cross-country to . . ."

"Prendergast, you say?" the old man interrupted.

Jason nodded. "That's right."

"An old lady with the same last name lived at that address for years," he said, gesturing with his head toward the door they'd knocked on.

"Really?" Tom said, at a loss for more words. *No way*, he thought, his heart beating in his stomach. *It can't be. It just can't be.*

"Is she dead?" Jason followed up, always the investigator.

The man shrugged. "I don't think so, but she's got a few years on me." He thought for a moment before pointing west. "Not too long ago, she moved into that retirement home across town." He placed his crooked index finger to his chin and nodded. "Rolling Hills, I think it's called."

"Impossible," Tom mumbled, looking at his brother. "It can't be."

Jason took a deep breath. "There's only one way to find out."

Tom snapped a few photos with his cell phone—the *Seattle Housing Authority* sign, as well as the number on the apartment—before hurrying for the SUV.

Within the confines of Rolling Hills Retirement Home, there was a peace most people could only dream of. Removed from the rat race of society, the tranquil surroundings were breathtaking. Hundreds of green plants filled the rooms, and a handful of birds chirped in harmony. The sun's rays engulfed the interior of the building and the same sweet melody seemed to play over and over on some hidden stereo. Tom listened carefully. There were also the muffled sounds of laughter.

Although torment loomed over each bed and death lurked behind every corner, Tom discovered a silent bliss. Most patients had reached the end of life's path and were finished with the denial, the negotiating with God, the anger. There was no battling the inevitable. Instead, the snickers of a friendly card game could be overheard, or the whispers of some treasured conversations detected. Peering into the patients' eyes was like gazing into a history book. For those who dared to open the cover, lengthy discussions would undoubtedly reveal years of hard lessons and the wisdom achieved. These teachers were old, they were sick and tired, but they had more to offer than anyone else.

"Miss Prendergast?" Jason asked the orderly.

"Mrs. Prendergast," the smiling man corrected him, pointing to an elderly woman sitting off in a corner; she was slumped over, almost sulking.

Both men took a deep breath before slowly making their way over to her.

"Mrs. Prendergast," Jason said, taking a knee in front of her. "We've come a long way and . . ." He stopped.

She was peering hard at them, her eyes darting back and forth, taking in every detail of their confused faces. As recognition registered in her eyes, her shallow breathing turned to hyperventilation.

There's no way she can be . . . Tom was thinking when Jason cleared his throat. Tom could tell his brother was struck with emotion, the very same he was now feeling.

"My name is Jason and he's . . ."

"Thomas?" she squeaked.

Tom took a knee beside his brother and grabbed her hand. "Yes," he said. "That's my name, Tom Prendergast."

Her eyes began to leak. "My . . . my boys' names were Jason and Tom," she stuttered between gasping breaths. "But they were taken from me so . . . so long ago . . . by their . . ." She couldn't finish and began to cry mournfully.

Instinctively, Tom took a whiff of her and was disappointed to discover that this woman smelled like an old lady and not how he remembered his mom—or thought he remembered her. In his fuzzy memories, his mother had curly auburn hair. But this ancient soul had thin white hair that barely covered her scalp; skin that was stretched over her skull. And Mrs. Prendergast's face was foreign to him as well—though his mother's face changed so much in his fragmented memories that he couldn't tell whether he had any true recollection at all, or just made it up in his mind to make her more real.

"I'd . . . I'd given up," she wept, her thin arms trembling.

No fucking way, Tom thought, struggling to take in air. Exchanging shocked glances, both Jason and Tom remained on their knees at the feet of the grieving woman, each holding one of her hands. Tom's eyes filled with tears, and he was having a difficult time stopping them from tumbling down his face. He could feel the woman's deep pain, shared in it. *Mom?* he thought. *Can you really be my . . . my mother?* He looked over at Jason to see a single tear running down the tough guy's crimson cheek.

Her body convulsing, her nose running past the awful sniffles, she finally looked up. "My boys," she said in a hoarse whisper. "You've . . . you've come back to me."

Jason and Tom looked at each other again. "That no-good son of a bitch," Jason muttered, putting each of their feelings toward their father into words.

Hugs—long, heartfelt hugs—were exchanged.

Pop lied to us all those years, telling us that our mother was dead, Tom thought, wanting nothing more than to cremate the bastard again.

For a long moment, Mrs. Prendergast's face—frozen somewhere between the suffering that follows a family death and the madness that accompanies a betrayed lover—locked onto her long-lost sons. "I've . . . I've prayed all these years that . . . that you'd come . . . home to me." She struggled for air like she was sucking it in through a crimped straw. "And . . . and I was starting to worry . . . that I'd pass before . . . before I ever saw you again."

This cannot be happening, Tom thought, while his brother's shoulders rocked back and forth to the rhythm of his quiet sobs.

Overcome with emotion, the brittle woman fought to take a few deep breaths—until she was able to speak. "For years, I . . . I hated your father . . . for taking you from me." Her mouth became tight in anger, creating a thin, taut line. "That bastard kidnapped you . . ." She began crying again, convulsing with each wail. "It's taken me a long time to understand . . . to understand how he could have been so cruel . . ." She had to stop for a moment to catch her breath. ". . . taking my baby boys away from me . . .the way he did."

"That evil prick," Jason muttered, his eyes filled with a wrath Tom had never imagined existed in him.

Their newfound mother looked off into the distance for a while. A few beats after it had become awkward, she nodded. "But I had a lot of problems back then," she said, trying to clear away the clog in her throat. "With all the drinking . . . and the pills." She shook her head in shame. "Truth is, I didn't come from the best family." Her eyes returned to the empty space before her, where she obviously tried to sort through her memories and rationalize her thoughts. "It's taken me years to admit it, but my family was no good . . . criminals that . . . that took advantage of decent folks." She looked at her grown sons. "My brothers, your uncles, were in and out of prison most of their lives. Two of your aunts sold their bodies for drugs and . . . and if I'm being honest," she solemnly confessed, "there was a time I did too." The tears began to roll again.

Holy shit, Tom thought. *Hoooooly shit!*

Jason knelt upright, clearly taken aback by the jarring news.

She began to weep in shame. "I've begged the good Lord's forgiveness for . . . for as long as I can remember."

As Jason placed his arm around her shoulder and gave it a supportive squeeze, Tom told her, "And I'm sure he forgave you long ago." He rubbed her leg. "You've clearly suffered enough."

Her eyes grew distant again. "I . . . I don't like being here," she said, her voice now sounding like it belonged to a little girl.

"Why, Mom?" Jason asked, making Tom's head spin at hearing the new title. "Is someone hurting you here?"

Mom? Tom repeated in his spinning head.

"No," she said. "They're good to me here. I just miss my home . . . the same home you boys were born in."

"On Milford Road?" Tom asked.

She nodded. "1165 Milford Road," she said. "After you boys were taken from me, I . . . I could never bring myself to leave that place . . . hoping you'd return to me someday."

Oh my God, Tom thought, shocked, *our mother's been alive all these years.*

Although the old woman vowed she felt overjoyed with the long-awaited reunion, her frail body was obviously suffering from the shock of it.

After agreeing to return in the morning, Jason and Tom walked out of the home. "In a really messed up way, this answers a lot for me," Jason told Tom, wiping his eyes without shame.

Tom looked at him, struggling not to fall to his knees and weep.

"The old man used constant negativity to inspire us to go in the opposite direction."

"He used to say," Tom said, jumping in, "'we can't help how we're wired, but we are responsible for our choices.'"

"This is what you call real irony," Jason said.

"How's that?"

"Pop stole us away to save us from the same degenerate behavior he displayed throughout our entire childhoods."

"What an asshole," Tom said, at a loss for a fancier word.

Jason nodded. "When I got the job in the prison, he told me, 'I always knew you'd end up behind bars.'"

"Messed up is right," Tom agreed. "I . . . I still can't believe any of this."

"Me either, Tommy," Jason said, his eyes glassed over with confusion and awe. "Me either."

chapter 11

THE FOLLOWING MORNING, Jason and Tom waited in one of the common living areas of Rolling Hills for nearly an hour before their mother felt well enough to receive visitors. As they approached, their mom was sitting off in the same corner, staring into nothingness once again.

On bended knees, the brothers greeted her as if they were all experiencing the previous day's discovery for the first time. The sickly woman mourned again—terribly. "Where's your father now?" she finally asked, her eyes turned to slits; she looked like she was already planning his murder.

"He's dead," Jason answered bluntly, happy to report the news.

"And we checked to make sure," Tom added with a smirk.

"It's about damn time," she said without emotion. "I suppose it won't be long before . . . before I'll be giving him a good piece of my mind."

She clearly has no problem throwing elbows when she has to, Jason decided. *At least I now know where I got it from.*

It wasn't long before they realized the frail woman was struggling just to sit up.

Tom grabbed her hand. "You should get some rest, Mom," he said, trying to soothe her.

Jason's head flew up at the word *Mom*. *That's obviously going to take me some time to get used to*, he thought.

Suddenly, she started in on a coughing fit that had two orderlies rushing to her aid.

"Breathe easy, Mom," Jason said, rubbing her skeletal back. "Try to relax."

"I'm sorry, gentlemen, but she needs her rest," one of the orderlies advised. "Do you mind coming back?"

The ancient woman shook her head in disapproval, but the hacking would not permit her to speak another word.

"It's okay, Mom," Tom said. "We'll come back later."

"We promise," Jason added, kissing her cold, bony cheek.

Continuing to live out of their suitcases, Tom and Jason stayed for a few days, learning about their deteriorating mother and the family they'd come from.

"When you boys were small, I . . . I used to dress you in matching outfits. You were so handsome," she reminisced, her eyes glassing over. "Your father . . . he never cared much for that, though."

"Of course he didn't," Tom said under his breath. "What did he ever care for?"

"Drinking beer and betting the dogs," the old woman answered, surprising them both.

"Which never changed," Jason told her.

She shook her head before allowing herself to drift off again. "We did have some good times, I guess. We . . . we used to play cards every Friday night . . . and everyone would come over . . ."

I remember that! Jason thought, a small door in his mind suddenly thrown open—revealing a small boy trawling beneath an old dining room table, searching for loose change. "I remember that," he said aloud.

Tom looked at him, shaking his head that he didn't.

Their mother smiled. "I'm so glad," she said, her voice cracking. "You were so young when . . . when you were both taken, I . . . I didn't think you'd have any memories of me."

"Oh, we do," Tom said, obviously lying to make her feel better.

Sprinkled in among the feeble woman's stories, Jason discovered that he and Tom had "a few tablespoons of Apache blood" in them, on their grandmother's side. They also learned that their grandfather had been shot dead for cheating at cards and that a lot of their relatives had passed on from cancer.

Looking at them both, she said, "I'm sorry, but pretty much everyone on this side of your family ends up dying from cancer."

"That's just great," Tom muttered.

Jason glanced over at him and shook his head, as if to indicate his name would not be on that list.

"Obesity and diabetes also run deep in your genes," she added.

Tom returned the glance, offering a nod that said, *I told you so.*

"I wish I could have cooked for you boys," she added sadly. "It's one of my regrets." She smiled, her entire face suddenly lighting up—the sparkle in her eyes offering a brief glimpse of a much younger woman. "You would have loved my chicken mozzarella dish," she said.

Each minute he and Tom spent with their dying mother, Jason soaked up every detail of her—right down to her scent—to take with him for the rest of his days. During their talks, he realized there was barely any evidence of a mother's touch in either him or Tom. *Whatever little sensitivity, compassion, or empathy we do have was picked up along the way through some tough lessons learned*, he thought, *and definitely not from Pop.*

As the conversation with their mom continued, Jason deciphered that she'd suffered from digestive issues most of her life.

That also explains a few things, he thought.

"And although we had a few relatives that were school-teachers," she said, "most of the bums were either serving time or overdosing on one drug or another."

Damn, Jason thought, *the prison is a family business.* "I hope you weren't alone all these years," he blurted, instantly fearing her reply.

"Oh no," she said. "Up until last year, I had my friend Shirley right by my side." Her eyes sparkled with love. "Shirley Luongo was her name. She was a wonderful woman."

Jason looked at Tom and—concealing his smirk—half-shrugged.

The old lady's sharp eyes caught it. "We were just friends," she said, shaking her head at the absurdity of it. "After being with your father, I was all done with men, women . . . whatever."

Both men chuckled at their mother's feisty spirit before sharing photos of their families. "I have a daughter," Jason said. "Miranda, your granddaughter. Her wedding's right around the corner."

"Isn't that lovely," she said, gawking at the photo like she was getting to know her estranged grandchild.

"My two are Caroline and Caleb," Tom said, handing his wallet photos to his mom. "They're both good kids . . . for the most part."

She chuckled. "They look like angels to me," she whispered, kissing the pictures. Suddenly, she looked up. "And your wives?" she asked.

Jason shook his head. "Divorced quite a few years ago," he said.

She looked at Tom.

"Unfortunately, it looks like I'm heading down that same road," he admitted.

She nodded, as though she wasn't surprised. "What about your jobs?"

"I'm a college professor," Tom answered.

"And I work in a prison," Jason said.

"You *work* there, right?"

Both men laughed.

"For almost thirty years," he said.

She nodded again. "I'm proud of you both," she said, slowly handing back the photos. "I wish I could have taken some of the credit but . . ."

"If it wasn't for your blood in us," Tom blurted, "we would have both ended up in prison."

"And not as correction officers," Jason added.

Her eyes filled. "Thank you," she whispered.

Before their conversation was completely swallowed by the woman's struggle to cling to life, they discovered their mom had been a seamstress for most of her life before collecting disability in her later years.

For whatever reason, Jason was happy to have learned that final detail. He thought about all the years he'd missed his mother's love. *Wow*, he thought, his mind drifting off. *I wonder why we never questioned anything about our mom's side of the family,* he thought, *or the fact that Pop didn't have the same thick New England accent we did.* He shook his head in disbelief. *Our mother and her family were never spoken of and, as far as I can remember, we never once questioned it. Even Miranda has never asked about her grandmother. That seems so odd to me now.*

Seated in Magoni's Italian Eatery—Jason's back placed flush against the wall—the young server waited patiently with her notebook in hand.

"Do you make a chicken mozzarella dish?" Jason asked the kid, hoping they did.

She nodded. "We have chicken parmigiana on a bed of pasta," she said, stepping sideways while a busboy delivered two glasses of water and a basket of rolls.

"I'll have that," Jason said, handing back the menu.

"Make it two," Tom said, doing the same.

As the waitress scurried away, Jason turned to his brother. "Have you ever imagined anything more screwed up than this?" he asked Tom, still trying to make sense of it all.

"Knowing Pop, we probably shouldn't be surprised," Tom said.

No shit, Jason thought. "That's something about having Native American blood in us, huh?"

Tom nodded. "Although I wasn't too happy to hear that cancer runs that heavily in our family."

"I know."

"And the obesity and diabetes—"

"I know," Jason interrupted, slathering a tab of butter onto the warm roll. "I get it."

Two hours later, Jason opened the front door to the Rolling Hills Retirement Home. They were seated once again in one of the common living areas being used as an improvised waiting room. "Your mom's having a difficult time of it this afternoon," the orderly said. "We're hoping she'll be ready to receive visitors soon."

Jason nodded. "We'll wait," he said.

"It may be a while," the man clarified.

"That's fine," Tom said. "It's not like she hasn't waited for us."

"We're here whenever she's ready," Jason told the confused orderly.

Jason looked around. They'd been seated among a few of the aged residents—catatonic and drooling—seated in wheelchairs that faced the sun-filled windows.

Another visitor—by all accounts from his condescending interactions with staff—was waiting to visit with his father, who was currently finishing up a kidney dialysis treatment.

After making two phone calls—both loud and patronizing—he turned to Jason. "So who are you here to see?" he asked with an air of pretentiousness that Jason rarely experienced in his corner of the world.

Jason smiled at him. "Our mom," he said, still finding the label strange.

"That's nice, and who's that?" the busybody probed.

"Mrs. Prendergast," he said, expecting their awkward discussion to end.

The stranger's face instantly changed, turning from pleasant—although fake—to repulsed.

Oh boy, Jason thought.

"Shame on you!" he hissed. "That poor woman hasn't had one visitor since she's arrived here."

"That's terrible," Jason agreed, sorry to hear it.

"Yes, it is terrible and you should be ashamed of yourselves," the man repeated, glaring at Jason.

"But . . . but . . ." Jason said, completely tongue-tied.

"After all she's done for you . . ." Snickering loudly, the man shook his head. "You don't deserve to visit with your mother." His beady eyes turned to snake-like slits. "How obtuse can you be?" he asked.

Tom popped up in his seat, while Jason searched his juvenile vocabulary. *Obtuse? What the hell does that mean?* he wondered, knowing it was anything but a compliment. Instinctively, his nostrils flared while his hands clenched into fists. *I can't hit him . . . not here,* he reminded himself, unable to find the words to properly defend himself.

"How *stupid* can *you* be?" Tom barked, sliding to the edge of his seat and staring the insulting man straight in the eye.

"Excuse me?" the stranger said, nearly spitting on himself.

That a boy, Jason thought, sitting back to enjoy the show. *Evidently, the asshole called me stupid.*

"Excuse you is right," Tom retorted. "If you knew anything about the situation, which there's no way you could, then you'd know we just found out our mother is still alive."

One of the elderly residents moaned.

"I . . . I didn't . . ." the nosy man started.

"If you didn't have your head buried up your backside, you would . . ."

"Excuse me?" the man repeated, his voice now garbled from emotion.

". . . then you wouldn't be jumping to conclusions on something you know absolutely nothing about." Tom shrugged. "If you ask me, that's the definition of ignorance," he added, verbally obliterating his poorly skilled opponent.

The stranger opened his smug mouth but nothing came out. Tom glanced at Jason. They swapped grins. The exchange seemed to inspire him to go for the frozen man's bared throat.

"A couple things you might want to remember, sir—if I can even call you that," Tom said, nearly sliding off his chair to further shame the pompous ass. "If it's not any of your business, then it's probably best to mind your own." He gritted his teeth. "Do you understand?" he asked, suddenly sounding just like his brother.

"I . . . I . . ." the red-faced man stuttered.

"It's not a difficult concept." He looked at Jason and smiled. "Besides, my brother just got out of prison, so he doesn't need someone like you shitting on him."

The same senior resident moaned again.

An orderly entered the room. "Mr. Reinhart," he called out. "Your dad's back and is ready to accept visitors."

Flustered, the embarrassed man got to his wobbly legs. As he huffed and puffed his way past the brothers, Tom shook his disappointed head at him.

Jason turned toward Tom. "Damn," he said. "Where the hell did that come from?"

"Not all confrontation is physical," Tom explained with a grin. "And you're not the only one who understands confrontation."

Jason nodded proudly. "For whatever it's worth, I appreciate what you did for me just now. I got stumped and . . ."

Tom waved him off. "Are you kidding me?" he said. "I'd never let anyone bully my brother." He grinned. "That would be *obtuse* of me."

They both laughed.

A few minutes later, the orderly entered the waiting room again. "Gentlemen," he said. "We've completed your mother's breathing treatment. You can see her now."

As they stood, Jason looked at Tom and grinned to himself. *Well, that answers that*, he thought. *Tom's definitely one smart son of a bitch.*

From the moment they saw their struggling mother, Jason knew it was time to say goodbye.

"Hi, Mom," Tom said. "You're not feeling well today, are you?"

In obvious pain, she gasped for breath before moaning like the ghost in the waiting room.

"Do you want us to get the orderly?" Tom asked. "Do you need medicine?"

The ancient woman rocked back and forth, her eyes staring off into space like some of the lifers Jason had known for nearly thirty years. "I'm dying," she said, gasping for oxygen every few words. "But for . . . for whatever reason . . . the good Lord's taking his time . . . calling me . . . home."

"Oh, Mom," Tom whispered, his eyes welled with tears.

Jason's heart filled with sorrow.

The apparition in the flesh forced a crooked smile. "I've . . . I've seen my boys again," she managed. "I'm . . . I'm ready now."

Tom shook his head. "We need to head home," he told her, kneeling at her lap like he'd probably once done, before he was old enough to remember. "Jason has Miranda's wedding, and I need to get back to the college." His voice was thick with sorrow.

Jason kneeled beside his brother. "But we'll be back to see you again soon, okay?" It was a lie.

"Sure," she said. "We'll see . . . each other again . . . I just know it."

In the next life, Jason thought, trying to make himself feel better.

Suddenly, as if they were the only three people in the world, the woman took a few deep breaths and began humming; it was the same song Jason remembered hearing as a young boy.

He grabbed her blotchy, paper-thin hand and held it to his face—washing it clean with his tears.

Tom began to cry like a child. "I'm so happy we got to meet you, Mom," he wept, grabbing her other hand and kissing it. "I can't tell you what a gift this has been."

Still humming, she pulled her hands away and grabbed for Tom's face. For a few moments, she flicked her arthritic thumbs on his cheeks just under his eyes—making him sob.

She then grabbed for Jason's face, doing the same. At that very moment, for reasons he could not understand or ever begin to explain, he felt an inexplicable peace—like a small boy being soothed by his loving mother. "Goodbye, Mom," he whispered. "I love you."

"And . . . I love you," she said between gasps.

Tom stood first and placed a soft kiss on the woman's white head. "Goodbye, Mom," he whispered.

Jason added a second kiss, surprised that he felt such raw emotion for a woman he'd only known for three days. *I've missed you my whole life,* he told her in his head, *but having only a few days with you seems like the cruelest joke Pop's ever played on us.* He looked at Tom, who was fighting off his own tears, and didn't know if meeting their mother had been a gift or a final punishment from their father. *We'll see you on the other side,* he told her in his thoughts before turning away with a broken heart.

As Jason and Tom walked out of the room, they looked back. The old woman was still rocking and humming.

"Let's go dump that box of soot," Tom said, referring to their father, "before I do end up pissing in it."

As they stepped into the parking lot, Jason thought about it. *All our lives, Tom and I have been intentionally isolated and self-con-*

tained, exactly what the old man needed to maintain control over us. He snickered. *Ironically, it's exactly how I've stayed alive in the prison for so many years.*

"No matter how you slice it, this whole thing is screwed up," Tom said, yanking Jason back into the moment.

"I just knew it," Jason said, focused on his own train of thought. "The old man couldn't care less where his ashes are spread."

"You're right," Tom agreed, looking back at the box. "Although I've had this strange feeling that his spirit's been tagging along this entire time."

"I know," Jason said, surprising himself when he said it.

"At least the son of a bitch was quiet during the trip."

Jason laughed. "Yeah, and not trying to shame either one of us."

"Or use us as his punching bags."

Jason nodded. "Overall, I'd say he's been very well behaved," he said, trying to lighten the mood.

Tom chuckled politely. "So where are we going to spread his ashes? The address he gave us was obviously intended for another purpose."

"Obviously," Jason agreed, thinking about it. "Like I said, I don't think he gives a shit where we spread the ashes . . . and neither do I."

"I agree, but we still have to dump him somewhere." They both gave it some thought for a few moments. Finally, Tom smiled. "I saw a dog track on our way here. I mean, think about it, the old man nearly lived at one of those when we were growing up."

"That's true." Jason nodded. "I imagine he'd be as comfortable at a dog track as anywhere else."

Tom grinned wider. "And even more importantly, we'll finally be rid of him."

Jason smiled, thinking, *Little brother's still filled with every ounce of hate the old man poured into him.*

It was already dark when they reached the dog track. Expecting to see the place lit up with floodlights, the entire area was in relative darkness.

"Dammit," Tom said. "They're closed."

"Yup, to the public," Jason said, slowing the SUV. "There's got to be some poor slobs in there slaving away, cleaning up the place." He rolled up to the front entrance, where they were met by a young security officer wearing more gear on his utility belt than Batman. *Oh boy*, Jason thought, *here we go*. He came to a complete stop and rolled down the driver's side window.

"You guys can't go in there," the kid said, leaning in the window like a veteran state trooper. "The track's closed."

Stifling a laugh, Jason took note of his shiny name badge. "Oh, we're not here to see the dogs run, Roy," he said. "We just need to drop off our father." He grabbed for his wallet, flipped it open and showed Roy his corrections badge. "We'll come right back out, I promise."

Nodding, the rent-a-cop looked into the back window. "Does your father work here?" Roy asked.

Tom leaned over his brother to get in on the fun. "You could say it's always been more like a part-time job for him," he told the kid. "He's kind of retired now."

Roy stood erect, adjusting his heavy belt. "Go ahead then. Just be quick and come right back out." He looked into the back window again—confused.

"You got it, chief," Jason said, rolling into the dimly lit lot.

They drove to the back of the track and, grabbing the wooden box and a couple of cold beers, found a break in the chain-link fence where they could squeeze in. Walking among the shadows, they managed to make it to the track's fourth turn where, appropriately enough, there was only a short distance to the finish line.

Jason opened the lid and peered in. The ash was a mix of pale and dark grey powder, like coarse sand—not the light and fluffy ash he'd expected to find. At that moment, he pictured his father being slid into a blazing furnace, a cremator—most of the old man vaporizing in seconds, all the water in his body evaporating, the bulk of him leaving the physical world through some exhaust pipe. He shook off the morbid train of thought and handed the wooden box to Tom. "Do you want the honors?"

Tom stood statue-still for a moment, locked in thought. He finally shook his head, unwilling to accept the box. "Pop never gave us shit," he blurted.

Jason shrugged. "Except for a backbone."

Considering it, Tom nodded. "Except for that," he muttered.

"The old man trained me well, though," Jason said, nodding. "I never once feared having to fight or even getting a beating, which has made me very good at my job." He nodded once more; it was an authoritative nod. "I figured no one could ever do to me what the old man did, you know?"

"I know what you mean," Tom said. "I've spent my entire life making sure I was the smartest person in the room."

Jason tipped the box a bit. "Ashes to ashes and dust to dust," he said.

Tom pulled out his cell phone and began recording the bizarre ceremony for the attorney. "From dust we arise and to dust we must return," he added.

"But the holy hell we can cause in the meantime," Jason said, tipping the box more—until their father's remains began pouring out, swirling around just above the ground. ". . . ashes, ashes, we all fall down," he mumbled, grinning.

"Isn't that the truth," Tom said.

For a moment, both brothers went silent.

As Jason continued to dump the ashes, he looked into his brother's eyes—feeling the defensive obligation of a protective older brother. "The old man's gone," he said.

"I know," Tom said.

"And don't you forget it, Tommy," he said, trying to alleviate his brother's deepest fears by calling him by his childhood nickname.

"I know," Tom repeated, swallowing hard.

Jason lifted his beer. Tom followed suit. Jason poured the first sip onto the ground. "Fuck you for all of it, Pop," he said before guzzling down the cold suds.

Unwilling to waste a drop of his own beer, Tom whispered, "Fuck you, you cruel bastard." And with that, he took a sip.

They both started laughing; it wasn't that anything was funny. Rather, they both felt a weight lift off of them and blow away. A moment later, the gray ashes that hovered above the ground began drifting along until leaping up into a small ominous cloud. Just as it seemed their dad had refused to leave, a strong breeze rushed over the cloud and dispersed it, sweeping it away forever—as easy as a whisper.

"Gone," Jason repeated, taking another sip.

"And it's about damned time," Tom said, echoing their mother's recent words. He shut off the video recording.

Amen, Jason thought, taking another sip of beer. He felt a strange sense of peace, like a heavy yoke had just been lifted from his heart.

As they walked back to the parking lot, Jason pitched the wooden box into the dumpster. Tom looked at him in disbelief. "What?" Jason asked. "It's not like Pop needs it anymore."

Tom nodded.

"And neither do we," Jason finished, though they both knew he wasn't referring to the box.

At the front gate, Roy—the young security guard—stood rigid in the middle of the exit, gesturing with an open palm that they stop.

Jason shook his head. "This kid needs a real job," he said under his breath.

Roy approached the driver's side window. "That took a while," he said. "I thought you said you were just dropping your father off?"

"We did," Jason said. "But it took a little longer than we expected." He shrugged. "The old man was one stubborn bastard."

"He won't be any trouble anymore, though," Tom called out from the passenger seat, grinning from ear to ear.

"Is he staying the night?" the kid asked.

"And then some," Jason said.

Tom laughed.

Trying to make sense of the situation, Roy placed his hands into the window and glared at Jason.

"Listen, Sheriff Roy," Jason said, his tone no longer friendly. "We're really tired. So if you don't get out of our way right now, I'm going to run you over. Do you understand?"

The kid instinctively pulled his hands out of the car window.

Jason punched the gas, squealing out of the lot.

"Did you really have to scare that poor kid?" Tom asked when they were back on the road.

Jason looked sideways and grinned. "I was just giving him a glimpse into the real world," he said, "where there are things he should be afraid of."

Tom shook his head and laughed. "Forever the brute," he said.

Nope, Jason thought, *I'm just the one who refuses to eat more shit than I have to.*

chapter 12

TOM WAS VERY TIRED, the kind of tired that mirrored physical illness. There was a dull ache in his head, some tiny percussionist playing inside his cranium, occasionally stomping on the bass drum just behind his eyes. He felt nauseous; maybe it wasn't so much nausea as the keen understanding that if he took a bite of food or a sip of drink—even water—he might actually vomit. He was drifting along, surrendered to the role of follower until he returned to his true self—rested and confident again.

The cramps in his abdomen grew sharp until he couldn't hold it in anymore and farted. He looked at his brother and waited for a reaction. *Payback's a bitch*, he thought, trying not to smile.

"What the hell is that?" Jason asked, his face showing every sign of being repulsed.

"Sorry," Tom said. "That was me."

"That's passive-aggressive, that's what that is!"

"No, it isn't. I wasn't hiding anything," Tom said, laughing. "I just realized I didn't get you anything for your birthday, so you're welcome."

"Yeah, thanks," Jason said, rolling down the window and filling the SUV with cold air.

They both laughed like they were little boys again.

As they reached the outskirts of the massive airport, the bank of dark clouds hovering over them became darker with each exit they passed. The rain fell hard, while the winds rocked the SUV back and forth in the storm. *We got rained on when we left, so it only makes sense we finish the trip the same way.* Looking out the smeared windshield, Tom realized, *Exhausted or not, this crazy ride is the first time I've felt alive in years.* He looked up. The overhead highway signs were busy with information, splitting traffic toward departures and returns, and then the multiple airlines. Tom took a deep breath. "Well, that's it then," he said, squinting to make out the car rental sign. "We survived the trip and . . ."

". . . and each other," Jason teased, also squinting to find their next exit.

Tom chuckled. "So have you decided where you're heading after this?"

Jason nodded but continued to focus on the slick road ahead. "I'm actually going to hop a plane south for a few days."

"South?" Tom repeated, surprised.

"My mentor, Lou, moved out to Southern California after he retired. I thought it would be a nice surprise if he found me sitting on his doorstep, begging for a meal."

"Lou was your boss in the prison?"

Jason shook his head. "Lou was much more than a boss," he said, firmly. "He was a leader." Just as they reached the blurry car rental sign, he looked at Tom. "There's a huge difference, you know."

"Oh, I know. Trust me."

"Why? Are you working for an asshole?" Jason asked, slowing the car in the heavy gusts.

Tom shook his head. "Not anymore, but I did for a long time." His eyes drifted off in memory. "His name was Robert Lawrence, the dumbest narcissist you'd never want to meet." He looked back at Jason. "Have you ever met someone who thought he knew everything but didn't know a damned thing?"

Grinning wide, Jason looked like he was going to bite off his tongue.

"It was amazing. The asshole could look you right in the eye and lie about anything." He nodded. "He got his in the end, though."

"They always do."

"There was too much suffering leading up to it, though," Tom said, fighting off a yawn.

"It looks like you survived it," Jason said, slowing even more.

"I did," Tom added, still trying to stifle the yawn.

"That's all that counts then."

"I suppose." They turned left into the car rental lot and parked behind a sea of red lights, each traveler waiting to return a car. Suddenly, the world went quiet—the heavy rain no longer pounding on the car's roof. While Jason sighed heavily with impatience, Tom's mind returned to Robert Lawrence. His fists involuntarily clenched tight. "What about you?" he asked Jason. "Are you going to stick it out for the next two years at the prison?"

Jason nodded. "I don't have a choice. The funny thing is, after that, I have no idea what the hell I'm going to do."

"From what I've read, Neil Armstrong and Buzz Aldrin had significant issues when they returned home from the moon," Tom said. "I mean, think about it: after traveling to the moon, where do you go from there?"

"I'd hardly compare my service in the prison to walking on the moon," Jason said, with gratitude in his voice.

"It's all relative," Tom said. "In many ways, the prison is your moon."

Jason thought about it for a few moments and nodded. "I guess," he muttered. "And then what?"

"What do you want?"

"I have no idea . . ."

"What have you always wanted to do?" Tom asked. "Where have you always wanted to go?"

Jason shrugged.

"No more excuses," Tom said. "For either of us. Our kids are nearly raised. Our careers are starting to sunset. We need to follow our passions and go get what we want out of life while we still can." He was talking mostly to himself.

"And what about you?" Jason asked. "Are you planning on making any changes when you get home?"

Tom felt a blanket of sorrow wrap tightly around his shoulders. "I don't see that I have a choice, do I?"

Jason shook his head. "Not from where I stand."

Tom knew he was on his way to being divorced. *Once I can summon the courage, that is.* "Why do you think it happened to the both of us?"

"What's that?"

"Divorce."

"Because we're both assholes, that's why."

"What?"

"I may be joking but you have to remember that we both have the old man's blood circulating in us, so it might be at least half true." He shook his head. "I thought that going to work every day and providing for my family was enough, but it wasn't, and it didn't take long before the job became my life—the vast majority of it anyway." He thought for a few moments. "When I did make it home, and wasn't out at the bar trying to drown my recent tragedy in some half-empty bottle, my wife would try to share her life. But I never listened. It just seemed so pale in comparison." He shook his head again. "I should have listened."

"I understand," Tom said. "But my situation's a little different, I think. My wife's been screwing around on me."

"You did mention that," Jason said.

Tom half-shrugged. "The kids will be fine," he muttered, as much to himself as to Jason. "At least they'll still have both their mother and father."

Jason nodded. "Exactly."

After turning in the SUV, they grabbed their bags and hobbled toward the airport terminal—the blood in their cramped legs just beginning to circulate again. As they reached the glass-enclosed bridge connecting the parking garage to the main terminal, the sound of pelting rain returned. Tom's eyes went wide. From the first time he'd ever flown, he loved the airport. It was so exciting to watch the constant hustle and bustle, people from all walks of life dashing off to exotic places in every corner of the world. The competing aromas of the food vendor kiosks awakened his senses, while the many characters—big and small, young and old—hurried past. From tearful goodbyes to the excited eyes of those escaping off to somewhere, there was so much to take in. He looked at his brother beside him, who was only starting to ease into a comfortable gait, and grinned. *This wasn't the worst trip after all,* he admitted to himself, knowing he would never openly share the thought.

Garbled PA announcements broadcasted one boarding flight after the next, while the eclectic names of passengers were asked to report to the customer service desk. After printing out his boarding pass, Tom checked the wall of monitors. "Terminal C, Gate 43," he said aloud, rechecking his ticket. "Do you have time for a drink?" he asked Jason, ignoring his own mind-numbing exhaustion.

After slipping his own boarding pass into his carry-on bag, Jason looked up at the monitors. "I guess I have time for one," he said, nodding.

They bellied up to the bar to share their final drink together. Tom scanned the short menu. *Fourteen bucks for a mixed drink?* he thought, whistling.

"I'll take care of it, you cheap bastard," Jason teased, before ordering a vodka and tonic for himself.

"Fine, but I get the second round," Tom said.

"Are you feeling okay?" Jason asked, concerned.

"I'm tired but I'm okay."

"Good," Jason said before looking at his watch. "If we're having two drinks then we'd better get started."

The young bartender—who looked tanned enough to be slinging cheap rum on some tropical island—delivered their drinks along with a small bowl of party mix, as if to lighten the blow of the bloated tab.

"Looks like someone's auditioning for a better tip," Tom whispered as she walked away.

Jason gawked at her and smiled. "As far as I'm concerned, she's got the job."

Tom took a deep breath, steeling himself for his body's adverse reaction to the first sip. "Yeah, she is," he said, swallowing hard.

They sat side-by-side in relative silence for a while.

"So you're spending a few days in California, huh?" Tom said, sorry he still felt the need to fill any silence between them.

Jason downed the last half of his glass, motioning toward the pretty barmaid to refill it. "Yup," he said, clearly uninterested in engaging in small talk.

As Tom tipped his glass, allowing the smallest sip down his throat, he noticed a warning banner drift across the bottom of the television screen above the bar: *FEMA has issued severe storm warnings for the area until eleven o'clock.* He turned to Jason. "Do you think it's smart to get on a plane right now?" he asked, rhetorically.

"Why not?" Jason said, grinning. "It looks like we might have some killer tailwinds behind us."

"Well, hopefully not *killer*," Tom said.

Jason turned toward him. "You need to chill out, little brother." He shrugged. "Stress is what's going to kill you." He laughed at the irony of it.

Considering it, Tom lifted his glass in some mock toast. "You're right."

As if it had just donned on him that he had to catch a flight, Jason suddenly checked his watch. "Shit," he muttered and stood, downing his second drink at the same time. "If you need me for anything, make sure you call on me," he said, placing one hand on Tom's shoulder. "You know where I am," he added, grabbing for his bag with the other hand.

"Always have," Tom said, nodding. "And you know where I am too, if you need me." Given where they'd come from, his brother's hand resting on his shoulder was like walking into the most intimate hug.

"I do," Jason said, slowly pulling his hand away. He smiled. "You got this?" he asked, motioning toward the drinks.

Tom nodded. "And I'm the cheap bastard?" he said.

"You're not a bad guy, Tom," he said. "And this time I mean it." He laughed. "I'll see you at the lawyer's office next week."

"I'll be there," Tom said, as his brother walked away. "And I'll see you at the wedding, too."

"I doubt it," Jason replied over his shoulder.

Laughing, Tom took another sip of his cocktail. Suddenly, he realized, *I'm alone.* He sat for a while, staring out the rain-smeared window that faced the tarmac. *I doubt we're ever going to be close again or even play any real role in each other's lives,* he thought. *But at least we made peace. It's enough.* There was no need for any Hallmark ending or ongoing bromance. *It's enough*, he repeated in his throbbing head.

He reached to grab for his drink but instinctively pushed the sweating glass away—feeling the weight of all the sleep he'd lost on the road. Although he'd slept over the past few days, it didn't feel like it. After getting his second and third wind, he was now a walking zombie—that was starting to lose its grasp on reality. Sounds were fuzzy. Smells were distant. There was a numb buzzing. He stood, paid the tab, and pulled his bag behind him.

Struggling to stay in the present, Tom checked his ticket against the boarding monitors once more. *I still have more than an hour*, he thought, dreading the wait ahead of him. Reaching Gate 43, he took a seat near the window. Even through the thick weariness, he wore a smile. With all the insanity he'd just experienced, he'd forgotten how much he missed his kids. *I can't wait to see them*, he thought.

His weighted eyelids fluttered, fighting off the darkness of sleep. He concentrated on doing some people watching. *Friendly people have great attitudes*, he decided, studying his neighbors. *It's all about perspective. Those who clearly carry the heaviest burdens still find the energy for a smile, while those who look worry-free are absolutely miserable.* Soon, his attention was commandeered by the giant window before him. Jets taxied up and down the black shimmering runways. Some vanished into the low-hanging storm clouds. Others delivered loved ones home. There was a real atmosphere of mystery at the airport. *I love anything mysterious*, he thought.

He nodded off once, fought his way back, and was succumbing again when he jumped to his feet. Like an expectant father, he eventually decided on a stroll. He walked past the gaudy souvenir kiosks and stuck his head into another of the terminal's tiny pubs. There were only two men inside and one was the bartender. Checking his watch again, he stepped in. *I have a better chance of staying awake in front of a TV than a rainy window*, he thought.

"How about a glass of water?" he asked the barkeep.

"Rocky Mountain spring water?" the stranger on the next stool joked.

Tom shook his head. "One sip of hops and barley and I'll be sleepwalking," he said, lifting the water glass to his lips for a long draw.

The well-dressed stranger extended his hand. "Name's Victor."

Tom obliged, introduced himself and grabbed the stool to the right of Victor. Above the glass bottles that cluttered the bar, there was a hockey game on the tube. Tom tilted his head to check the score. *Maybe I should catch a game with Caleb when I get home*, he thought.

"So what do you do for a living, Tom?" Victor asked.

Evidently, my new friend isn't interested in sports, Tom gathered.

"I'm a college professor, and I do some online trading at night," he said, realizing how ridiculous that sounded. "Stocks, bonds, mutual funds," Tom added with a hint of indifference.

Victor's eyes lit up. "Finally, a man I can talk shop with."

Tom cringed. *I don't want to get into it,* he thought, hoping to burn away the half-hour with a glass of water. Reluctantly, he nodded.

"Have you ever used an investment manager?"

Tom grinned. "A brother and sister team, Caroline and Caleb Prendergast. Ever heard of them?" *At least someone should get a laugh out of this,* he thought.

Victor's forehead folded in thought. "No, I don't know them," he said. "They must be with Merrill Lynch or another firm." Before Tom could let him in on the joke, the stranger pressed on. "I'm an investment manager myself. I've been with Fidelity for almost ten years now."

Tom nodded. *I really wish Victor liked sports.* He stood. "It was a pleasure to meet you, Victor, but you'll have to excuse me. I need to jump on a plane and go check on my two biggest investments."

Tom returned to his gate to fight off the Sandman while he waited for his flight.

Tom returned home to the welcome he expected—nothing. *So this is what the bottom feels like,* he thought.

"So you survived the trip with that gorilla brother of yours, huh?" Carmen said, already dozing off on the couch.

"He's not so bad," Tom said, his voice weaker that he would have liked.

"What's that?" she asked.

Tom studied her for a moment—every detail—and felt an invisible fog of sorrow engulf him. *We could have had a great life together*, he thought, ignoring her question, *but that's over now.* He felt himself get angry. *You cheating bitch*, he thought, asking, "Where are the kids?"

She shrugged. "Your guess is as good as mine."

Wow, he thought, watching as she drifted off to sleep. *It looks like I've really been missed around here.* He started for the bathroom to take a shower.

"Your dinner's in the fridge," she called out. "You just have to heat it."

"No thanks," he said, never looking back. *I need a lot more than dinner.*

Jason wheeled his custom pickup truck into Attorney Russell Norman's lot and parked between a Lexus and a BMW. *Tom's already here*, he thought. Remembering how their journey had begun together, he smiled. *It's amazing how much things can change in only six days.*

He'd only spent a week with his brother, but he still realized a great deal had changed. He now understood that he'd only experienced a fraction of life—of the world—and that there was so much more for him to look forward to and experience. Even visiting his mentor, Lou, was something that seemed like an impossible venture just weeks before. *It's time to live and not just wait to die at fifty-four*, he thought, committing himself to beating the abysmal statistics.

Jason took a few deep breaths and started for the front door. He hated lawyers' offices; his only exposure to attorneys was in the prison, when the inmates were trying to sue him for excessive force or some other foolish accusation. As he reached for the doorknob, his skin was already crawling with the need to get out of the place—*as soon as possible*, he thought. *Not to mention, this mouthpiece is one creepy son of a bitch.*

"Are you feeling okay?" Jason asked his brother upon entering the waiting room.

Tom nodded. "Better now that I'm back on my treatments and have gotten some rest."

"That's good," Jason said, taking a seat beside him.

"Mr. Prendergast," the secretary called out.

Both brothers stood.

"Attorney Norman will see you now."

This time, they walked in together.

After the obligatory handshakes, Attorney Norman wasted no time in getting down to business.

Jason and Tom exchanged smirks. *Attorney Norman wants this over with too*, Jason thought, remembering how he and Tom had shocked the man during their first visit.

Without hesitation, Tom shared the video footage on his cell phone—proof that they'd followed the old man's final wishes and spread his ashes in Seattle. As the lawyer's face cringed and contorted, Jason listened to the audio and tried not to laugh.

"From dust we arise and to dust we must return," Tom said.

"But the holy hell we can cause in the meantime," Jason said. There was a pause. ". . . ashes, ashes, we all fall down," he added in a mumble.

"Isn't that the truth," Tom said.

For a moment, there was silence—and then Jason said, "The old man's gone."

"I know," Tom replied.

"And don't you forget it, Tommy."

"I know," Tom repeated.

After another pause, Jason said, "Fuck you for all of it, Pop."

Tom followed, whispering, "Fuck you, you cruel bastard."

Jason looked at Tom to exchange proud grins. Shaking his head, Attorney Norman handed the cell phone back to Tom. "And how do I know you spread his ashes in Seattle?" he asked.

"Where the hell do you think we spread them?" Jason asked. "At the local dog track?"

Before the man could answer, Tom showed him several photos that were taken in Seattle—proving they'd made the long trip.

Disgusted but satisfied, the lawyer revealed a white envelope, lifting it for both brothers to confirm it was still sealed. "When your father discovered he had terminal cancer and didn't have long to live, he had my office investigate whether or not your mother was still alive."

Jason looked over at Tom again. This time, his brother rolled his eyes.

"When we discovered she was still living in Seattle, he drafted this letter and . . ."

"Just read the damn letter!" Jason blurted, beyond his limits with this charade.

Attorney Norman cleared his throat and read, "Jason and Tom, if you're reading this letter, then you've both been to the West Coast and have met your mother. I realize it must seem like bullshit now, but I wanted you both to meet her before she passed over—and for her to see you again before she died. I know I was tough on you, but I had my reasons. And I did the best I could with the two of you. Had we stayed in Washington, you both would have grown up to be lazy, shiftless criminals. Instead, you both turned out to be decent men . . ."

Tom coughed, as if choking on the last sentence.

While the lawyer looked up from the letter, Jason stood—like their father was standing in front of them. "Fuck you, old man," he said through gritted teeth. "We became who we are in spite of you, not because of you."

"Ain't that the truth," Tom said, in the spirit of his older brother's crude vocabulary.

Filled with rage, Jason reclaimed his seat.

The attorney waited another moment to see if the outbursts had concluded. When he was satisfied, his eyes dropped back to the letter: "It never meant a piss hole in a snowbank to me where you boys spread my ashes. I just figured you should meet your ma before it was too late."

"Mighty kind of you, Pop," Tom blurted, his words thick with contempt.

Attorney Norman sighed heavily, his patience having already run out.

"Just go on and finish it," Jason growled, staring the mouthpiece down.

"I know you both hate me," the lawyer read. "That's never been any secret. Truth be told, I don't blame you. But like I said, I did the best I knew how. Well, that's it then. Look after each other and I'll see you on the other side. Pop."

"No land deed," Tom muttered, thinking aloud. "The forty acres was nothing but one of the old man's twisted fantasies?"

The attorney half-shrugged, his face surprised at the mention of land.

Un-fucking real, Jason thought. *The old man had nothing to pass down—no big score at the dog track—nothing except the need to make himself feel better on his way out.*

Tom stood. "This is bullshit," he said angrily. "That bastard doesn't get to end it like this." He looked toward his brother. "He doesn't deserve a pass or any forgiveness whatsoever."

"No, he doesn't," Jason agreed. "And let's be honest, he didn't send us on this trip for our benefit. He did it for himself—just like everything else he ever did—to make himself feel better." He shook his head. "I doubt either one of us will be seeing him on the other side." He nodded. "We have higher expectations than that."

Norman dropped the letter onto the table and folded his arms.

"Are you shitting me?" Jason asked.

"I shit you not," the lawyer said, wearing the subtlest smirk.

"That's it?" Tom asked, checking to be sure. "No money? No land?"

"That's it," the man said, like he enjoyed delivering the news. "This letter is everything your father left you."

Jason stood. "What a waste of fucking time," he barked, starting for the door.

Tom also stood, following him out.

"Do you want the letter?" the attorney asked, calling after them.

"You can shove it up your ass," Jason said, looking back at the man long enough to deter any clever comeback.

The brothers marched out into the sun before turning to each other. "Well, that's it then," Jason said, echoing his father's empty words.

Tom nodded. "That's it then," he repeated. "Oh, I received the invitation to Miranda's wedding. I appreciate it." He nodded. "I'll be there."

I'll? Jason thought, deciding not to question it—yet. "Sure, brother."

"I will," Tom said.

As Jason jumped into his pickup truck, he laughed. "Hey, by the way, they tortured me over the dented fender on the rental, claiming the damage was done after we took it."

"That's bullshit," Tom said. "Why didn't they say anything at the airport when we dropped it off?"

Jason shrugged. "I guess they didn't spot it until after we left."

"Did you clear it up?" Tom asked.

Jason grinned. "It's been taken care of, believe me."

"Oh, I bet it has been," Tom said, laughing. "I'll see you at the wedding."

Jason grinned. "Sure you will," he said, before driving off.

The following morning, Jason and Miranda arrived at Blake's Formal for the final fitting of his tuxedo. As they waited in the foyer, Miranda whispered, "I still can't believe Grandma's been alive all these years. Are you sure she doesn't have much time left? I was thinking maybe Mario and I . . ."

"Just remember her in your prayers, sweetheart," Jason said. "Trust me, it won't be long before I receive a letter telling us that she's passed away too."

Miranda sat for a few minutes in thoughtful silence. "So how was it, really?" she asked.

"How was what?"

"The trip out to Seattle with Uncle Tom."

"Well, we didn't murder each other. That's something, I guess."

"I guess," she repeated.

Jason sighed heavily. "I'd be lying if I said it wasn't a long trip, but . . ." He grinned. "Spending time with him wasn't half as bad as I thought it would be."

"Really?" she said, surprised. "Did you get to see anything good in your travels?"

He shook his head. "Nothing worth talking about," he said.

She looked at him for a few long moments. "Did you make peace with him, Dad?" she asked reluctantly.

Jason shrugged. "In our own way, I guess. Lord knows we've had our differences, but we're brothers, Miranda." He grinned. "Nothing can ever change that."

"What about with Grandpa?"

Jason sighed again. "He no longer has the power to hurt me, if that's what you mean."

"Good," Miranda said, smiling brightly. "I was hoping you would find peace on your trip."

"Why?" he asked. "Did you think I needed it?"

She nodded. "Yes," she said honestly.

"Mr. Prendergast, we're ready for your fitting now," a voice called out from inside the shop.

While Miranda waited, Jason stepped into the fitting room and tried on the traditional black tuxedo. *Oh shit*, he thought, *this isn't good.* The tux was much too tight. *This is isn't good at all.* He looked into the mirror. *I look like ten pounds of shit stuffed into a five-pound bag*, he thought, shaking his disgusted head. *Miranda's going to kill me.* Steeling himself with a few deep breaths, he slowly drew open the black curtain and stepped out.

"Oh no," Miranda blurted.

Shit, Jason repeated in his head.

"There must be something wrong," the flustered tailor said, pulling the tape measure from his scrawny neck and going straight to work. Within seconds, he'd wrapped the plastic tape around Jason's waist, chest, and neck. Jotting down the new measurements, he checked his paperwork. "My apologies, Mr. Prendergast," he said sheepishly. "They must have measured you wrong six weeks ago. The numbers are off."

"They are?" Jason asked, playing the best victim he knew how.

"Dad," Miranda said, her voice disappointed. "It looks like you ate good on your trip, though."

He looked at her, widening his eyes enough to ask for her silence.

Still scratching his head over the error, the tailor cleared his throat. "I'll put a rush on the size you need, Mr. Prendergast," he promised. "And I guarantee we'll have it in the store in plenty of time for you to try it on before the wedding."

"I really appreciate that."

"Again, I'm sorry," the man said sincerely.

"No worries, we all make mistakes." Jason chuckled. "Who knows, maybe I even put on a few pounds?"

Miranda glared at him, her eyes filled with concern.

Again, he begged for her discretion with his pleading eyes.

She smiled at him—like he was a little kid—and placed her hand on his arm in a show of solidarity.

That's my girl, Jason thought.

As the tailor walked away, Miranda squeezed his arm. "You put on more than a few pounds," she whispered, sounding like the mom he'd needed as a child.

"You're right," he said. "And I'm sorry. I promise I'll lose some weight for the wedding and . . ."

"I don't care what you look like at the wedding, Dad," she said in her normal voice. "I care about you. You need to start taking better care of yourself." Her eyes were even more pleading than her words. "Please, Dad."

"I know," he said. "I will."

"Do you promise?" she asked, turning her pursed lips into the cutest pout; it was an indefensible skill she'd perfected as a little girl, melting his heart each time.

"I do," he said. "I promise."

She slid her arm into his elbow. "Let's get out of here," she said, smiling.

"Do you have time for lunch with your old man?" he asked.

She nodded. "If we're ordering salads, I do."

His eyes went wide. "Perfect," he said, too excitedly. "I love salads, especially if they have cranberries and walnuts and goat cheese and . . ."

Laughing, she slapped his arm. "I'm just asking that you try—for your health, okay?"

"I will," he said, and meant it.

"Then let's go," she said.

As they stepped out into the sunlight, Jason looked at his daughter and could feel his eyes fill. *Thank you, Lord, for this beautiful kid. Life just wouldn't be worth the trouble without her.* He coughed once, trying to clear the emotion from his throat. *But I'd better toughen up quick,* he thought, *or I'm going to be a blubbering idiot at the wedding.*

chapter 13

D<small>AYS</small> <small>PASSED</small>—long, thoughtful days—before Tom was able to steel himself for the inevitable showdown with his wife.

Carmen was standing in the kitchen, making herself a cup of herbal tea.

"Where are the kids?" he asked.

She stirred a spoonful of sugar into her dainty cup. "Caroline's at the library studying," she said, shrugging. "God only knows where Caleb is."

Maybe I should give her one more chance, he thought, but the cowardly idea made him feel like vomiting. *Just get it over with!* he screamed in his head.

"What's wrong with you?" she asked, her tone overflowing with condescension and empty of compassion.

Fuck you, bitch! he told her in his thoughts. "We need to sit down and have a family talk—and the sooner the better," he said aloud.

She stopped stirring. "Oh yeah, and why's that?"

"Because the kids need to know their parents' marriage is over and that it's absolutely no reflection on them or anything they've done," he said, feeling ill; his greatest fear had finally been put into words.

Dropping her spoon, Carmen glared at him. Her eyes said it all.

I've seen that look before, he thought. *It's the same hateful look Pop used to give me.*

"Are you sure about this, Tom?" she asked, an evil smirk working its way into the corners of her smug mouth.

He nodded. "What are you smiling about?"

"I'm just surprised, that's all," she said, picking up her tea and taking the first sip. "And, if I'm being honest, I doubt very highly you'll go through with it."

"Then you have no idea who the fuck I am," he barked, shocking them both. "And please spare me on the idea of you being honest, Carmen. You betrayed me in our own home. Even if I could forgive it, I'll never be able to forget it—nor do I want to. I could never trust you again. And if we're really *being honest*, we both know you have no intention of ever being faithful to me again."

"So you're going to try to turn the kids against me because I made a mistake, Tom, is that it?" she asked, more concerned about how she was perceived than the fact that her marriage had just died.

"That's not the plan," he said. "Besides, you'll end up taking care of that all by yourself. You're too selfish not to."

While her eyes widened, her lower jaw drooped. "What . . . what happened to you—"

"For too long, I've forgotten who I am," he interrupted, expecting her to explode. Instead, something much worse happened. Carmen smirked again; it was the kind of grin that announced she was no longer capable of feeling anything for him. *Indifference*, Tom decided. Deep down, he wished she would scream at him, maybe even scramble to provide some false promise of fidelity. But she only smirked. And that's when Tom knew they were at the final stage in their relationship. *It's really over*, he realized.

She studied him for a while longer before shrugging. "Whatever, Tom," she said. "But you're the one who needs to move out." Her demeanor instantly changed from surprised to defensive. "The kids and I aren't leaving this house, so you can go wherever . . ."

That seems fair, he thought sarcastically, *you screw around on me and I lose everything*. He started laughing, cutting her off from a long and painful rant. It had been years since he'd felt any self-respect, and he really liked the new feeling. "I'll trade this house in for my balls any day of the week," he told her, heading for his study. "Let me know when the kids get home. I'd like to get this over with as soon as possible."

As he stepped out of the kitchen, he could feel Carmen's eyes burning into his back. A wave of new and confusing emotions ripped through him. He pictured his brother's face. *I don't know whether I should thank Jason for saving my soul*, he thought, *or curse him for destroying my life*.

The Prison Administration had officially deemed the death of Inmate Andrew Pires a suspicious one. According to the autopsy, Pires' suicide may have been "assisted." Essentially, they believed someone had strung him up and pulled down on his waist. An investigation was ordered. Everyone snickered. There was no such thing as a truthful investigation behind the wall.

Lieutenant Paul Robinson arrived from Boston and reviewed the case. Sergeant Jason Prendergast had been in the small interrogation room with him for nearly two hours before his patience had been completely exhausted and he stood. "I've found more than my fair share of dead inmates through the years. Is that the crime you're trying to pin on me?"

Robinson sat speechless. "I'm . . . I'm not trying to . . ."

"In this place, it's called doing your job," Jason barked. "Now unless you plan to charge me with a crime, we're done here!" He tossed his unlit cigar onto the steel table between them.

Robinson's mouth hung open. Jason took it as a sign to leave and returned to his assigned block. *Just two more years to go*, he thought.

After picking up a six-pack of cold pints at Mucky's Liquors, Jason was two blocks from home when his cell phone rang. *It's Miranda*, he thought, immediately answering. "Hi beautiful, are you ready for the big day?"

"I am," she said excitedly. "But are you?"

"Of course I am. I've been waiting my whole life to—"

"Please don't cry, Dad," she interrupted, "or you'll make me cry."

Jason smiled. "I'm a hardened correction officer, sweetheart. I don't cry."

"Do you want to make a bet?"

He smiled wider. "I would, but I've given up gambling. It's a terrible vice."

"Sure you have," she said. There was a long pause. "Listen, Dad, I just wanted to say thank you for . . ." Her sniffles gave away her depth of emotion. "For everything you've done for me and Mario."

While his eyes welled with tears, Jason could feel his throat constrict. "You're welcome, sweetheart," he said, just as soon as his voice would allow. "I'd do anything for you."

Returning home after being away for two weeks, Jason finally got a chance to check his mail. There was a thick envelope in the pile, sent by Eric Denson, the second shift counselor at the Howland Detention Center, DYS. *Oh yeah*, he thought, remembering their brief telephone conversation while he was on the road. After spending several years volunteering his time at DYS, Jason was seriously starting to question his impact. On more than one occasion, he'd even considered calling it quits.

He opened the thick envelope and started reading, discovering that Eric Denson had hosted an essay contest for the boys. The assignment: *Write one to two pages explaining how Jason Prendergast's presentation on adult incarceration has impacted your life.* He'd sent Jason copies of the end results.

Through surprised, misty eyes, Jason took a seat and read one wonderful example after the next:

> . . . *My fists were clenched tight of fear from Jason's horrific real life stories about life in state prison. He told stories about people getting raped, killed, and getting the crap kicked out of them and it made me scared to go to prison. Jason also taught us that we still have time to change our lives around . . .*

> . . . *Jason's stories really made me think of all the stupid things I've done in my life. I hate the pain I've put on my family and friends. I'd like to thank Jason for inspiring me to change and believe in the power of hope.*

There were twenty-six essays in total, each one proving to be a new lesson in hope. Jason finally got to the contest winner's touching piece. It was written by a loud-mouthed twelve-year-old named Raul. There were two ink stamps on the copy. One read: *I'm PROUD of YOU!* The other: *If you can DREAM IT, you can DO IT.*

It read:

> *Well I never thought about jail like that until Jason came in. I always thought of jail totally*

different then what he said. I never thought that they had people with aids. After that group I started feeling sad just thinking about what my brother must of went through. All the things that I heard from Jason weren't so nice. He got to my head so good that it made me think twice about life. It made me think how my future is gonna end. Following my brothers path like I'm doing or get my shit straight. Jason whenever he comes back he will have my full attention again, cause this guy knows what he's doing. When he first walked in I thought that he was just another guy talking about things he knew nothing about. But he proved me wrong. He totaly blew my mind. Every body always told me about jail but I didn't care. I didn't think about it like Jason made me think about. I believed every word that came out of his mouth. He's worked there for a long time. I always told people that I'm not scared to go to jail. After this with Jason it realy had me thinking. I don't want to go be some place where I'm always watching my back, always worried about who wants to mess with me. I wouldn't make it in there. Always thinking about something. And if it comes down to a fight, you'll realy be in trouble cause you could get extra years in there. And me in the hole for two-three months, I'll go nuts. I don't wanna have that type of future. I have a loving family who is there for me. I got a little brother to look out for, and right now I'm not setting a good example for him. My older brother didn't set a good example for me and look what I'm doing. The same thing he was doing. He used to call home and regret that he chilled with his boys instead of listing to my mothers advice. But now its to late for him to chang. To me I think

Jason's class is realy helpful. It realy made me think twice about life. I already told my mother that I would not end up like him. I don't want to call my mother some day in the future when it is to late to turn back. That's why I have to make a chang in my life now that I'm young. Thanks Jason. The end.

Jason drew in a couple deep breaths. *No big deal, Eric?* he thought, remembering what the man had told him on the phone. *I'd say this is a gigantic deal.* A smile overtook his face. *This seals it for me*, he thought. *I'm going to do whatever it takes to make the move.*

He picked up the telephone and dialed. Eric Denson answered. "Eric, it's Jason Prendergast. I just wanted to thank you for sending along the copies of those essays. I just finished reading them."

"You're very welcome, Jason."

"So what did Raul win for placing first in the contest?"

There was a pause. "From the look of his essay," Eric said softly, "I'd say his adult freedom."

Jason choked back the ball in his throat. "Let's hope," he said, thinking, *I need to share this story with Tom.*

"So we'll see you next Monday?" Eric asked.

"It's funny you should ask," Jason said.

"Please don't tell me you're quitting," Eric said.

Jason smiled. "Just the opposite, Eric," he said. "Is there still a full-time position open?"

"Are you kidding me?" Eric said, his voice changing from concerned to overjoyed.

"I'm going to talk to the central office about transferring over this week."

"You realize we make a lot less money here, right?" Eric said.

"I do, but I'm not concerned about the hourly rate at this point in my life. As long as the DYS time will count toward my retirement, I'll be thrilled to make the move."

"Really?" The growing excitement in Eric's voice made Jason smile wider.

"Who knows," Jason said. "Maybe I have even more than two years left in me."

"I hope so," Eric said. "The kids really need you, buddy."

I'd say it's the other way around, Jason thought. "I'll see you Monday night and let you know what the central office has to say about it."

"Fingers crossed," Eric said.

"Toes too, my friend."

The white stretch limo pulled up, a dramatic pause preceding the gray-haired chauffer opening the rear door. With a gloved hand, he politely helped the new Mrs. Mario Arruda out. Immediately, Miranda and Mario were met by a wave of applause. Yet, all eyes were glued on the bride. Some of those eyes watered. Others gazed dreamily from wishing themselves the same happiness.

Tom's niece was rapturous, the perfect picture of beauty. Her makeup had been professionally applied; her permed hair, two hundred dollars prettier than the day before. Yet, it was the gown that stole the breath of the well-dressed mob that milled about. Miranda wore pure white, the lace and frills falling to a train that stretched ten feet behind her. *She could not look more beautiful,* Tom thought.

As he watched his full-grown niece from a distance, equal amounts of joy and guilt fought for his attention. *At least you're here now,* he told himself.

As Miranda's mom—Jason's ex-wife, Janice—fluffed her gown, the rest of the wedding party arrived. Betrayed by playful giggles, they'd already toasted the new couple more than once. The bridesmaids and Maid of Honor were dressed in pink chiffon. Like the bride, each wore tiny white flowers in her hair. Mario's best man and ushers strutted in black tuxedos with tails. The hats and canes added a touch of formal elegance. *For the wedding of such a young couple, it's quite chic,* Tom thought.

Although it was the rainy season, the forecast promised a calm day. One could only hope. As the sun set on the water's flat horizon, the large wedding party gathered at the rustic gazebo to take pictures. Everyone beamed, especially Miranda. She constantly grabbed for Mario and stole every kiss she could.

Different poses and combinations of people were stiffly ordered by the photographer—*all done, only to be placed in an album and thrown on some closet shelf to collect years of dust,* Tom thought, feeling sorry for himself. Still, in the unseasonably warm breeze, the wedding party took turns smiling. Miranda and Mario made sure that even years from now, they'd have concrete proof that on at least one day of their lives they'd experienced perfection. By the end of the shoot, a full moon broke through to shimmer on the bay's rippling water. Smiling, Tom started for the bathroom.

Luna Bella Harbor hosted only the most prestigious and important functions. One step inside removed all questions as to why. The foyer welcomed visitors with a floor of white marble and plush green plants. It was gorgeous, with high-vaulted ceilings, antique moldings, and a wall of enormous windows that faced the ocean. Waves crashed off jagged rocks and continually sprayed the glass with sea mist. *I can taste the salt,* he thought, licking his lips. Crystal chandeliers lit mahogany- and brass-accented bars that sat beside fireside alcoves. A winding staircase led to the function hall upstairs. Just past the coat check, an arrow pointed to some sinfully indulgent bathrooms. Tom quickly stepped in to relieve his throbbing bladder. Inside, a doting attendant offered cologne and fluffy towels.

Amid the luxurious sophistication, a buzz filled the room. While a few men pulled at their ties, others whispered excuses for sneaking off to the bar. Awaiting compliments on their lovely dresses, women used spit to clean their children's faces. The kids who were able to escape their mothers ran around with untucked shirts and runny noses, and did what all-normal kids do: they explored and screamed in delight at each new discovery. The adolescents simply scanned the room in search of their prey. Weddings always moved stagnant hearts and inspired romance, even in the boys who were shy.

There were flowers everywhere, most of them out-of-season lilies that needed to be flown in. *Jason spared no expense in sending off his little girl,* Tom thought. No doubt, the best caterer in the western hemisphere had been hired to prepare a virtual cornucopia of delights. From cheese and fruit arrangements to the detailed ice sculpture of two smooching angels, the main course promised filet mignon, glazed baby carrots, and some type of potatoes no one could pronounce. For dessert, Miranda's childhood favorite would complete the menu: fresh strawberries and cream.

It was an open bar, with as much beer and wine as anyone could consume. Jason had wanted a live band and Tom knew for a fact he would have gladly paid the extra two thousand. But, if only for the sake of her friends who loved to dance, Miranda had insisted on a DJ. *It's Miranda's big day and she got everything she wanted,* Tom thought, chuckling to himself. *And why not? Weddings are different for girls.* While grooms-in-waiting played baseball and chased frogs, their future wives were already preparing.

Bottles of expensive wine sat atop each table, while teenage waiters saving for college poured half-glasses in preparation for the toast. Wedding favors had also been put near each place setting. In honor of Mario and Miranda, they were no less than fancy white boxes filled with M&M's, half plain and half with peanuts. *Months of thought have gone into every detail,* Tom decided.

Three linen-covered tables were set up across the dance floor from the DJ. The first held a giant wishing well, constructed to collect the cards. Tom watched as it quickly filled, happily adding to it. The table in the middle held a three-tier cake, with a running fountain in the middle and a young couple on top. The tiny plastic lovers actually appeared to be looking down into the reflections the fountain created. The final table was used to gather presents, neatly wrapped gifts covered in white and silver that overflowed onto each other.

Everyone Mario and Miranda ever loved was on hand to celebrate the joyous occasion. From what Tom could tell, the guest list—exceeding well over three hundred—also included many they didn't know. The receiving line looked as if it would never end. While a quartet provided some soothing background music, the newly married couple shook hands, laughed falsely, and kissed relatives they'd never set eyes on before. Cousins long-removed, friends of their parents, perhaps even strangers passing by, got in on the festivities. Nobody cared. The day was too perfect for such menial concerns.

Tom jumped into the receiving line. Filled with emotion, he approached Miranda. Her eyes searched his, while her mind clearly scrambled for his name. He squeezed her hand. "I'm your Uncle Tom," he quickly announced, allowing her raised eyebrows to relax.

"Oh my God," she said, sincerely excited. "Does my dad know you're here?"

"He will soon enough," Tom joked, pointing down the line to his oblivious brother.

"Miranda, I just want to say I'm sorry that I haven't . . ." Tom began to apologize.

She grabbed him with both hands, pulling him in for a strong hug. "I'm so happy you made it, Uncle Tom." Grabbing his hand, she said, "I want you to meet my husband." She stopped. "That sounds strange, *my husband.*"

"I'm very happy for you," Tom said, his eyes misting over.

They turned toward Mario. "Babe, this is my Uncle Tom," she said proudly.

Tom shook the young man's hand. "Congratulations," he said, looking back at Miranda. "I'm so happy I'm here."

"We are too, Uncle Tom," she said, looking down the line at her grinning dad.

Whether he tried to conceal it or not, Jason's face lit up when Tom approached him. "So you came," he called out.

Tom remembered that same proud face and his brother's same words when they were kids and he'd returned to Jason's side at the cemetery in Salem. "Congratulations, tough guy," Tom said, shaking his brother's beefy hand. "Just so you know, I caught you crying during the service."

"Are you crazy?" Jason asked, trying to conceal his grin. "That church was dusty as hell."

Tom laughed. He knew better; he knew it was as though Jason's entire life had been spent preparing to give away his little girl's hand. It was almost a life's accomplishment that could not be put into words. "Congratulations," he repeated.

Jason nodded his appreciation. "So you actually made it," he repeated. "I would have never thought . . ."

"I told you I'd be here," Tom finished for him. "Which proves once again that you have no idea who I am."

Jason extended his hand. They shared another firm shake. "It's my kid's wedding," he said. "You're not going to bust my balls today, are you?"

Tom shrugged. "I can't make any promises," he said. "I learned from the best, you know." He then gestured toward the quartet. "They're really good," he said.

"They should be for twelve hundred bucks," Jason replied, his face suddenly getting serious. "How are you feeling, Tom?"

"Not bad," he said.

"When do you finish your treatments?"

"Not for a while yet," Tom said. "But the doctor thinks I'm doing well." He shrugged. "We'll see when they test me again."

Jason nodded. "I want to go with you for that."

"You don't have to . . ."

"I want to go with you," Jason said, definitively.

Tom nodded. "I appreciate that."

Jason looked behind Tom. "No Carmen?" he asked.

Tom's chest filled with pride. "She's not here," he said.

Jason studied his face. "What's up?"

"I gave our talks a lot of thought on the plane ride home," Tom said, lowering his voice. "I finally found the intestinal fortitude to put our marriage out if its misery."

"Are you shitting me?" Jason asked rhetorically. "Good for you."

Tom shrugged. "Yeah, good for me," he muttered, thinking, *Now what?*

Jason nodded that he understood. "How did Carmen react when you dropped the hammer?"

"Well, she let me know she's keeping the house."

"Good for her, the nasty bitch," Jason said.

"I told her, 'That's fine because it's a small price to feel my balls again.'"

"Good for you," Jason repeated, proudly. He studied Tom's eyes for a moment. "So are you okay?"

Jason nodded. "In some ways, I've never felt so lost." He shrugged. "But in all the ways that count, I've never felt better."

"Do you have a place to stay?" Jason asked.

"I'm all set," Tom said, unsure whether it was an invitation. "Thanks."

There was quiet between them for a moment. "I miss her, though," Tom said. "I miss her voice, even when she's screaming at me to get in the last word."

Jason put his hand on Tom's shoulder. "It'll pass, brother. Trust me, it'll pass." He stepped out of the receiving line and started making his way toward the bar, gesturing for Tom to follow him. "Let's go get a drink to celebrate."

"But aren't you supposed to . . ."

"Let's get a drink," Jason repeated.

As they walked past two ice sculptures of angels kissing, Tom commented, "It looks like you pulled out all the stops for Miranda."

Jason shrugged. "There's no egg white frittata with goat cheese on the menu," he said. "But I'm guessing you'll enjoy the meal just the same."

"I'm sure I will," Tom said. "So what did you end up getting Miranda for a wedding gift?" he asked.

"The wedding," Jason said, smirking.

"Is that it?" Tom teased.

"Actually, I promised her that I'd start losing weight." He patted the girth around his midsection. "I'm down seven pounds already."

"Where?" Tom asked. "Behind your ears?"

"Please don't make me put you over my knee and spank you in front of all these people, Tommy," he joked. "Not here."

Tom laughed, recalling that very same threat at the beginning of their quest. *Only he was serious then.*

Jason lowered his voice to a whisper. "I hired that artist, Brian Fox. Have you ever heard of him?"

Tom laughed. "I might have," he said. "As I recall, they had one of his pieces on display at a studio we walked past in Youngstown. His work's amazing."

"Did they?" Jason teased, slapping his brother's arm. "As you suggested, I commissioned Brian to do a portrait of Miranda as a little girl. It came out beautiful." His eyes filled. "Brian titled it *Life's Joy*. Wait until you see it."

"That's fantastic," Tom said. "See, you have become cultured."

Jason shrugged off the compliment. "Brian said he was willing to push off Steven Tyler to do the piece in time for the wedding, so how could I go wrong with a guy like that?" Jason smiled. "We're going to unveil it for Miranda at the end of the reception."

"I can't wait."

As they reached the bar, Jason turned to the bartender. "I'll have a vodka and tonic," he said. "And give my brother whatever he wants."

Now there's a new one, Tom thought. "What about you?" he asked, ordering the same cocktail. "Two more years in the prison and you're a free man too, right?"

"It's funny you should bring that up," Jason said, wearing a giant smile.

"What's up?" Tom asked reluctantly.

"I just transferred to DYS, full time."

"You're kidding me?"

"Nope," he said. "I finally escaped."

Tom tapped his glass to Jason's. *Good for you,* he thought before they both took a sip. "When things slow down for you, let's get together and take a look at your retirement plan."

Jason nodded. "Thanks, I really appreciate that." He took another sip of his drink. "Listen, now that I'm in the new position, I thought you might want to . . ." He stopped.

"What is it?" Tom asked.

Jason shrugged. "I know this is a long shot, but I was telling my new supervisor about you and we both think the boys might really benefit from your knowledge and experience."

"And how's that?" Tom asked, not knowing what to think.

"We were hoping you'd consider coming in once a week and—"

"Once a week?" Tom blurted; his initial reaction was to decline the offer right away—*whatever it might be.*

"Or whatever works for your schedule to start a writer's group with the kids. We're thinking that most of the little punks love rap music, so writing poetry might allow them to express their . . ."

As Jason's words drifted off, Tom's head immediately filled with one idea after the next—his mind racing with the thrilling possibilities. *I could introduce culture to the boys from a different perspective—through street poetry. The program would encourage self-expression while providing a cathartic means to release their demons. I could create a safe and trusting environment so that each student feels free to express his own voice—maybe even his soul—while building confidence and a sense of accomplishment.*

Tom tried to refocus on his grinning brother, but the ideas continued to fire away inside his spinning head. *We could create an anthology of student works based on some common theme we pick at the onset and maybe even present the kids' work to the community, proving these boys can still bring value to society.* He could feel himself smiling. *Respect will be the foundation of our group, as we put it out there and express our deepest feelings and thoughts. We could do an anthology and a poetry slam. I could try to get some of their work published in local and Internet publications, teaching them the value of success. I could even bring in guest speakers and . . .* Tom emerged from his fog to find Jason waiting for him—and smiling.

"Well?" Jason asked.

"I'll do it," Tom said, feeling an intense commitment to the kids before even meeting one of them. "But with one condition."

"And what's that?" Jason asked.

"That I never have to get into another vehicle with you again."

"Done deal," Jason said, extending his hand.

Tom grabbed it and gave it a firm shake, both men holding on a few moments longer than usual. "You know what's a real shame, brother?" he said, looking around the room.

"What's that?" Jason said, taking a drink.

"I'd give anything for that egg white frittata with goat cheese right now."

Jason laughed enough to choke on his drink, splashing his tuxedo jacket. "You bastard," he said.

Acknowledgments

First and forever, Jesus Christ, my Lord and Savior. With Him, all things are possible.

To Paula, my beautiful wife, for supporting my dreams.

To my children—Evan, Jacob, Isabella, and Carissa—for inspiring me.

To Mom, Dad, Billy, Julie, Caroline, Caleb, Randy, Philip, Darlene, Jeremy, Baker, Aurora, Jenn, Jason, Jack, the DeSousa's—my beloved family and foundation on which I stand.

To Lou Aronica, my mentor and friend, for helping me to share my stories with the world.

To Brian Fox for sharing his incredible talent and painting *Life's Joy* for this project.

About the Author

Steven Manchester is the author of the #1 bestsellers *Twelve Months*, *The Rockin' Chair*, *Pressed Pennies*, and *Gooseberry Island* as well as the novels *Goodnight, Brian* and *The Changing Season*. His work has appeared on NBC's *Today Show*, CBS's *The Early Show*, CNN's *American Morning*, and BET's *Nightly News*. Recently, three of Manchester's short stories were selected "101 Best" for the *Chicken Soup for the Soul* series.